Lord Something

Lord Something

UNEXPECTED HEIRS
BOOK THREE

LOREA T. HARTWELL

This is a work of fiction. Any resemblance to incidents or persons living or dead is purely coincidental.

For Alfie and Tamsen

Contents

Chapter One

"We cannot afford the slightest breath of scandal. Not after..." Lady Sophronia trailed off. "Well. I certainly do not have to tell *you*."

Charles Keynsham, Sixth Viscount Alford, would have answered his grandmother, but he felt the same choking sensation that had been afflicting him ever since the library incident. He tried to swallow.

"And it could be worse, of course. At least she is an heiress." Lady Sophronia nodded to Holt, her butler. He, in turn, opened the door and signaled the footmen to bring in the tea things.

Lady Sophronia's posture was perfectly erect. Her pale blonde hair, now streaked with white, was perfectly coiffed. She was still wearing half-mourning for her son, the fifth viscount, and her lavender gown's standing lace collar perfectly framed her delicate features. But the events of the past year had weighed on her, just as they had on Keynsham.

The footmen unloaded their trays. Lady Sophronia

measured tea into a white and gold Meissen teapot and poured in the hot water. One of the footmen offered Keynsham a tray of macarons and *petits fours* topped with candied violets. "No thank you, Robert," he managed to choke.

"Very good, your lordship."

At another signal from Lady Sophronia, the servants withdrew. They were left alone in the drawing room, with its pale grey silk walls and enormous gilt-framed paintings. His grandmother's miniature spitzes—Carlo, Duke, and Viper—wandered through this elegant setting, their toenails clattering on and off the edges of the thick Aubusson carpet. Carlo, the ringleader, kept snorting and giving Keynsham condescending looks.

He scowled back. Yes, it was his own fault that he'd been duped by Miss Spry. But to be judged by a *dog*? That was the outside of enough.

He still couldn't believe that it had happened at all. A ball... a note requesting a meeting in the library... the shadowy approach of a girl with whom he'd scarcely exchanged two words in his life...

Oh, God. What a fool he'd been. And it wasn't even as though the plot had been original! If he'd been on his guard—as he ought to have been—he'd never have been taken in.

But he hadn't been on his guard. He was exhausted after months of late nights poring over the estate ledgers. And so, when he'd received the unsigned note, he'd assumed that it was from one of his late father's many unsavory creditors, prepared to threaten public exposure unless Keynsham met with him at once.

It certainly wouldn't have been the first such note

that he'd received. In fact, the irony was that if Miss Spry had had any idea of his family's real financial circumstances, she'd never have set her cap for him at all.

"Well, at least the money will not go amiss." Lady Sophronia sighed and handed him a cup of tea. "Though one could wish that the family... Well. They say that the father is a hard man. But then, I suppose that he has had to be. No matter how rich he is now, we cannot expect from him the manners of a gentleman." She took a sip of tea and sighed again. "Have the solicitors reached an agreement?"

That was what Keynsham didn't understand. "Er, no. There seem to be... sticking points. Mr. Spry asked to see the estate's books. The marriage settlements have not been signed."

"How irregular." She frowned. "But you *have* bought the ring."

"Yes." It was in his breast pocket—a large and rare pink spinel of spectacular clarity, surrounded by diamond brilliants and set in a gold band.

"And tonight is to be the night."

"Yes." Tonight was the night when his future would be sealed to a giddy, spoiled girl eleven years his junior, with whom he had nothing in common, and to whom he had nothing to say.

It wasn't what he'd hoped for. But then, hope was for fools. He ought to have learned that by now.

After all, he'd spent the past year living on the hope of a future with a very different lady—a lady named Miss Catherine Ryder. That hope had sustained him right up until last week. In fact, he'd clung to it until the very moment that he'd been stupid enough to open the library door.

And now there would be no Miss Ryder. Now, he would marry Miss Spry.

"It is most unaccountable." Lady Sophronia rang the bell. "In cases such as this, the engagement is *always* announced immediately, so as to hush up any talk. But Spry seems to be more concerned with protecting the girl's financial interests than her reputation! I suppose that is because he is a cit."

Mr. Spry had invented Spry's Rose Lotion, which was sold in bottles with pink labels and touted in advertisements as the secret to a pimple-, wrinkle-, and freckle-free complexion. He was a widower, and his daughter, Miss Arabella Spry, was the heiress to his fortune.

Miss Spry always dressed in pink, to match the Rose Lotion label, and claimed to prefer pink above all other colors. And so, as the marriage settlement was being hammered out by opposing teams of solicitors, Keynsham had pink orchids and pink roses delivered to his future bride in order to preserve the appearance that this was a real courtship. Appearances were everything to the *ton*.

His most successful gift had been a pair of pink coral earbobs. Given the several minutes that Miss Spry had spent unwrapping and cooing over them, he'd managed to stave off excruciating silence for almost half of the fifteen-minute call.

The clocks struck half past six. He rose and made his grandmother a bow. "My appointment with Miss Spry is set for seven. I must take my leave."

His grandmother rose as well and surprised him by

taking his hands. "None of this is what I had hoped for you, of course." Her piercing blue eyes searched his face. "But I know that you will do your duty. You always do."

* * *

The carriage swept north toward Grosvenor Square. A fog was coming up from the river, and the passing buildings were growing hazy... unless that was Keynsham's vision. He blinked to clear it.

The trouble with his breathing had come back, only worse than before. He cleared his throat. He put two fingers between his neck and his neckcloth and tugged. It seemed too tight. He was becoming lightheaded.

Was he dying? After all, his father had died young—of an apoplexy, in the arms of his mistress. That pointed to a constitutional weakness. Perhaps Keynsham had inherited it.

He felt briefly hopeful. Dying wouldn't be so bad. At least then he wouldn't have to stand up with Miss Spry in St. George's, Hanover Square, and be joined together in holy matrimony, and...

Dear God. He pounded on the ceiling. "Stop!" His voice was hoarse. "Stop the carriage! *Stop!*"

The carriage stopped. A moment later, the coachman opened the door. "Your lordship?"

"Let me out," gasped Keynsham.

He all but tumbled onto the pavement, where he stood with one hand on the side of the carriage and the other at his neck, fighting for air. He was bathed in sweat. His skin prickled. He tore at his neckcloth and succeeded in loosening it. It didn't seem to help.

"My lord! Are you ill? Do you need a doctor?"

With difficulty, he focused on the worried face of his coachman. Young. George Young. He was hard-working and kind and reliable. He didn't take unnecessary risks or curse at other drivers, and he never grumbled—as some coachmen did—at having to take the family out in foul weather.

And George Young was just one of the hundreds and hundreds of people who depended on him—Charles Keynsham, Sixth Viscount Alford—for his livelihood. He couldn't fail Young. He couldn't fail any of them. He couldn't fail the housemaids, the footmen, the grooms, the stable boys, the gardeners, the groundskeepers, the housekeeper, the scullery maids, the cook, the gamekeepers...

Dear God. It was starting again.

He forced himself to breathe through the choking sensation. It was nothing. It would pass. It was his *duty* to take the chance that fate had thrust upon him. He must marry Miss Spry and use her thirty thousand pounds to un-mortgage the farms and pay the servants' wages and make the estate profitable again and find a husband for his sister and...

"Sir! Sir! Can you speak?"

He took a rattling breath. It didn't seem to fill his lungs. "Yes."

"Shall I drive you home?"

Home. He wanted nothing more. "No. I must keep this appointment."

"But, your lordship, if you are unwell..."

"I am not unwell." What was the matter with him? "I—I was in need of air." He forced himself to straighten up—and caught sight of his reflection in the carriage window. His face was drawn and yet somehow puffy at the same time. His forehead was shiny with sweat. His neckcloth hung limp and loose.

He couldn't call on Miss Spry looking like this. Her father would assume that he was drunk.

But... he was expected.

He pulled out his pocket watch. He had less than twenty minutes before he was due in the Spry sitting room, pink spinel ring in hand.

"I shall walk."

"I beg your pardon, your lordship?"

He cleared his throat. "You may follow with the carriage. I shall walk the remainder of the way."

"Very good, your lordship."

Young waited on the box while Keynsham, with fingers that were trembling to a degree that made him furious with himself, did his best to re-tie his neckcloth.

He was not ill. He was fine. He'd led his men into battle at Waterloo. He'd had his horse cut out from under him by rifle fire. This was nothing. *Nothing.* He'd always done his duty. He would continue to do his duty now, and that was final.

He mopped his face with his handkerchief and replaced his top hat. The foggy air was damp and cool. Perhaps it would put a stop to this dreadful sweating. It must. This disgraceful loss of nerve could not become known.

He set off. Young followed, keeping the carriage to a walking pace.

* * *

To the outside world, Keynsham appeared to be a most eligible bachelor. He was young, titled, and—so people said—handsome. And as far as most people knew, he was rich.

Few suspected the truth. Keynsham himself knew only as much as he'd been able to unravel. He hoped that he'd come to grips with the worst of it. But it had cost him a year of tense meetings with managers and solicitors, and sleepless nights poring over the estate ledgers. And—because his late father had had the habit of cramming random invoices and dunning letters into drawers and folios and even the backs of books—it was always possible that there was still some unpaid bill awaiting discovery.

What he knew for certain was that his father had secretly sold several terraces of houses whose rents had provided the estate with a good income for nearly a century. He'd sold the stock in the East India Company that the third viscount had bought. He'd mortgaged the estate's farms at ruinous rates of interest.

And then—just when he'd apparently been certain that he would become the first man in history to borrow his way out of debt—he'd died.

Since then, every day had been a juggling act in which Keynsham moved the remaining money around to try to stave off disaster. A partial payment here, a renegotiation of loan terms there... even the calculations required to balance the trickle of money coming in with the torrent still going out were exhausting.

But he had to keep doing it. If he were to fail, the full extent of the debt would become known. All their creditors would demand payment at once, and the whole desperate enterprise would collapse.

He glanced ahead. Mount Street. He checked his watch. He had six minutes. There was the corner of

Grosvenor Square. If he cut across it, he'd arrive exactly on time.

A few smart equipages rolled past, their lanterns already lit against the early gloom. Fog hung between the buildings, rendering the far side of the street indistinct.

"I shall walk directly across," he called to George. His own voice sounded oddly muffled by the fog.

"Very good, your lordship." George clucked to the horses and the carriage sped up to meet him on the far side of the square.

The gate in the iron railing that surrounded the square's central park was not yet locked. As he opened it, he had the odd feeling that something was about to happen.

But nothing was about to happen. Or at least, he knew exactly what was about to happen: He was about to shackle himself to Miss Spry... for the rest of his life.

The footpath led him into a dense grove of evergreen rhododendrons and laurels. Above, the bare branches of the elm trees were ghostly in the fog. Fat drops of water dripped onto his hat and jacket. At the center of the square, the paths converged beneath the familiar gilded statue of George I. He chose the path that led north toward the Sprys' impressive foyer.

Or at least, he *thought* that he did. Instead of leading straight out of the square, the path took him into heavy shrubbery. He stopped in confusion. He must have taken a wrong turn.

But that was impossible. One could not become *lost* in Grosvenor Square—fog or no fog. If he continued in a straight line, he was bound to reach a street—any street, it didn't matter. He set off again.

He realized that he could call to Young—who must by now be stopped before the Spry mansion. The answering halloo would tell him if he were walking in the correct direction. Yet some sixth sense made him suddenly reluctant to reveal where he was.

He forced himself to be rational. "Young!"

The fog seemed to muffle his voice. There was no answer.

He cupped his hands around his mouth. "*Young!*"

Still no answer. And this time, the skin between his shoulder blades began to creep. What was the matter with him? He wasn't walking into a French ambush! He was in the middle of Mayfair—the wealthiest, most civilized neighborhood in the wealthiest, most civilized city in the world.

A wet branch slapped him across the face, temporarily blinding him. At the same instant, he collided with someone—someone warm and solid in the cold fog. He staggered back. "What the"—

The person said, "Shh!" and made a shushing gesture with one hand. All he could see of her—she was a woman—was the back of her shabby bonnet and pelisse.

"I *beg* your pa—"

She made another shushing gesture, this one more violent.

What? He was a viscount! He had an important appointment! He would not be stopped or shushed by a random, shabby woman lurking in Grosvenor Square! "Madam, I really must insist—"

She whirled around. And everything changed. Because it was *her*. Her heart-shaped face, the sweep of her long lashes, the curve of her lips, her warm gaze...

Her eyes softened. Her expression transformed—from tight anxiety to shocked disbelief to happy recognition. Her lips moved soundlessly, forming his name: *Keynsham*?

Relief and joy flooded him. For the first time in days, weeks, months—maybe his entire life—he could breathe properly. "*Miss Ryder?*"

He reached for her. She took a half step toward him. In another moment, they would be touching.

And then she froze. Her face went still. She raised a gloved finger to her lips and held her other hand up, palm out, in the gesture that meant *stop*.

Stop? At the very moment when he'd finally found her again?

And then, from the fog behind him, he heard the crunch of a boot on gravel.

Miss Ryder grabbed his hand and whispered a single word: "*Run.*"

Chapter Two

They ran.

He pulled Miss Ryder along with him as they dodged between the dripping shrubs. He didn't know why they were running, or in which direction. Then, just ahead, he thought he saw the iron railing that surrounded the garden.

Yes. They were almost out of the...

Wham. Something hit him in the side of the head.

Everything went momentarily black and starry. He sank half to his knees.

Fortunately, he was accustomed to shaking off blows. He straightened and turned in one fluid motion. The man who'd hit him stepped back, dismayed. It was plain that he'd expected Keynsham to go down and stay down.

Keynsham didn't bother to square up. He simply looked for an opening. The man was huge. He swung hard—a big, obvious swing. Keynsham ducked easily and returned a solid blow to the man's stomach. The big man sucked in air but lurched forward anyway. His flailing fist smacked into the side of Keynsham's mouth.

But that was just the opening that Keynsham wanted. His own fist shot up and caught the big man solidly under the chin—a perfect uppercut. *Crack.*

For a moment, his assailant's momentum continued to carry him forward. But that moment passed. The big man's eyes rolled up. He crumpled face first onto the wet lawn.

Miss Ryder was pulling at Keynsham's arm. "He is coming! We must go!"

Who was coming? There was no time to ask. They shoved their way through the shrubbery. His feet skidded on gravel. A path. "This way!"

A few steps more led them to a gate. They stumbled out of the square onto the pavement. The roadway before them was empty. Ghostly lights shone from windows through the fog. How surreal it was, to think that they were surrounded by candlelight in drawing rooms and dining rooms, the soft clink of silverware on china...

"Young!" Surely the coachman would hear him. "*Young!*"

"No!" Miss Ryder clutched his arm, out of breath. "He will hear you! I am certain that he is coming!"

"*Who*?"

Her face was taut with panic. "You do not understand!"

They paused under a streetlamp. He'd lost all sense of direction. He couldn't see the nearby buildings well enough to identify them. Unless... Ah. That great grey pile was the home of the Earls of Scarfe. He'd gone in a circle. They were back where he'd started.

Miss Ryder let go of his arm. "Look out!"

The man who loomed out of the fog was tall and fair and elegantly dressed in a flapping greatcoat and a black top hat. His eyes gleamed beneath its brim as he paced deliberately toward Keynsham. "Give her back."

"I beg your pardon?" Keynsham moved instinctively between him and Miss Ryder.

"You heard me. Give her back."

"I advise you to remember that this is a civilized country."

"Oh yes?" The man's mouth drew into a sneer. A jeweled stickpin in his neckcloth winked in the lamplight. "And I advise *you* not to make yourself part of something that you do not understand."

Keynsham narrowed his eyes. "What I am part of, sir, is defending an innocent lady from villainy."

"An innocent lady?" The man smirked. "I do not see one of those here. What I do see is a gentleman who knows nothing about what he's got himself into."

Keynsham drew himself up. The man's eyes widened for a bare second as he recalculated his size. "Apologize to the lady, sir."

The man gave a short laugh. Then, without warning, his fist flew at Keynsham's face. Keynsham dodged —but not quickly enough. The blow connected with his cheekbone.

This man was a more cunning fighter than the other thug had been. He closed quickly, using his feet to try to hook Keynsham's feet out from under him. Keynsham, hard pressed, broke away. They closed again. Blows hammered his ribs and back. They struggled from the pavement into the middle of the street.

Keynsham nearly went down. He broke away and

landed a solid punch to the man's chest, followed by a facer to his nose that sent the man staggering back.

The blow would have knocked many men unconscious. But his opponent, though sputtering blood, righted himself. "You'll regret that," he said. A pistol appeared in his hand.

"Wilkes! *No*!" shrieked Miss Ryder.

The drumming of hoofbeats broke through the fog. With a curse, the man flung himself to one side. "Whoa!" shouted Young, as Keynsham found himself directly in the path of his own carriage. "Whoah! Whoah!"

The horses shied and reared in their traces, whinnying in fright. Hooves flashed in his face. He reeled backward, his heart pounding and his arms windmilling. Young struggled with the reins. "Whoa, whoa, whoa!" The horses snorted and danced as he brought them under control. "Your lordship! What happened? Are you hurt?"

Keynsham caught his balance and looked around. His opponent had vanished. The foggy street was empty and quiet. Everything had happened so quickly that for a moment he half doubted that it had happened at all. Then he realized that he could taste blood. His lip was split and beginning to throb.

Miss Ryder! He turned, saw her wobbling on her feet, and lunged forward and caught her before she could fall.

And for a moment, nothing else mattered. He could have held her forever. He gazed down into her face. After more than a year apart, it was her. It was really her. Her eyelashes fluttered against her pallid cheeks.

Young sprang down from the box. "Who was that man? What happened? We must call the Watch!"

Keynsham came back to reality. "Help me get her into the carriage."

They propped her on the seat. He pulled off her gloves, took her icy hands in his, and chafed them, willing her to open her eyes and speak. Was she hurt? What had the bastards done to her?

"Your lordship?" Young's voice was low, and his face was wary. "I believe that that... *gentleman* is still in the square. Watching."

They had get out of here. But he couldn't take Miss Ryder home. She required rest and peace—and his mother, who still ruled at Alford House, would make a never-ending fuss about having a strange young lady in the house, about whose family she knew nothing.

And besides, there was his forthcoming engagement to Miss Spry to consider.

"We will go to Grafton Street."

"Your lordship?" The young coachman's expression was shocked.

"It is close by, and she will be safe there. That must be the only consideration."

* * *

The lamps in the carriage illuminated her face. Her skin was greyish, and her eyes were still closed. "Miss Ryder?"

She made an indistinct noise.

"*Miss Ryder.*"

Her eyes fluttered open. Slowly, they focused on him. She gave a shriek.

"Miss Ryder!" He laid a hand upon hers. "It is I. Keynsham. Do you remember me?"

She swallowed.

"You are safe now."

Her pale lips moved. "*Keynsham.*"

"Yes. You know me." She'd recognized him in Grosvenor Square. Why did she seem confused now? Had she hit her head? "Remember?"

"Yes." Her voice was a whisper. "You—you helped me get back my pocketbook."

"Yes. Good."

But she must remember more about him than that! If she didn't, that would mean... well, that would mean that he'd imagined the connection between them. And that couldn't be possible. He refused to believe that one heart alone could bear the weight of such powerful emotions.

She glanced about the interior of the carriage. He remembered her as brave and defiant. Now she seemed fearful—even cringing. "Where are you taking me? Whose carriage is this?"

"Please do not be afraid. You are safe. We are going to a house owned by... well, by my family. Would you like me to call you a doctor?"

She drew herself up and shrank away from him at the same time. "Why are you here?"

"What do you mean?" Perhaps she *had* hid her head. "I live here. I live in London. Do you not remember?"

She took a shaking breath. "What I mean is... Were you following me?"

"*Following* you?" He blinked, affronted. "No! Of course not!"

"But you were in the square. You walked into me."

"Because I was taking a shortcut on my way to a... Never mind." He couldn't think about any of that now. "Miss Ryder, you are plainly in some serious trouble. Tell me what is the matter. Please allow me to help."

She gave a quick shake of her head and looked out the window, refusing to make eye contact.

"You knew those men. They were not merely ruffians out to rob passersby. Why were they chasing you? I heard you call the well-dressed one Wilkes."

"No! Do not say his name!" Her face was anguished. "Forget that you ever heard it! You cannot become involved."

"I am already involved. Surely you do not believe that I would walk away and abandon you after such an episode! Why, what would you have done if I had not happened to be walking through the square?"

She bit her lip. "I do not know."

"Where were you going?"

"I was not *going* anywhere. I was trying to hide!"

"Then where had you come from? You did not drop into Grosvenor Square from the sky."

She shook her head. And before he could press her further, the carriage slowed. They drew up before an elegant double-fronted house. He leapt out first and checked up and down the street as far as he could see through the fog.

His throat was tight, as though all the things he wanted to say to her were trapped there. Fate had brought them back together. There could be no other explanation. But for now, his one and only duty was to ensure that she was safe.

* * *

"What *is* this place?" Miss Ryder stared up at an enormous Rococo-style painting of a lady whose porcelain-skinned, naked breasts were displayed above the bodice of the pale pink silk robe *à la française* that was inexplicably slipping off her body.

"Your lordship!" A footman hurried into the foyer, buttoning his jacket as he came. "I beg your pardon! We weren't expecting you! Betty! Come light the candles! His lordship is here!"

"Good evening, James." Keynsham glanced at Miss Ryder. "Come with me to the library, and I will explain."

After a moment's hesitation, she followed him across the hall to the library—or what passed for a library in this house. The only books in it had been purchased by the foot. He knew this because he'd paid the invoice from the company that had supplied them.

The housemaid bustled about lighting more candles and laying a fire. He cringed inwardly as he saw Miss Ryder's eyes lingering on the lewd statuary that decorated the room. He hadn't considered the impression that the place would make on her.

A moment later, the elderly housekeeper appeared. "Master Charles! Your lordship, that is! Dear me—what has happened?" She held a candle up. "Why, you are hurt!"

"It is nothing."

"Oh no it is not!" She frowned up at him. "I do not like the look of that eye! And your jacket is torn as well! You have been brawling!" She looked suspiciously at

Miss Ryder, as though she might be responsible for Keynsham's injuries.

"Merely a minor altercation." But now that the excitement of the fight had begun to wear off, he felt the throb in his cheekbone and lip and the ache in his sides. He would be sore tomorrow. "Miss Ryder, allow me to present Mrs. Barley. Mrs. Barley, Miss Ryder is an... old acquaintance. She has become separated from her companions and has suffered a great shock. As she has nowhere to stay in London, I suggested that she would be comfortable here."

"Of course, your lordship." Mrs. Barley made Miss Ryder a curtsey, though she still looked suspicious. "Let me take your jacket, at least. I shall brush and sponge it." She hurried off.

The moment that they were alone, Miss Ryder leaned forward, her eyes wide. "Is this a... a *brothel*?"

"Good God! No!" He cleared his throat. "But it was my father's... Well, it was the home of his... close friend."

Her eyes widened still further.

It was not good *ton* to acknowledge the existence of mistresses. Indeed, it was not a subject which a gentleman ought to discuss with an unmarried lady—or really, any lady. Still, he had to say something to explain why he had the keys to this gaudily decorated house. "My father was not... He was not what one would call a family man."

"Oh."

"His, er... light o' love vacated the property a few months ago. I have had to station several servants here to ensure that she does not return and help herself to any more of the furniture. They are all completely trustworthy. Mrs. Barley—the housekeeper—was my nurse when I was a boy. No one else knows that this place exists."

In truth, Keynsham hadn't known that it existed himself... at least, until some inexplicable half-yearly bills had arrived via his banker. After some investigation, he'd traced them to a large house on one of the most exclusive streets in Mayfair. And then, to his surprise, he'd learned that—via a fictitious company incorporated by his father—he was its owner.

Unlike most of the properties belonging to the Alford estate, the house wasn't mortgaged. But when he'd tried to visit it, he'd found that it was occupied by his father's most recent mistress, Miss Aurora Celeste.

Miss Celeste had been reluctant to leave. She swore that his father had left her penniless (apart from all the presents of jewelry and money that he'd made her, of course.) However, she told Keynsham, she was luckily in possession of some very, very, *very* personal letters sent to her by the late fifth viscount. And a kind publisher had offered her a very generous fee to print them—which would be enough to secure her future.

In the end, it had cost Keynsham a great deal of money that he couldn't afford to buy back the letters—and to relocate Miss Celeste to an establishment of her own in Brighton... with the deed in her own name, as per her stipulation. Miss Celeste was only nineteen, but she was no fool.

He wrenched his eyes away from a particularly explicit statue and cleared his throat. "I—I am quite confident that you are safe here. There is no obvious connection between me and this house. Its ownership is —well, my father took steps to conceal it."

"Oh." She stared at him. "But he will not come here… will he?"

"Who?"

"Your father."

"Good God, no! He died over a year ago. Only a few days after we… we met, in fact." Why did he sound so confounded awkward?

"Oh! I am very sorry to hear it." Her heart-shaped face flushed. "That explains why the servants are addressing you as…" She broke off and frowned. "I am sorry. I do not know your title."

"Viscount Alford. But of course, I am still Keynsham to friends who knew me before I acceded to the title."

"Viscount!" Her face fell. "Oh."

"Now, the men who were chasing you…"

Mrs. Barley bustled back into the room, bearing his jacket. "I am warming up some of what we had for dinner, and Betty will make up one of the guest rooms for Miss Ryder."

"Thank you, Mrs. Barley. I cannot stay to eat, however. I have…" Did he still have an appointment? It was now past eight o'clock. "Well. I have an obligation elsewhere."

When the housekeeper had gone again, an awkward silence fell. He knew that he ought to leave. He knew that he was only looking for a reason to delay his departure. But he couldn't seem to make himself go. He couldn't seem to stop drinking in the sight of Miss Ryder.

He could have spent hours memorizing her face all over again... the play of candlelight on her light brown hair, the delicate lines of her brows, and the dark sweep of her lashes along her cheeks. He wanted to ask her what had happened in every moment of every day that they'd been apart—where she'd been, what she'd done, what she'd thought, whether she'd ever thought of him...

He cleared his throat. "I trust that you will be comfortable. You may, of course, stay here as long as is convenient for you. But please—promise me that you will not go out alone. Not until we can be assured that it is safe."

She looked down and swallowed. "Thank you."

"Tomorrow, when you are rested, we will discuss what is to be done about this man Wilkes. His actions cannot go unpunished."

Her eyes went wide again. "No! Please! Do as I ask, and forget his name! I require no assistance."

He couldn't help himself. He smiled. "Miss Ryder, you *always* say that you require no assistance, even when it is plain that you do."

She looked at him in blank confusion.

Oh. He felt his face warm under the bruises. Apparently, of the two of them, it was only he who'd mentally replayed every word of their conversations from a year ago. He was making a cake of himself.

He cleared his throat again, realizing as he did that he must sound as though he had the catarrh. "Well. I shall call upon you in the morning. I trust that you will be comfortable."

Wait. He'd already said that. He forced himself to rise and move to the door before he could embarrass himself further, although part of him feared that if he took his eyes off her for so much as a moment, she'd vanish again. "Good night, Miss Ryder."

She raised her eyes to meet his. He couldn't read their expression. "Good night. And... and thank you."

Chapter Three

Oh, why did it have to be *him*?

For over a year—when she'd been bent over some embroidery, or playing the piano for her employer, or walking to the village to do errands, or pouring tea—her body had been in one place and her mind had been somewhere else.

Somewhere with Mr. Keynsham.

She wasn't stupid. She'd known almost from the night that she'd met him that there couldn't be anything between them. But somehow, that hadn't stopped her from dreaming. He had become her ideal of the perfect gentleman.

And of course, she'd never see him again. So what could be the harm in thinking about him? Maybe someday, he'd fade from her thoughts. But in the meantime, no one would ever know.

His wit, his manners, the way that he'd protected her... the way that he'd looked at her... She'd spent hours obsessing over their one extraordinary night together, and many more hours—dozens, hundreds, perhaps thousands!—having imaginary conversations with him.

She remembered every detail of their one kiss: the way the morning stubble around his mouth had prickled her lips, how much warmer his body was than hers, the strength of his arms when he'd drawn her closer, and the scent of Castile soap on his skin.

And... well, she'd imagined what it would be like to kiss him again. It was mortifying to remember these fantasies while sitting in the same room as him—so mortifying that she'd scarcely known what to say to him.

"Miss Ryder, you are quite clearly in some sort of trouble." His voice was exactly as she'd remembered it, only better: low and with a certain rumble to it, despite his cultured accent. It was a voice that belonged to a rich man who indulged in bare-knuckle boxing. It was a voice that—even amidst her terror—seemed to warm her whole body.

But he was a viscount now. And what was she? An out-of-work lady's companion. And as if that weren't bad enough, now she'd dragged Wilkes and his gang out of whatever dark hole they inhabited and straight into Keynsham's life.

She hugged her elbows and stood before the little fire, wishing that it could melt the chill and fear from her muscles. She couldn't seem to stop the deep shivers that wracked her body. They were from more than the damp chill of the evening. They were from her nerves. Her mind kept replaying the terrifying, disorienting flight through the wet shrubbery, the realization that she was trapped in the square...

And then there was her terror at seeing Wilkes again

—the way that he'd appeared out of the night, his great-coat flapping like the wings of a bat... and the sickening crack of his fists hitting Keynsham.

And the instant that she'd seen the pistol in his hand.

She found herself squeezing her eyes closed, trying to shut out the sheer horror of the moment when she'd believed that Wilkes would murder Keynsham.

And yet, it made no sense. Why was Wilkes still pursuing her? It certainly wasn't because he was in love with her. He'd never loved her. When she'd run away she'd assumed that if she disappeared, he'd quickly forget about her.

Well, it appeared that she'd badly misread the situation.

Her mind wouldn't stop whirling through the list of bewildering questions: How could Wilkes have known that she was in London almost the instant that she'd arrived? And why would he bother to send his men after her? Any business that he'd had with her father was long since ended. After all, he'd been dead for over a year—as Wilkes well knew. He was the one who'd told her of his death.

She caught sight of her reflection in the gilt-framed mirror over the mantel. She looked dreadful, with pale cheeks, a reddened nose, and anxious eyes. She certainly wasn't such a prize that a man would lose his head and scour London for her. Yet for some reason, Wilkes had.

She'd arrived that morning by stagecoach. Though she was hungry and tired, she'd gone directly to the first of the employment agencies on the list that she'd made. She couldn't afford to be out of work for more than a few days.

But the proprietress hadn't even looked at her character reference. Instead, she'd stared down her nose at her costume and said that she must dress more smartly if she hoped to make a respectable figure in some London lady's sitting room.

Mustering all her dignity, she thanked the woman and left, trying to persuade herself not to mind. She might not possess any fashionable gowns now, but she was patient and thoughtful. She read aloud, played piano, answered and filed correspondence, and never complained about being sent on tiresome errands. Those were the qualities upon which she ought to be judged—not her wardrobe!

She raised her chin, squared her shoulders, and walked on toward the next agency on her list. She was too agitated to notice, at first, that a man who'd been loitering across the street looked familiar. It took her a few minutes to realize that he bore a strong resemblance to a certain petty criminal from the Hampshire town in which she'd grown up.

That was odd. Then again, there were more than a million people in the capital city—and she'd never actually seen the man—Dick Fenton—up close, much less spoken to him. Perhaps her mind was playing tricks on her. She hurried onward. And when she checked the street again after leaving the next office, she saw no one at all.

Fine. She had more pressing matters to think about.

But a few streets later, she realized her mistake. She was being followed—and not just by the first man, but by another man, too, one she'd never seen before.

Wilkes. The thought flew into her mind from seemingly nowhere, but she knew instantly that she was right.

Her heart pounding, she hurried up one street and down another. The faster she went, the faster they chased her. Fear made her feel sick and weak. A sudden fog was rising, and she had no idea which direction she was facing.

She hadn't seen Wilkes in over a year! She had nothing that he could want! This wasn't fair! Her brain chanted these futile thoughts in time with her hurrying footsteps. But the men kept following, and the thickening mist and her unfamiliarity with London made it impossible to know where she was. And then, dimly ahead, she saw trees and palings. She thought that she must have reached a park—and decided that she could hide in it.

It didn't take long before she realized that she'd made yet another mistake. The "park" was only a square—large and densely planted but bounded on all four sides by streets. She'd thought that she could outsmart the men. Instead she'd outsmarted herself. She was trapped.

And if Keynsham hadn't come...

But he had. She only wished that she could be happy about that.

She dropped her eyes. The mantel of this overdecorated bedroom was lined with a collection of enameled silver snuff boxes whose painted lids depicted eighteenth century beauties in the style of Fragonard. Scarcely thinking what she was doing, she picked one up.

The hinged lid swung open, revealing a different picture on its underside: The same smiling lady, but now with her skirts hiked above her waist and a kneeling gentleman... She gasped and dropped it back on the mantel as though it had burned her hands. What on earth...? Did people really...?

Curiosity got the better of her. She picked up the next box. On the outside, a coy beauty held a rose that matched her pink lips and lace-trimmed gown. Inside, however, she was bent forward over a bed, naked, while the frock-coated gentleman who stood behind her, his breeches pulled down, was...

"Your bath, miss."

She jumped away from the mantel. The housemaids entered with huge pitchers of steaming water and filled the tub. When they were gone, she took off her damp and dirty gown and sank into the hot water, closing her eyes against the images of the silly erotic pictures that she'd just seen.

In what world were people rich enough to buy such costly, vulgar little trinkets?

Well, Keynsham's world. Which wasn't her world—and never would be. And she would do well to get that through her head for once and for all.

And the Keynsham—or rather, *Lord Alford*—who'd rescued her tonight had changed subtly over the past year. He seemed weary, cynical, older—maybe even bitter. His clothes, his carriage—not to mention the way that he'd been so matter of fact about this luxurious house and his father's mistress... all of it only served to emphasize the gulf between them. He was a man of the world. And that world was a different world than hers.

She tried to concentrate on scrubbing the grime of travel from her pores. She must stop thinking about him... and the way that the slight rumble in his voice seemed to tickle her spine... and focus her mind on her next steps. It was plain that there were many things that she didn't know. The only thing that she *did* know was that coming to London had been a mistake.

She'd known that Wilkes had been expanding his business into London. She'd heard it from their housekeeper, Mrs. Ryder. But almost everyone in the town had known, because Wilkes was—or had been, anyway—a braggart.

No doubt he was doing well for himself here. Indeed, judging by the look of his clothes, he was wealthy. But until today, she hadn't given him or his criminal career much thought in over a year. So why was he still so interested in her?

She didn't want to stay to find out. She must find a new position in some country town or isolated house and leave as soon as she could—tomorrow, if possible. The one comfort was that unless Wilkes had a gang the size of an army, he couldn't search every corner of the kingdom. And as it happened, it was easy for a lady's companion—expected to be a gentlewoman, but to efface herself like a servant—to disappear into the woodwork.

And, of course, she must never see Keynsham again. To be near him was to put him in danger. And until she could master her emotions, to be near him was to put her heart in danger too.

She sat before the fire, drying her hair. Keynsham had told her to stay in the house tomorrow until he could come. What he didn't understand was that it would be far better—for both of them—if she did not.

She blew out the candles and slipped between the

heavy, luxurious sheets. If there were one piece of comfort to which she could cling, it was that Wilkes couldn't possibly know who Keynsham was.

And she would make certain to disappear again before he could find out.

* * *

Wilkes melted back into the shadows as a lone carriage rolled past. Fog filled the street. The lit windows in the house opposite were squares of light in the gloom.

Ordinarily, a job like watching a house was one that he sent his men to do. But this was Celia. Celia was not an ordinary job. Besides, his men had already let him down several times today. They were far too stupid to be reliable—as recent events had shown. The day had been nothing but a series of their cockups.

He had informants at all the principal coaching inns. After all, it was often necessary to ensure that a debtor didn't make a run for the Continent. So, when a boy had arrived with the message that a young lady traveling alone and matching Celia's description had arrived on a public stage from Lincoln, he'd dispatched Fenton and Gooley to bring her in.

How difficult could it possibly be for two grown men to snatch one young woman off the streets of London? And yet, they hadn't managed to follow her for even a few minutes before she spotted them! One of the street urchins he paid to spy on his men and carry messages had come pelting to his office with the news that Celia was on the run.

Wilkes was downstairs and in his carriage almost before the boy had finished speaking. He ought to have handled this himself from the beginning. Well, soon it wouldn't matter. Soon, Celia would understand that running from him was futile.

The thing that he hadn't counted on was that someone would come to her rescue. And not just any someone—but a gentleman who had training in fighting.

Wilkes had always prided himself on being a quick study when it came to the ways of the gentry, but until he'd moved to London, he hadn't realized how popular boxing was with a certain set of young aristocrats. It would have made him laugh, if he'd been the sort of man who laughed.

Which he wasn't.

Didn't these overbred fools understand that being rich meant not having to do your own fighting?

And what had the young lord been doing in Grosvenor Square on a damp, foggy March evening, anyway? What impulse could have led him to help Celia? It was impossible that there could have been any previous connection between them. She knew no one in London. Was he merely a drunken young aristocrat out looking for a brawl?

That would have been the most likely explanation... but for one thing: the gentle way that he'd lifted Celia into his carriage when she'd fainted. There had been something so unmistakably tender—almost *possessive*—in his manner that Wilkes's blood had boiled as he stood in the shadows of the square's garden, watching.

Because Celia was his. And he would teach the overbred fool that lesson the hard way. He was looking forward to it, in fact.

He folded his arms and studied the house. It was a

huge, creamy stone affair with a porticoed front and a stone wall that separated the semi-circular drive from the street. As his father would have said, it wasn't the sort of crib that would be easy to toss.

Of course, Wilkes had moved on from housebreaking… mostly. There were far easier ways to get what he wanted. Still, if there was one thing that his father had taught him, it was that every house had its weakness. Sometimes that weakness was a broken window latch, and sometimes it was a bribable servant. You never knew until you looked.

It hadn't been at all difficult to find the place. After all, London's wealthy could never resist a chance to announce who they were. The family coat of arms—surmounted by a gold viscount's coronet, of course—was right there for all to see, painted on the door of Lord Alford's very new, very expensive carriage.

The instant that Wilkes had his name, it had been an easy enough matter to learn the location of his house. And if there'd been any remaining doubt, the very same coat of arms appeared upon the glossy painted iron gates.

Ah. There was movement in the house. Someone—a servant, probably—was shutting the curtains in the windows on the first floor. He wondered who else lived here besides the viscount. A wife? Children? He'd find out. He knew people who knew things. And many of them owed him money.

This miserable fog sent its cold tentacles everywhere—down his collar, up his already-aching ribs. The young lord was a bruising fighter. Fortunately, there was a remedy for that. It was called a pistol.

He shifted his weight and drew his greatcoat closer

about himself. It had, of course, been made by Weston. His hat was from Lock & Co. and his boots had been made by Hoby. The fact that he looked like a gentleman made his clients trust him to behave like one—a trust that, to a man, they came to regret.

Moving his operations to London had been a good decision. Not only were there richer clients to fleece, but in the teeming capital city—where everything was available for a price—a man could reinvent himself. People in the city had much shorter memories than they did in a country town, and money took on a self-cleaning property: When you had enough of it, people were eager to overlook how you'd got it.

Which was just as well, because he'd done any number of things that wouldn't bear scrutiny. For that matter, he was still doing them.

And that, of course, was why he couldn't allow Celia to slip through his hands again. As long as she was wandering about loose, there was a chance that she might discover the truth. It was only a small chance—she was only a woman, after all—but it was a chance nonetheless. And he never left anything to chance.

What he still couldn't understand was how she'd managed to run away in the first place. She was a sheltered girl who'd never been farther from her home than Chichester! She hadn't the slightest idea how to survive on her own. So how had she managed to defy him, slip out of his grasp, and disappear for an entire year?

Had the viscount helped her then? Was she his mistress?

No. It wasn't possible. Besides, it was plain enough from her shabby clothes that wherever she'd been, she hadn't been living well.

That would change when he married her. He liked to see a well-turned-out lady. She'd never want for new gowns—although, unfortunately, he'd have to keep her quite isolated. After all, he couldn't risk her chattering to other ladies. That would lead to gossip... which would lead to questions... which would lead to suspicions.

Which was why Lord Alford's chivalrous impulses—assuming that that was all that they were—were so dangerous. Celia didn't need anyone putting ideas into her head and making her believe that she could escape the destiny that had awaited her since she was thirteen. Whether she liked it or not, she was just as much Wilkes's as his ruby cufflinks were.

A carriage rolled slowly past, the driver keeping the horses to a walk in the dense mist. It was a cursed cold evening for March. If it hadn't been for this uncanny fog, even Fenton and Gooley wouldn't have lost Celia.

Well, now that she was in London, he'd have her back soon enough. He'd struck a bargain with her father, after all. And he wasn't in the business of forgiving debts. He was in the business of collecting on them... as young Lord Alford was about to discover.

Chapter Four

Keynsham had at least one misgiving after he rapped on the Sprys' door. But he shoved it down. A few darkened windows in a house meant nothing. It was only half past eight, after all—not late by the standards of the aristocratic class, which often didn't rise until well past noon in town. And surely Spry couldn't be so gauche as to maintain tradesmen's hours now that he was one of the wealthiest men in England!

But the footman who answered the door looked cross, and his powdered wig was askew, as though he'd just clapped it onto his head. When he saw Keynsham, he straightened immediately and looked—if Keynsham were not mistaken—*frightened*. "Oh! Your lordship!" He held the door open the merest crack and glanced nervously behind himself. "I—I… that is, the household has been…"

"Who is it, Job?" shouted someone within.

Job winced. "My lord, perhaps it would be best—"

“I said who is it!” And someone seized the door from the unlucky Job and wrenched it open.

It was Spry himself—Miss Spry’s father—clad in a gold damask banyan and a matching cap. “Why, you...” He squinted, taking in the bruises on Keynsham’s face and his damaged jacket. “What is this? Have you have been out brawling?”

“Sir, I—"

“You have, haven’t you? You have been out with your drunken friends. How dare you? How dare you come here now, at this hour?”

Was this how Spry would talk to him when he was his father-in-law? If Keynsham hadn’t been honor-bound to marry Miss Spry, he would have left instantly.

“I had not thought that half past eight was late, sir. And I have not been brawling. I was on my way here for this appointment when I was forced to chase off a pair of ruffians who were lurking in this very square.”

“Ruffians? In Grosvenor Square? Pah!” For a moment, Spry looked as though he might spit on the doorstep. “A likely story!”

But at this Keynsham drew himself up. His father might have nearly bankrupted the family. His estates might be mortgaged to the hilt. His sister might never have a proper London season, for all she was the daughter of a viscount. But he was still a gentleman—and Spry had just called him a liar. “I am afraid that I must have misunderstood you, sir,” he said, quietly. “For a moment I almost had the impression that you doubted my word.”

Spry had been about to say something else, but he checked himself. His face passed from rage through to indignation to doubt and thence to an expression that was at least in the general vicinity of embarrassment. "I—I am sorry for it, your lordship," he muttered. "I did not mean—that is, my manners are sometimes rough. And of course, Arabella..." He cleared his throat. "Well. I am certain that I need not tell *you* how unpleasant she can make things."

Keynsham hadn't yet seen this side of his future bride. He wasn't looking forward to it.

Spry shook his head. "Ah, well. Since you are here, you may as well come in." He paused in the open doorway and gave the dense fog in the square a long, suspicious stare. "Ruffians! The Watch must be told of this. I have long said that there is far too much undergrowth in that garden! After this, I shall personally see to it that all those trees and shrubs are cut down and the place laid to grass. I have not paid a fortune to live in Grosvenor Square to have to worry that footpads are skulking about my very door!"

Keynsham followed him through the gilt-encrusted front hall and into his library. The draperies at the French doors hadn't been drawn and the white fog seemed to press against the glass, as though seeking a way inside. At the same time, he could see nothing but their reflections in the lit room. Anyone outside would be able to see them... without being seen in return.

These weren't thoughts that would have occurred to him ordinarily. But Miss Ryder's obvious terror of Wilkes had given him pause—though no doubt her fears were overblown. The thug couldn't possibly be as all-powerful as she seemed to believe.

Spry followed Keynsham's gaze. "It is a foul night indeed, if nothing else. *Job!* Draw these curtains at once."

The hapless footman hurried to obey. Spry glared irritably around the room as though all of it displeased him. "Well, well. Sit down, sit down. May as well have a coze, now that you are here." He waved a hand toward a pair of armchairs in front of the fire.

Keynsham was puzzled by his manner. Spry seemed ill at ease—almost as though he couldn't look Keynsham in the eye, for some reason. It was as though... it was as though he were embarrassed. But why?

He sat down. The library was the most homey and least pretentious room that he'd seen in this house. It was clear that Spry used it as his office. The books in the bookcases looked as though they'd actually been read—which made an interesting contrast to those that his own father had bought by the foot.

"Port?" Mr. Spry went to the sideboard and sloshed liquor into two glasses. He handed one to Keynsham and stood holding the other, grimacing like a child anticipating a bad-tasting medicine. "I dislike alcohol myself. Until recently I abstained, you know."

"Do not feel that you must drink on my account, sir."

"No, no." Spry shook his head. "Arabella says that I must acquire the taste for it, if I am to mingle in society. I am behindhand, you see. I am not in the fashion. But my butler orders the wine, so you may be assured that it is of the first quality." He took a sip and drew his lips back from his teeth. "Gah!"

Keynsham sipped as well. "It is excellent."

Spry looked glum. "When I was a 'prentice, our master always said that alcohol was poison. Leave it to the gentry, he said. Let *them* pickle themselves. All the more business for us. No offense, your lordship," he added, hastily.

"I took none." In fact, Keynsham was beginning to like Spry—his rough manners notwithstanding.

Spry dropped into the armchair that faced Keynsham's and stared despairingly at the port in his glass. He was a distinguished-looking man—hawk-nosed and barrel-chested, with dark hair dashed with silver and a firm jaw. In his luxurious, old-fashioned banyan, he put Keynsham a little in mind of his grandfather, the fourth viscount. He supposed that Lady Sophronia—who, though she had many fine qualities, was a snob—would be deeply shocked if she knew that such a thought had crossed his mind.

"That is a lovely portrait of your late wife." Keynsham already knew what Miss Spry's mother looked like, as there was another portrait of her in the pink sitting room upstairs.

"Aye, and it ought to be—for what I gave for it." Spry set his barely touched glass on a side table and folded his arms. "Now then, your lordship. Before I say anything else, I may as well tell you that I like you. *Your* conduct has been beyond reproach—which is certainly more than I can say for... Well." He cleared his throat. "I am sorry. It has been a bad business—but I hope that it will not long trouble you."

What was he apologizing for? Keynsham waited for him to explain. Spry's jaw worked for a moment before he tried again. "What I mean to say is that the rules of high society are all very well—but not when they make more problems than they solve, if you take my meaning."

Keynsham did *not* take his meaning. But Spry gave a

decisive little nod, as though a matter had been settled, and visibly relaxed. “Well, now, your lordship! I must say that your face is rather less pretty than it was the last time I saw you! That is not a blacked eye, however. It is a contusion upon your cheekbone. And to make matters worse, I should say that the man who struck the blow was wearing a ring.” He squinted at it. “Yes. I shall give you an ointment to take down the swelling.”

Spry had been a prosperous apothecary with his own shop before the success of Rose Lotion had taken London—and then the whole country—by storm. He crossed the room to a battered cabinet that didn’t match the other furniture and hunted around on its shelves before presenting Keynsham with a small tin. “Pot marigold, comfrey, and hyssop. Apply this to the bruises as needed. It will constrict the vessels and prevent the blood from stagnating.”

“You are very kind, sir.” Keynsham turned the tin over in his hand. “Thank you.” He had the strange feeling that Mr. Spry had just given him... a parting gift? A consolation prize?

“Papa! Papa!” Miss Spry came flying into the library, her raven ringlets artfully unbound. She stopped mid-flight, one delicate hand at her throat. “Oh! Why, Lord Alford! Why—I had not—I have only just awoken—I did not realize!”

Miss Spry might be very pretty and very rich, but she wasn’t a very good actress. Even her own father merely smiled indulgently on her performance as she pretended to be astonished to find Keynsham in the library, despite the fact that his carriage was drawn up in the square outside, clearly visible from every one of the windows on the front of the house.

She was attired in an evening gown—which, it went without saying, was pink. She was also wearing large pink sapphire ear bobs. Despite her loose hair, both of these things made her claim of having been asleep unlikely.

The ring box grew heavy in Keynsham's jacket pocket. Now that the moment was here, how could he do it? How could he propose to her? Spoiled and flighty as she was, she wasn't yet eighteen. He was certain that she—or perhaps one of her friends—had sent the note about the library meeting without thinking through the consequences. She didn't love him. And he could never love her. Indeed, after tonight he was even more certain that...

But no. He must not even allow himself to think that way. He must do what he'd come here to do—his duty. He cleared his throat. "Miss Spry, will you do me the honor of granting me a private inter—"

Her mouth dropped open. She gasped theatrically. She put one hand to her throat. "But what has happened to your *face*? Oh, Lord Alford! You have been in a fight! A dreadful, violent fight! Oh dear! Oh! Oh! It is too shocking!" And—with a quick glance behind her to make sure that there was no furniture in the way—she crumpled gracefully to the thickly-carpeted floor.

"Job!" Spry sounded resigned. "Fetch the *sal volatile.* Miss Spry has fainted. *Again.*"

"Air! Give her air! Stand back!" The butler, a housemaid, Miss Spry's French maid, and Job all bustled around Miss Spry's prone form. Keynsham wondered if he ought to offer to help. But it appeared that the household already had a routine for these circumstances and that he would only be in the way.

Spry beckoned him away from the furor, nearer to the window. "I can tell you from experience that this will go on for some time."

"Oh."

"But now you see how it is. She has a mind of her own. I would have forced her to go through with it—but it will not fadge, sir. It simply will not fadge."

Job passed the *sal volatile* under Miss Spry's nose. It had no effect.

Her father sighed. "Well, it is a shame. The fix that you have been left in is no fault of your own. And *I* should not be in the least surprised if you make good yet—mark my words!"

What was he talking about?

"Well, we understand each other. And I am glad of it, your lordship. A little plain talk is always enough to settle such matters—without the slightest need for fainting and theatrics."

Plain talk? Keynsham glanced over at the scene by the door. "Miss Spry seems, er... very shocked by my appearance."

"Pah!" said Spry, unfeelingly. "Bruises heal. She's seen your fizzog without 'em. No, no—let us not sugar-coat matters. She has put everyone to a great deal of trouble and expense. And for what? A momentary fancy that has come to nothing."

Keynsham wished that he hadn't been punched in the head before this meeting. He seemed to be having unusual difficulty understanding exactly what Spry was driving at. He would almost have said that he was hinting that Miss Spry no longer wished to marry him.

But that was impossible. When a young lady claimed to have been compromised, marriage was only remedy for the situation. So, it could not be that. He cleared his throat. "Ladies may be easily overset."

Spry snorted. "Oh, Arabella used to be a level-headed enough girl, before she got so high in the instep." He set his still barely touched glass of port down on a corner of his desk with a bang.

The hubbub around Miss Spry increased. It appeared that two footmen were preparing to carry her unconscious form from the room.

"Are you certain that she is quite well?" Keynsham was a little taken aback by Spry's casual assumption that his daughter was playacting.

"Oh yes. Healthy as a horse. She has taken a fancy to these fainting fits, that is all." He raised his voice so that his daughter would hear him as she was carried out. "Swooning, she thinks, gives her the appearance of great sensibility and refinement!"

Miss Spry kept her eyes determinedly closed. The footmen who were carrying her maintained their stoic expressions. One of the housemaids shut the door behind the retinue of servants.

The sudden silence was a relief.

"Well, that is that." Spry sighed again. "Once she takes it into her head to be unconscious there is no telling how long it will last. Some say that I am too lenient with her—and perhaps I am. But since the death of Mrs. Spry...Well. It is a hard thing to lose one's wife and helpmeet, sir—a hard thing. I hope that you never experience such sorrow."

Keynsham couldn't imagine that anyone would ever describe Arabella Spry as a "helpmeet." He bowed. "I shall send for word of Miss Spry's health in the morning."

"I assure you that there is not the slightest cause for concern, your lordship. She has had her fainting fit now and cannot want for another for a few days, at least."

"I shall send a note, regardless."

Spry gave him a look that seemed to mingle pity and incredulity. "Well, please yourself—although after the shabby way that she has treated you, I should say that you are taking fine manners a deal too far, your lordship—a deal too far indeed!"

He sucked air through his teeth and shook his head. "I had my doubts about you at first—I do not scruple to tell you so. But you have proven yourself an out-and-outer. You did your best, sir. You did your best." He clapped him on his shoulder. "And that is the most that any man can do."

* * *

Keynsham tried and failed to find a comfortable position against the squabs. His ribs ached where Wilkes's blows had fallen, and pain radiated from his left cheekbone.

The whole evening had taken on a surreal quality. Miss Spry's unconvincing fainting fit was the least of it. Spry had been attempting to communicate something important, he was certain—and yet, he still couldn't grasp what it was.

And above all, Miss Ryder's face haunted him. There had been such fear in those wide eyes with their long, dark lashes. Why had she refused to tell him who this man Wilkes was, and why he was chasing her? Surely she didn't believe that she could manage the situation on her own!

In the single night that they'd spent together, over a year ago, he'd noticed her talent for becoming involved in chaos wherever she went. But this was something different. This was something serious and sinister.

The carriage drew up before the steps of Alford House. Despite his sore muscles and aching ribs, he sprang out and was up the stairs before Young could even climb off the box. He must not fail to compose a note enquiring after Miss Spry's health before he went to bed, so that a servant could deliver it first thing tomorrow morning—along with a pink bouquet for the invalid, of course.

Then, while the note and bouquet stood in for him, he would go to Grafton Street, press Miss Ryder to explain why Wilkes was pursuing her, and make a longer-term plan for her safety.

The past year had taught him to juggle more than just money. He'd become an expert at very nearly being in two places at once and—through relentless attention to detail—almost managing to satisfy everyone's demands.

But the problem of how to help Miss Ryder, while not failing in his obligation to Miss Spry, was a complex one. And as he entered his house, he didn't notice the fog-shadowed figure of a man in the mouth of the mews across the street.

Chapter Five

"Well? Is the deed done?" His younger sister, Pomona, was occupying the library in much the same way that Napoleon's army had occupied large swathes of Europe. Her resupply operation—stacks of paper, spare quills, a plate of cakes, a pot of tea—was evident all over the big wooden worktable.

"Er... well... no."

"*No?*" Her face lit up. "Then you came to your senses?"

"Pomona."

"Or she came to hers? Though I grant you that *that* is unlikely."

"*Pomona.*"

"Well, for heaven's sake! What happened?" She threw a ball of crumpled paper at him. It bounced off his arm. "You look dreadful. I should never have suspected Miss Spry of having such a strong right arm."

"Hah." Keynsham flopped down into a large leather armchair and put his hand over his eyes. "As a matter of fact, I am not certain that I myself know what happened."

Pomona rose and held a candle closer to his face. "Oh dear! It is worse than I realized. There is blood on your lip *and* on your cheekbone. Shall I ring to see if cook has some ice?"

"No, but I would not say no to one or two of those rout cakes." He hadn't had a chance to eat all evening.

She brought him the plate. "I thought that gentlemen were not supposed to hit each other above the neck or below the belt."

"I was not fighting gentlemen. I was fighting ruffians."

"Ruffians?" She narrowed her eyes at him, apparently trying to work out whether or not he was serious. "Oh. I see. You are bamming me. But I suppose that that is all you will tell me."

"You suppose correctly." He hadn't realized how damaged his face was until he tried to eat and found that his swollen lower lip wouldn't move properly. "How goes the book?"

"The book is... Oh, I suppose that it is nearly done. Do not change the subject. If you were not with Miss Spry, where were you? You have been gone hours."

He wished that he could tell her about Miss Ryder. But Pomona was a romantic. She was bound to become impassioned and entreat him to follow the urgings of his heart, or something equally poetic and impractical.

Besides, he couldn't tell her about the Grafton Street house. Pomona didn't know—at least officially—that their father had kept mistresses... although Keynsham suspected that she wasn't quite as ignorant about such matters as their mother hoped.

"I did see Miss Spry. But before I could propose, she fainted and had to be carried from the room."

She narrowed her eyes. "No, but really."

"That is what happened."

"What?" She began to laugh. "How perfectly ridiculous! What did Lord Lotion say to that?"

Keynsham frowned. "I know that many in the *ton* call him that. But he is a decent man, and—well, it is nothing but snobbishness."

"Yes. You are right. I am sorry." She considered. "But it *has* been dragging on. Has it not? It is all very odd." She frowned. "Do you know—I have the strangest feeling that the marriage will not come off after all."

"Well, the solicitors are hard at work drawing up the marriage settlements, so that seems unlikely."

She sat down again and began sorting through a large stack of closely written pages. There were ink stains on the heels of her hands. Her brown hair was haphazardly fastened into a knot, and she wore a plain gown of dark figured calico. "Well, if mama suspects that there is any difficulty she will fall into hysterics. She spent most of dinner talking of how Miss Spry's thirty thousand pounds is to be spent—on a ball, on adding a conservatory, and on hiring more servants and a French maid for me."

He snorted. "It certainly will not. It will be spent to redeem the mortgages and put the estate to rights. Why is she talking of a ball? And why does she wish you to have a French maid?"

She sighed. "She said that I look a quiz. She said that I always look a quiz and that I have humiliated her long enough. She said that Great Aunt Theodosia has turned me into a bluestocking, that bluestockings are ladies who are too lazy to do their duty and marry and bear children, and that she will not suffer to have me lolling about imagining that I am a writer. Oh, and that if I am still thinking of Mr. West I may think again. It was a perfectly lovely meal."

Keynsham frowned. "Have you been crying?"

"No." She looked down at her papers.

Keynsham stared into the fire. He would have to ensure that their mother stopped scapegoating Pomona... and that his sister's future was a happy one. But how?

A little over a year before—just after Keynsham had met Miss Ryder, in fact, and just before the death of the fifth viscount—Pomona had announced that she had fallen in love and wished to marry. The happy man was to be Mr. Gabriel West. He was the stepson of Sir Randolph Graham, M.P. and aspired to a career in politics himself. And he'd been part of Keynsham's circle of friends since Cambridge.

But when Lady Alford learned of the attachment, she was furious. West had good prospects but little money. And Sir Randolph was only a recently-created knight, and not wealthy. She called West a fortune hunter, and ordered Lord Alford to forbid the marriage.

The couple eloped—but their disappearance was discovered after only a few hours. Lady Alford sent Keynsham after them with the promise that if Pomona would come back to London, she and West could be married properly, and all would be forgiven.

But that was a lie. When Keynsham brought Pomona back, Lady Alford had punished her. "Gretna Green! How *common*! I shall never forgive her. *Never!* I only pray that this may be hushed up." And in just three days she'd had a weeping Pomona packed onto the next ship for Ostend, on her way to live with their Great Aunt Theodosia in Augsburg, Germany. Keynsham had tried to prevent it. But Lord Alford, who found the entire matter tedious, refused to intervene.

And then, only a week later, Lord Alford had died unexpectedly, after a night of heavy drinking at Cheltenham, where he'd traveled for the races. The family solicitor had paid the new Lord Alford an urgent visit. Learning for the first time of his father's mismanagement, he'd been plunged into a desperate scramble to save the estate.

Meanwhile, if Lady Alford gave any thought to her daughter at all, it was to imagine her in a most miserable European exile—perhaps not *exactly* like the Prisoner of Chillon, but... well... not entirely *unlike* him, either.

Eventually, however, disturbing information began to filter back to London. Instead of starvation and sorrow, it seemed that Pomona's days were filled with concerts, literary *salons*, and dressage lessons on a very pretty Hanoverian mare. Lady Theodosia had taken her great-niece to Salzburg. They had attended a lecture by someone called Mr. Goethe.

Lady Alford made inquiries, and learned that he was German who had had several children out of wedlock. "It is not suitable!" She'd stormed into Keynsham's study, waving a letter from an acquaintance who was visiting Germany. "Theodosia is *spoiling* her! I did not send Pomona to Augsburg to *enjoy* herself!"

Keynsham had looked up from the ledger books with a sigh. "What can you wish me to do, ma'am? Forbid her to smile?"

Lady Alford applied a handkerchief to her face and pretended to cry. "It was your father's fondest wish that she be well married!" (If Lord Alford had ever given a thought to his daughter, it was news to Keynsham.) "It is very hard for me now that he is gone, and... and I am a widow! Besides, Pomona must have a London season. I only want what is best for *her*! It is my duty! I am her *mother*!"

Despite Keynsham's misgivings—not to mention the seasickness involved in a winter crossing of the North Sea—she sent for Pomona and brought her back to England.

Keynsham had been worried about his sister's low mood ever since. "I still do not understand why she is talking of a ball. She knows that we must be very careful with our expenses at the moment."

Pomona sighed. "She says that I *must* have one for my come-out. But my friends came out last year or the year before—and are married now, besides."

"Well, that does not signify. You will not be the first lady to make her debut late, after a death in the family."

"But I do not want a ball at all! *She* is the one who wants a ball. All I want is for her to leave me in peace so that I may finish my book—and to stop throwing West in my face. I never wish to see him again in my life! I am sick of his very name!"

"But West is not to blame for—"

"Yes, he *is*. And that is the last I will say about it." She gathered her papers and stalked to the door. "Good *night*."

* * *

For five generations Alford House had been the home of the Viscounts Alford. Yet as he toiled up the sweeping marble staircase, his body bruised and aching, Keynsham wondered how much longer the family could afford to live in it.

Once, he'd been an optimist—a believer that hard work could solve any problem. But a year of sifting through the rat's nest of bills that his father had left behind, trying to understand exactly how bad things were, had ground him down.

He found his bedroom in near darkness, the curtains still open. The fog was as thick as ever. The streetlamps were dim orbs illuminating nothing, and the other side of the street had all but vanished in the dense mist.

He was about to turn away when he had the sudden premonition that someone was out there in the dark watching the house. The intuition was so strong that he froze. *There.* At the mouth of the alley across the street, a shadow moved—the corner of a well-cut greatcoat, perhaps.

He didn't know why, but he had no doubt that it was Wilkes. He burst out of his room at a run—his aches temporarily forgotten—and charged down the stairs. He nearly skidded across the entry hall floor, flung open the front door, and was down the steps and nearly at the gate before he even had time to think. Did he hear footsteps—or only the echo of his own pounding feet?

He came to a stop, listening. His pulse was pounding in his ears. "Your lordship!" A lantern bobbed down the steps, borne by Martin, the first footman. "What has happened?"

The lantern illuminated nothing but swirling white vapor. Yet there was a charge in the air—the same sense of watchful malice that he'd felt in Grosvenor Square. The last time he'd seen Wilkes, the man had been holding a pistol. And the lantern made him—or rather, Martin—an easy target.

"Nothing. That is, I thought that I saw something. Let us go back inside."

Martin checked the locks. "Old Partridge thought that he saw someone hanging about the stables—not long before your lordship returned. But when he went to check, there was no one."

"I see. Thank you."

He went back upstairs. It could be coincidence, of course. Or it could have been Wilkes. If he'd traced Keynsham here already, he was dangerous indeed.

The only consolation was that if he'd been lurking outside Alford House, he hadn't followed them to Grafton Street.

* * *

The bruises on his ribcage and lower back throbbed as he sank into the steamy water of his bath and closed his eyes. His valet, Rogers, took his ruined jacket—with exclamations of dismay over his bruised and swollen face—and left him alone at last. His mind was suddenly overwhelmed with exhaustion.

When he spoke with Miss Ryder tomorrow, he must be careful to make no more references to things that she'd said over a year ago on the night that he'd met her. It would make him seem... unhinged. Obsessed. Sad, even.

He covered his eyes with his hand. Well, he'd brought this upon himself. He was the one who'd allowed himself to moon over Miss Ryder—even when he'd known that it was a bad idea.

It had begun on a night not long after his father's sudden death, when he'd discovered a wad of unpaid bills hidden in the back of an old ledger book—which itself had been hidden behind another book at the back of a shelf in the study.

He'd sat smoothing the bills with his hand, mentally reeling. It appeared that the fifth viscount had been single-handedly keeping the capitol's jewelers in business. Garrard. Charman. Grey's. Antrobus. Rundell, Bridge and Rundell. Every one of them was owed hundreds—if not thousands—of guineas.

He began mechanically sorting the bills into stacks. One part of his mind kept a running tally of the total. And the other... well, the other wandered into a tempting thought: What would it be like to simply close his eyes, go to sleep and simply... not wake up again? Would it be so very bad?

After all, there could be no shame in dying in his sleep. No one could blame him for that. Instead, they'd shake their heads and say how sad it was that he'd been driven into an early grave. He'd be buried respectably in the Alford family vault—not in the unsanctified corner of the churchyard with the suicides and the un-baptized infants, the way he would be if—oh, just for example—he were to put a pistol in his mouth...

He propped his head on his hands, closed his eyes, and prayed earnestly for the mercy of sweet oblivion.

But for some reason, instead of Death, the figure who appeared in his mind was... Miss Ryder.

He wondered later if his exhaustion had been so great that he'd actually drifted off to sleep sitting at his desk. If he had, in those few moments, slipped into the most vivid dream of his life. He found himself back in the long-ago inn yard in which he and Miss Ryder had said goodbye to each other. The chaos of shouting ostlers and porters, clattering hooves, and impatient passengers seemed to surround them once again. And once again, she threw her arms about him and kissed him.

He could have sworn that something happened as her lips met his. Strength seemed to flow into him. His whole body felt lighter—even warmer. She put her mouth to his ear and spoke one word: "Courage."

His eyes flew open. He returned to reality with a jolt. What in God's name...? He was still seated at his desk, the candles burning low. But the warmth of her embrace seemed to linger. The painfully tight muscles in his shoulders and neck had loosened. He felt, for the first time in weeks, as though there were some tiny chance that he might actually survive this.

Over the months, the fantasy Miss Ryder became the one person in whom he could safely confide. And what had begun as mental relief became a habit. He seemed powerless to banish her from his thoughts. She was always with him. She always laughed at his jokes. She *believed* in him.

Was he going mad? Well, maybe a little... or a lot. Still, having an imaginary friend was better than blowing his brains out. And by the time he realized that was making himself more—not less—lonely, it was already too late. He wanted Miss Ryder—and only Miss Ryder.

And that was the reason that his fantasies turned... heated.

He'd imagine what she would say if she could see his latest awful discovery. "My father sold off three Vermeers—and yet he bought his mistress a diamond and sapphire parure and did not pay the bill," he'd tell her, for instance.

The fantasy Miss Ryder wouldn't flinch. Instead of wringing her hands, she'd lighten the moment with a teasing reply. "Indeed, darling? But you would do the very same for me, I have no doubt." The candlelight would catch the soft curve of her cheek as her dimples flashed.

He'd say... hmm, what would he say? In his fantasies he always thought of a witty rejoinder. So, he'd say that yes, of course he would—if only his father had left him with so much as Vermeer to sell.

She would say that she did not long for jewels—because she already had him. And he would say that she was the most beautiful woman in the world—with or without a matching tiara, necklace, earrings, bracelet, and shoulder clasps.

"Shoulder clasps!" she'd tease. "You did not tell me that there were *shoulder clasps*. That puts rather a different face on things, I must admit."

"Is that so?" He'd rise from his chair, draw her to him, and kiss her soft lips until her breathing hitched and her body was pliant against his. "But if you were wearing shoulder clasps, I might not be able to do this." And he'd kiss his way down her neck and begin to ease her gown from her shoulders.

"That would be terrible," she'd breathe.

"Yes. It *would* be terrible." He'd push her back onto

the desk, scattering the cursed papers to the floor. His lips would travel from her neck to her shoulders as he rucked her skirts and petticoat upward, his hand traveling over the soft skin of her thighs until...

Good God. This had to stop. He snapped back to reality and climbed out of the bath. He would never have taken such liberties with the fantasy Miss Ryder if he'd known that he would see the real Miss Ryder again.

And now she was here. And he would see her again tomorrow. And he was no longer free to claim her.

Chapter Six

"You play piano?"

"Yes."

"Speak French?"

"My French is passable."

"Arithmetic? Geography? History? Needlework?"

"I—I believe that I am reasonably furnished with information and accomplishments."

"Then, Miss"—she glanced down at the letter—"Ryder, tell me: Why do you not seek employment as a governess? I could send you to speak with at least two ladies in need of governesses this very day! Families in the very first circles of society! Elegant houses! French cooks! Liberal terms! Everything that is comfortable and fashionable!"

The proprietress of the employment agency, Mrs. Lewes, was a middle-aged lady with crimped grey hair peeking from beneath a claret-colored velvet turban. "Surely you realize that a lady's companion is a position all too often filled by poor relations—or friends of friends. The allowance paid is always small. There is no security, no"—she waved her hand—"*prestige.* A governess, on the other hand, has a recognized standing."

"I had not considered it," she lied.

"Well then, I advise you to consider it now."

"I—I have no training as a governess."

"Nor do most young ladies, when they become governesses!" Mrs. Lewes was beginning to look annoyed. "Think! Your position in the family would be respected. Your wage would be fair. Sundays off! And if you are afraid of the hard work of managing children—well, I have personally seen all too many ladies' companions treated worse than servants! Shouted at, expected to work without respite, and to run errands in all weathers. Why did you leave your position?"

"Mrs. Allenby had an attack of kidney stones. Her physician suggested the spa at Harrogate. She went to stay with one of her nephews. His wife said that there was no room for me."

"Ah. Meaning that she did not want a pretty young lady in the house." She looked knowing. "You quite prove my point, Miss Ryder. You quite prove my point! A lady's companion is in a precarious position. But a governess—ah, a governess may make a life for herself. You must consider your future security."

Future security? She suppressed a bitter laugh. After yesterday, she no longer hoped for security... or a future.

"Perhaps you do not fully comprehend the advantages that you are so heedlessly dismissing. I shall read to you from some of the letters which I have recently received." She turned and began searching through the cubbyholes of a cabinet pushed against the wall behind her. "Why, a Mrs. Abernathy wrote to me only this week! Her letter is just here. Four girls on Cavendish Square. Only imagine the elegance! *Cavendish Square!*"

The second floor office was above a fashionable linen draper, and the murmur of voices rose through the floorboards. Celia's eyes fell on the desk, where an opened letter lay partially concealed by other papers. "Companion," she read, in a crabbed black scrawl. Her hand shot out, twitched the letter from its position in the stack, and slipped it into her reticule before she could think about right and wrong.

"Here we are!" Mrs. Lewes turned to face her, waving a letter in the air. "A charming schoolroom—new furbished and carpeted, and with a fireplace! Use of a piano, and Wednesday and Sunday afternoons quite at your own disposal! Really, Miss Ryder, if *this* is not up to your standards, I cannot imagine what would be. *Cavendish Square!*"

"I—I do not like children." That was another lie. How many lies would she have to tell?

"*Do not like children?*" Mrs. Lewes stared at her. "Is *that* all? *That* is scarcely a reason not to be a governess! I myself was a governess for many years—and I loathe them. What I am explaining to you, Miss Ryder, is that you have yourself to think of." She spread her hands. "Look around! I was able to put money by from my salary and open my own employment agency!"

She felt as though she could scarcely breathe. "I—I am afraid that I simply cannot."

"*Well.*" Mrs. Lewes refolded the letter of reference and handed it back to her. "I must be frank, Miss Ryder. I do not at all care for obstinate young women. I shall not help you. My fee is paid by employers when I fill a position. You have wasted my time. Good day."

She'd been dismissed. "Thank you," she choked, and rushed down the stairs to the street.

The cold fog was just as thick as it had been when she'd slipped away from Grafton Street early in the morning. She felt a fool. Mrs. Lewes had only been trying to give her advice. And of course, it would be preferable to be a governess in Cavendish Square! Yet Wilkes's reach had grown long. If he were to find her, the safety of any children in her charge would be at risk. The possibility was too terrible to contemplate.

Her vision swimming with tears that she tried to blink back, she followed a pair of ladies into the busy linen drapery. At least there, breathing the sweet smell of new cottons, she could take a moment to collect herself.

There were other employment offices, she reminded herself. And she had the purloined letter too—though she would wait until she was alone to read it.

But her fears had come tumbling out of the corners of her mind where she usually crammed them away. Her father was dead. Her family's money was gone. Her efforts to recover from these blows were but pitiful flailing—the struggles of a fly hopelessly caught in a spider's web.

And the spider was Wilkes.

She stepped out of the way of a pair of fashionable ladies hurrying past her to examine a bolt of striped damask. Richly colored velveteen... airy printed muslins... deep laces... At one time, she would have loved to visit this shop. But she must not linger here now. She must go on to the next agency on her list.

She only hoped that Keynsham would understand why she'd left—and forgive her.

"Excuse me." A bosomy lady pushed past her, jostling Celia out of her sad reverie. "It is *that* bolt of muslin that I mean. No, not *that* one. The figured one, in the window! With the puce sprigs, at eight shillings the yard. No—the *other* one with the puce sprigs!" The harassed clerk finally landed on the correct bolt and lifted it out, leaving a narrow gap in the crowded window display.

In the gap there was an eye. And the eye was staring directly at Celia.

She jerked back in fright. The eye disappeared.

Her heart began to pound. It couldn't be! Anyone might be looking into the shop. Besides, there was no way that they could have found her.

She edged toward the side of the large bow window. From this angle she could see past the bolts of gaily printed muslins and out onto the pavement. There was a man there, his nose nearly touching the glass.

He was the smaller of the two thugs who'd followed her yesterday.

At once she saw how foolish she'd been to underestimate Wilkes. If only she'd listened to Keynsham and stayed in the house! Now that it was too late, she realized that the independence that she'd been forced to develop had led her into a dangerous situation.

She tried to think. Well-dressed ladies, followed by maids or footmen carrying parcels, bustled in and out of the shop. Perhaps she could attach herself to a group of ladies as they were leaving and escape that way.

"May I help you, miss?" It was the same clerk who'd pulled the bolt of muslin out of the window. He stared down his long nose at her.

"No, thank you." She turned away, hoping that he couldn't tell that she was terrified.

"Are you certain that you require no assistance?"

"Yes, thank you. I... I am merely browsing."

"I see." He continued to stare at her. She felt her face warm. He was watching her... as though he thought that she were about to steal something!

For a moment, she considered telling him that she was hiding from a man outside and asking him to help her. But this was London, and she looked poor. If she seemed likely to cause trouble, he would simply throw her out.

"Excuse me. *Excuse* me!" A lady glared at Celia as though she were purposely monopolizing the shop clerk. "I require five yards of the rifle green granite cloth."

"Very good, madam." With a last glare at Celia, he was forced to go assist the customer.

She checked the window again. The man was still there. Worse, he'd been joined by Dick Fenton! Her knees went weak with fear. So much for her idea that she could somehow slip away. If she stayed here much longer Wilkes's entire gang would be assembled on the pavement.

She edged backward until she was pressed, uncomfortably, against the shelves that held more bolts of fabric along the wall. Her hand was at her throat. She tried to force herself to breathe—to think.

"Miss, if you are not going to buy something, I must ask you to leave." The clerk was back—this time with another man.

"I—I am here to look at laces."

The two men exchanged a look. The clerk pursed his lips. "We have nothing for you here."

In the background she heard the bells on the door jingle. Suddenly there was a hand on her arm. She leapt sideways with a half-suppressed scream.

"There you are." Keynsham stared down at the two men, his eyes narrowed. "I hope that you are finished your shopping?"

She couldn't speak. She couldn't breathe. She'd been so certain that he was one of the thugs that her voice had gone.

"Good day… your… lordship?" The clerk took in his impeccably tailored jacket and gulped. "Why, if this young lady…"

"My cousin."

"We are honored indeed!" He twisted his face into an obsequious smile. "May I suggest that you may wish to examine the fine muslins that arrived only this morning from Manchester? Just twelve shillings the yard."

Keynsham glanced down at Celia. Their eyes met. In the midst of everything she felt, again, the sensation of rightness that she'd been trying to tell herself wasn't real. It rang through her like the chiming of a bell. For one deranged moment, she wanted nothing more than to throw her arms around his neck, right here in this shop, and kiss him.

"Thank you. I am afraid that we have another appointment. How *unfortunate* it is that you were not able to be helpful to her whilst she had the time." He tucked her hand into the crook of his arm and turned toward the door.

Everything seemed to slow down. The clerk rushed ahead to hold the door. The manager was bowing and saying something about hoping to be of service in the future. Keynsham's coachman was only two or three yards away across the pavement, holding the horses' heads. The thugs fell back in dismay, as though they expected Keynsham to attack them right there in the Strand.

He handed her into the glossy carriage, sprang in after her, and shut the door. A moment later, they were moving off down the busy street. She put her hands flat on the leather seat and tried to breathe.

She wasn't sure how Keynsham had found her—but he'd rescued her yet again. She must still be in shock, because all she could do was stare at him. The bruises and swelling on his face weren't as bad as she'd feared. But his ordinarily pleasant, open countenance was tight with fury. She opened her mouth to speak, changed her mind, and shut it again.

"You *lied* to me." His voice—that cultured rumble—was the crack of a whip.

"I—I..."

"I asked you to stay—to wait for me. You said that you would. You *lied*." His eyes were blazing. "How could you put yourself at risk in this way? Do you not understand the danger in which you find yourself?"

"I did not lie." As soon as she said it, she knew that her argument was childish. "I did not agree to wait for you. Not in... well, not in so many words."

His eyes narrowed. "That is nothing but a lie by omission, and we both know it. And a lie by omission is as damaging as any other lie. Why, my father..." He broke off. "I do not care to be lied to. Not by you. Not by anyone."

She swallowed. In all the conversations that she'd imagined them having, never once had she thought that Keynsham might become angry with her.

"If I had not come looking for you this morning—and if I had not chanced to recognize those thugs loitering outside the shop—what would have happened?"

"I—I do not know."

"Yes, you do. The moment that you attempted to walk away from that shop, those men would have snatched you."

"I… well, they would have tried."

"*Tried!* What would you have done to stop them? Do you not see what a foolish risk you ran? How did they know that you were there? Were they following you?"

She stared down at her hands, twisting in her lap. "I—I do not know. I do not think so."

"Well, perhaps you will tell me how many more times I will have to come to your rescue before you will admit that you need help—and trust me enough to tell me what is happening."

She fell silent. The carriage smelled of the fine leather that covered the squabs. It was so well-sprung that they seemed to float over the cobblestones. Keynsham was rich. He would never be able to understand how she'd arrived in this position. And he was already injured, and Wilkes had almost shot him—because of her.

"I do not wish to involve you. I could not bear it if…"

The carriage lurched violently. The coachman shouted something. There was a crash and a jolt as something struck the side of it. She gave an involuntary little scream.

"What the devil?" Keynsham lunged for the window but was thrown back against the seat as something collided with the carriage's side again. "Is this fellow mad? Can he not see us in the fog?" He pushed down the window. "You there!"

Abruptly the other carriage came level with them. Someone inside shoved down its window... and pointed a pistol at them.

She couldn't move. She couldn't breathe. All she could do was stare at the black circle of the pistol's muzzle. There wasn't the slightest doubt in her mind about who was holding it.

The whip snapped and their carriage leapt forward, swinging perilously as they took a corner too quickly. She was thrown hard against its side. Someone was shouting.

The carriage accelerated through the traffic and the fog, and the shouts were lost behind them. A low, stone wall that she recognized as the abutments of a bridge flashed past. The carriage swayed violently as they took another sharp corner. She felt sick. Keynsham reached across to grip her hand. "Once we are out of this traffic, we can outrun him."

"Where—where are we?"

"Just south of the river."

They swerved right, then left. Now the road seemed wider, and they were going faster. A gunshot rang out. She clapped her hand to her mouth to suppress a scream. Keynsham flung himself on her, pushing her flat on the seat.

A moment later, there was another shot, and the

glass of the rear window shattered. She shut her eyes tight. Wilkes would kill them both… and it was all her fault.

Keynsham cupped the side of her face with his hand. "Miss Ryder. Look at me. Miss Ryder."

She forced herself to open her eyes. His face was only inches from hers. "Stay down. Miss Ryder? Listen to me. *Stay down.*"

The carriage tilted sickeningly as the coachman turned right again. They must surely be on two wheels. At any moment they would crash. They would die in a carriage accident—exactly like her father.

Silent tears trickled from the corners of her eyes. Each moment seemed to consist of tiny, precise details: Keynsham's weight upon her. The cedarwood smell of his woolen jacket and the buttons digging into her breastbone. The warm strength of his body. The glittering shards of glass on the seat all around her. The pounding of the horses' hooves and the rattles and squeaks of the carriage.

They slowed unexpectedly and swung hard right again. One window went momentarily dark. The carriage's side scraped against something. They came to an abrupt stop.

For a moment, all was unnaturally quiet, apart from her pulse pounding in her ears and her own sobbing breathing.

Then, far too close, she heard hoofbeats. "Damn your eyes, Begley, you useless bastard! You lost them!"

It was Wilkes's voice. She shut her eyes again in terror.

"It's this cursed fog, boss!"

"It's not the fog! It's your incompetence! You turned the wrong way at the last corner."

"I'll catch them up, boss."

"You're damned right you will—or you'll regret it!"

They lay motionless. A second later, Wilkes's coachman spoke to the horses. "Walk on."

The sound of the carriage wheels receded. "Miss Ryder." Keynsham's thumb stroked the side of her cheek. "Miss Ryder?"

She opened her eyes.

"They have gone. They did not see us." His thumb continued to caress her face. "You are safe."

Her eyes focused on him. She found herself searching his face—from his warm blue eyes to his firm chin, from the livid bruise on his cheekbone to the cut on one side of his lower lip. His big hand was still cradling her cheek. His eyes fell to her lips. She knew that he was about to kiss her. And suddenly, she was drowning in a wave of desire. Her shaking hands rose by themselves, as though she would pull him down to her...

There was a thump as the coachman leapt off the box. Keynsham jumped, pulled back, and sat up. The carriage door banged open. "Your lordship! We lost 'em!" The young coachman was beaming, silhouetted against the grey light.

"You mean *you* lost them." Keynsham turned to help her up. "The credit is yours, Young. You have saved all our lives."

She brushed shards of glass off her pelisse. Her hands were still shaking—though whether that was because of the ordeal of the chase, or because she'd almost kissed Keynsham, she couldn't be certain.

"Careful." Keynsham handed her down out of the carriage.

They were in what seemed to be a muddy wasteland, surrounded by an eerie maze of red brick walls that rose into the mist. "Where—where are we?" Her voice shook.

"It appears to be some sort of building site. And we must be somewhere in Kent."

Oh. The brick walls were the unfinished shells of buildings, missing their roofs and windows. Young had driven them through a narrow gap between two buildings and hidden the carriage behind. The deep, crisscrossing ruts left in the mud by the workers' carts concealed the new ones made by the carriage.

All was silent. Keynsham, peering through the fog toward what must be a road, let out a low whistle. "They were only a few yards away."

And then, from the fog, came the sound of footfalls.

Chapter Seven

Keynsham flattened himself against the side of the coach, drawing Miss Ryder with him and placing his arm across her body. He'd protect her with his life, if it came to that.

But first he was going to kill that bastard Wilkes.

The footsteps stopped. Whoever was coming had seen the horses and carriage. There was a long, tense pause. A man spoke. "Who's there?"

Miss Ryder had one hand over her mouth. Tears of terror stood in her eyes. Young, on his other side, already had his fists raised.

"I said, *who's there*?" The footfalls began again, squelching through the mud. One of the horses snorted and stamped. He heard the man pat it. "Steady there. Aren't *you* a fine fellow!"

Keynsham frowned. That didn't seem like something that one of Wilkes's thugs would say.

"Good God!" The man came around the front of the carriage, saw them and leapt back, clapping a hand to his chest. "What the…?"

He was tall, broad shouldered, and wore a blue workman's tunic. His gaze traveled suspiciously from the fine matched pair of greys, to Miss Ryder, to the long gouges in the side of the expensive carriage, and finally to Keynsham's bruised face. "Who the devil are *you*?"

At this, Young took offense. "Now see here..."

The man noticed the coat of arms on the coach door. He studied it, then let out a whistle. "Well, I'll be! *Lord* something, eh? I thought you was one of them damned banker fellows—begging your pardon, your ladyship!" He doffed his cap, made Miss Ryder a surprisingly passable bow, threw back his head, and began to laugh. "Was I about to give you a piece of my mind!"

Keynsham felt himself beginning to relax. It would be almost impossible not to, around this man. "I assure you that I am no banker."

"No more you are, your lordship! No more you are! Oh, this is something! Why, afore I saw you wasn't one of *them*, I was fit to knock you down! Can you credit it? Me, knocking down a lord?" He shook his head. "Ah, well. But none of us has been paid, you see."

Considering everything that had already happened today, Keynsham wouldn't have expected that a conversation with a random man in an abandoned construction site would be the most confusing thing of all. "Paid? Paid by whom?"

"Them fellows what put up the money for all these houses. They've scarpered. That slick banker come round this morning. 'Money's gone,' he says. 'No wages for you, lads.'" He put his cap back on. "The other fellows didn't know what to say, so I spoke up. 'In that case,' I says, 'what gives you the right to be here?' He saw what I was driving at, and took himself off in a hurry."

Keynsham frowned. "Do you mean to say that the investors in this project have disappeared without paying you?"

"Aye—you've hit on it, your lordship. That they haven't. Not for the past fortnight. I only came back to fetch me tools. Who'll finish building these houses now, I'm sure I can't say. And with families going without roofs over their heads too! 'Tis a sin."

Keynsham noticed the tools scattered about the yard—a mason's hod, a wheelbarrow half full of bricks, a ladder. Without the slightest regard for precedent the man stuck out his hand. "Downey. Tom Downey."

"I am Charles Keynsham—Viscount Alford."

They shook hands. Downey's grip was almost painfully firm. "*Viscount*, eh?" His eyes glinted with amusement. "Well, well. Never seen one of *them* before."

"Are you the foreman? What is the name of this place?"

"Foreman? Me?" Downey guffawed. "No. I'm just a mason—though they had me checking the plans, seeing as I can read and write. These here new streets is what they're calling Grange Grove. Or as I call it, 'No grange, no grove.'"

It was an inconvenient time to have an idea. Nevertheless, Keynsham had one. "Are these all to be houses?"

"Aye. This terrace is twenty-eight houses—and was to be finished within the fortnight too. Other side of the street, thirty-two." He waved a muscular arm. "And over yonder, three more streets and a square was to be built next. I've copies of the plans—all drawn up official-like. Hundreds of houses. Them money men talked a big game, all right. All us masons and carpenters and glaziers and roofers was to be in work building for at least the next year or two."

The idea was beginning to take shape in Keynsham's brain. He tried to push it away. It persisted. "What does this terrace of houses require?"

"Not much. Roof tiles and windows and doors. Kitchen stoves. Plaster. Paint." Downey shrugged.

Miss Ryder must be inspiring him... because suddenly Keynsham's mind was filled with thoughts and plans. Gentlemen did not engage in trade. But as it happened, there was a very large asterisk next to that statement when it came to property development...

Of course, this wasn't some stately Knightsbridge square of townhouses for the wealthy. Nor was he standing on a tract of land that he'd conveniently inherited in Mayfair. And he'd have to persuade someone to loan him money...

But he could do this. He knew it. "I should like to discuss this with you further, Mr. Downey, but I cannot leave my, ah... her ladyship standing in this mud. Here is my card. Tell me your direction, and I shall be back to speak with you."

Downey turned his card over in his large, callused hands. "Discuss what? Begging your pardon, but if you will speak plain, I'd appreciate it. I've had all I can take of double talk and no pay."

"I—I may be able to involve myself in financing the building of these houses."

"*Financing*, eh? And here I thought we just needed money." Then Downey's tanned face split into a wide white grin. “I’m joking! Well, well. Just when I told the missus that money doesn’t fall from the sky, here you are to prove me wrong, I suppose.”

Keynsham hoped that he wouldn’t disappoint him. “I cannot promise that it will come off.”

Downey folded his massive arms and studied him. “No more you can. But I’ve a good feeling about you, Lord Something.” He clapped him on the shoulder—a friendly blow that nearly sent Keynsham staggering sideways. “Any man with bruises like those ones doesn’t back down from a fight.”

* * *

They trudged down the road. Young led the horses. Keynsham and Miss Ryder followed behind the carriage. One of the horses had lost a shoe in the deep mud of the building site, and they couldn’t risk laming him. Downey had directed them toward a farrier a mile or so farther south, where they could have him re-shod before the drive back to London. According to Keynsham’s watch, it was already mid-afternoon, although the thick fog blotted out the sun.

Miss Ryder was silent.

The moment in the carriage weighed on Keynsham. He’d nearly kissed her. He’d nearly imposed his private fantasy version of Miss Ryder on the very real, very vulnerable woman walking next to him. What was wrong with him? He wasn’t free to court her. He was as good as engaged!

Yet even now his palm seemed imprinted with the warmth and curve of Miss Ryder’s cheek. And something had shifted in his thoughts, too. His mind—dull sludge for over a year—was suddenly alight with ideas and plans and possibilities. How he would get the money to finish building the houses, he didn't know—yet. But now that Miss Ryder was here, he felt as though he could overcome almost any difficulty.

Except, of course, the difficulty concerning Miss Spry.

A carriage was coming up from behind. He stiffened. There was no chance that they'd lost Wilkes and his thugs for good. No, he'd still be hunting them, looking for a chance to strike again. Now that they were on foot, they were easy targets.

But the carriage passed them without slowing. Keynsham let out a breath that he hadn't known he was holding.

"You were right." Miss Ryder startled him by speaking. "I—I ought to have waited in the house as you asked me to do. This is all my fault." Her voice broke.

"*This*? This is not your fault! Miss Ryder, I..." How he wished that he could tell her how he felt! "No. Wilkes is a madman! He fired on us on a public roadway! Unless... does he have some reason to believe that he may operate with impunity?"

Out of the corner of his eye, he saw her clamp her lips together, as though she were afraid that words might slip out.

"Will you not tell me why he is pursuing you? What is it that he wants?"

She shook her head. Another carriage passed them. They had to get off this road. "Miss Ryder..."

"I do not know! I did not know that he was still looking for me until yesterday. It does not make sense.

I…" She stopped herself, as though she'd already said too much.

The carriage in front of them slowed. "This must be the place," Young called back.

The blacksmith's workshop was a low building with a gated yard outside. Unfortunately, the farrier—according to the apprentice who ran out to meet them—had gone to a wake that afternoon and wouldn't be back until after nightfall.

Keynsham and Young unhitched the horses, examined them, and found another shoe loose.

"His lordship can stay at the inn," suggested the apprentice.

"Inn? Does it have horses for hire?"

"No, your lordship. For that you have to go to The Bullock, where the stagecoaches stop. It's three miles away—over to the London road."

"Ah." He looked at Miss Ryder. His heart was racing. He'd have more time with her.

She avoided his eyes.

"Well. The inn it is, then."

* * *

They left the carriage and horses in the farrier's stables and walked through the tiny village to the inn—a square, whitewashed building whose front wall directly abutted the road. At first, a servant told them that they were full for the night. But when Young made a point to refer to him as *Lord Alford*, a room suddenly became available "for you and her ladyship."

Young said that he would see to the horses and sleep in the carriage, and went into the inn's snug for an early dinner and a pint or two.

Keynsham didn't dare look at Miss Ryder as they were led upstairs, away from the noisy public rooms. It was this or nothing. She folded her arms as she surveyed the low-ceilinged room. "I shall sleep in the chair. I grew accustomed to sitting up with Mrs...." She stopped, as though she were keeping a state secret.

"I insist that you take the bed. I may just as easily sleep on the floor."

She sighed and took off her pelisse. "I shall take the chair."

Before they could resolve the argument, several inn servants arrived with a meal. The fare looked much better than they could have expected at most coaching inns, and explained the crowded dining room below. Soon, the small table was loaded with plates of buttered new peas and roasted parsnips, sliced ham, pickles, a salmagundi of cold chicken, chopped boiled eggs, capers, and anchovies, and more.

When they were alone, he piled food onto a plate for her and tried not to think of all the things that he wished he could say. He wished that he could promise her that he would always be by her side. That he would keep her safe, and that she need not face Wilkes—or anyone else—alone, ever again.

But he couldn't—not truthfully. For a moment, he imagined the empty promises that his father must have made to his many conquests, and was revolted to realize how easy it would be to lie. He cleared his throat. "Well. Let us eat."

She picked up her fork, but rather than eating,

pushed some of the pickled beets a half inch across her plate. "He… he knows who you are. I am certain of it. And he must have worked out that I—" She broke off. "That is to say, he seemed to know where I might go next."

"Yes. I believe that you are correct. I believe that he may have been watching my house last night."

She gasped. "*Last night*? But that is everything that I… How can you be so calm?"

"I am quite capable of taking care of myself." *And you too*, he wished he could add. "You may have noticed that Wilkes did not win today. Or last night."

"But we did not *win*! We barely escaped!"

He shrugged. "Winning and escaping are often the same—at least, in war. I do not mind a fight, Miss Ryder. I should have thought that you would have realized that by now. What I do mind is seeing a bully get his way merely because no one is willing to stand up to him."

Her eyes flashed. "This is not some—some entertaining diversion from your life. He is *dangerous*."

"Yes. So I have gathered." He poured some wine into her glass, met her eyes, and gave up his resolution not to speak of the past. "Miss Ryder, when I met you, you did not strike me as a lady who would give up easily."

"Well, that was because I was a fool."

"Perhaps you were not foolish, but brave."

She pursed her lips in a momentarily bitter moue. "And perhaps it was easier to be brave when I did not know that he would pursue me, and that even after a year of hiding and…" She broke off and ate a butter-drenched parsnip.

He didn't think that she was aware that she was eating. Well, so much the better. "He is a thug. He cannot be allowed to dictate what you can and cannot do."

She set down her wine glass. "If you think that Wilkes is a mere thug, you are much mistaken. You may be certain that powerful men in London are already in his debt."

"Then he is a moneylender?"

Her face grew guarded. "He is many things. He has always been… well, a man of great ambition and no scruples."

"Ah. Then he is either a crime lord or a politician."

Unlike his fantasy Miss Ryder, she didn't laugh at his joke. "I shall say nothing else."

"You make it difficult to help you."

"There are some situations that cannot be helped." She ate some salmagundi. "You would not understand."

"Are you certain of that? You are not the only one in this room who is in a difficult spot."

"Oh yes? What can be your complaint? Gaming debts?" Her tone was caustic.

"No, in fact." He took a deep breath. "Well. As you will tell me so little about your situation, I will tell you something about mine instead—something that almost no one knows: My father, the late fifth viscount, left the estate nearly bankrupt."

Her eyes widened. Slowly, she set her fork down.

"If he had not died when he did—well, even another year of his spending would have left my mother and sister with nothing. And so, since his death, I have spent nearly every waking minute attempting to rescue the estate. This… this escapade, today?" He gestured at the room. "This is the first time that I have been more than a mile or two from my desk and my ledger books in over a year."

She stared at him. "But you are a viscount. You... you drive a new carriage."

"My father ordered that carriage. It was delivered only the week before he died. And he had not paid for it. It was left to me to find the money to pay the bill."

"Oh." Her voice was small.

"I am managing to make all the payments that I must make—for now. But I must find a new source of income so that I can begin to redeem the mortgages on the farms. If the truth gets out before I can do that, the lenders will all call in their loans and my family will be ruined."

She was silent a moment. "But that proves my point."

"What point?"

"That you ought not to involve yourself in my situation! You have troubles enough of your own. You cannot afford more."

"I assure you that I am quite capable of helping you and managing my own affairs at the same time." He folded his arms. "So. It appears that we are at an impasse."

"I have not asked for your help. You cannot simply... *impose* yourself on my life." Her slightly pointed chin was quivering in indignation. "I have made my own plans."

"Really? Do those plans involve being abducted the moment that you return to London?"

She glared at him. "I shall go about things differently now that I... Well. I shall take precautions."

He opened his mouth to make a retort. But on at least one point, she was right. He had no claim upon her, and no say in her decisions.

And yet he was more and more certain that she was the only woman he could ever... No. He must not even think the word.

He stared into the small fire. This was all wrong. He ought to be able to take her into his arms, stroke her hair, kiss her face, reassure her that he'd solve all her problems, and promise her that he'd protect her for the rest of his life.

But, because he'd been stupid enough to open that library door, he couldn't.

"Have you no family that you might go to?"

"No. My mother died when I was a child. My father died last year—the day before we met, in fact."

"I am very sorry. I had no idea."

She looked down. "No." The corners of her mouth tightened for a moment. "You see, he had..." She stopped. "At any rate, I am alone."

Alone. It broke his heart to hear her say that. "And your father did not provide for you in his will?"

She stiffened. He could see that he'd hit a subject that was painful. "No." There was a silence. "I—well, I suppose that I must tell you the truth."

But then she said nothing for a long time. Splinters of light glanced off the old wavy glass of the windowpanes as someone carried a lantern across the inn yard. The window was darkening with the onset of evening and the heavy fog. "I do not know how to tell the story, or where to begin." She was hugging her own elbows. "I have never told it before."

She paused. "Perhaps I should begin by trying to

describe my father. When I was small, I—I idolized him. I thought that he must be the most important man in the world. He was so clever! So lively! So handsome and popular! But then I grew older, and I realized that he was..." She trailed off and swiped at her cheek with the back of her hand.

She was crying.

"Please—take my handkerchief."

She dabbed her face. "You may not... you may not like me very much, when you hear all of it."

"There is nothing that you could say that would make me like you less, Miss Ryder. *Nothing.*"

It was perilously close to an admission of his feelings—but there were only so many times that he could playact.

She took a shaky breath. "Then the first thing that I must tell you is that my father promised my hand in marriage to Wilkes. And the second is that my name is not Catherine Ryder."

Chapter Eight

"Promised your hand to... *Wilkes*?" His face changed slowly—from surprise, to confusion, and then to something almost like disgust.

She couldn't bear to have him look at her that way. But what else had she expected? The sordid details of her history were scarcely the sort of thing with which a viscount would be familiar.

"I did not wish to marry him, of course." Her words came out in a rush. She didn't look at Keynsham. "I had always disliked him. But my father had agreed to it, and I had never disobeyed him."

Her father had pleaded, and cried, and clutched his chest and said that his weak heart couldn't withstand the disaster that would come if she didn't marry Wilkes. They would be tossed out into the street. He would be sent to debtors' prison. He would die of the cruel treatment there—he was certain of it!

"I believed that I would be helping my father. But I did not understand..." Her face began to heat. "That is,

I had not fully considered what would be... required of me. And I could not bear..."

Her voice faltered for a moment. Keynsham was still silent. She risked one glance at him. His square jaw was set and in the gathering shadows of the small room his bruised cheekbone and cut lip looked alarming. His arms were folded, and he was gripping his own elbows, making his muscles strain against his jacket sleeves. His knuckles were white, as though he were barely restraining himself.

"Perhaps I should have explained that my father was considered the village squire. He lived in the style that he thought accorded with—well, what he thought was his importance in society. But he outran his income. I learned later that he was borrowing money."

"Of Wilkes." His voice was flat.

"I do not know when it started. But Wilkes never seemed to be far away. For the last few years, he had been spending more and more time in London with his —well, his enterprises. But he had attached himself to my father long before that, and often came to dine and spend the evening."

"*Enterprises*. He is a criminal."

"Yes. But although my father was snobbish, he treated Wilkes as an equal."

"Because he owed him money and wished to borrow more on easy terms." His tone was still expressionless.

"I suppose." When she'd been young, Wilkes had been only a figure glimpsed from a window—a loud voice late at night, a bustle in the hall departing before the arrival of her father's more respectable friends. He'd been sent away to be educated—which was surprising, as his father was merely a petty criminal. When he returned, he was dressed in the first stare of fashion, and cut a swagger about the village in a top hat of shining beaver. Gold rings flashed upon his fingers.

Both he and her father enjoyed flashy clothes, fast horses, and fine wine. They often stayed up late together, their voices growing louder as the hours passed. Sometimes she'd hold a pillow over her ears and try to pretend that Wilkes wasn't in the house. Because... well, the way he looked at her made her skin crawl.

"So. Wilkes had made money through thievery or some other racket. And then—clever enough to realize that he could make a good deal more money, at far less risk to himself—he began lending it out?"

"I know nothing of his... his business arrangements. I always kept away from him when he visited."

"I see. And so then a few years later, your father—to preserve his own comforts—bargained you away. How old were you?"

"Eighteen."

The muscles in his jaw clenched. "And how long do you believe that he had planned this?"

"Wilkes?"

"No. Your father. When do you think that your father realized that the easiest way to afford the mode of life that he enjoyed would be to sell you to a criminal?"

She went cold, then hot with shame. "You cannot... My father was a gentleman! I—I think that he simply did not realize the extent of his debt to Wilkes. He would not have..."

And yet... was it possible that he had really been so completely ignorant of his financial position?

Keynsham merely looked at her. "Many bargains are struck for marriage. Not all of them are honorable." His face was grim. "Well. But you managed to escape."

"Yes. A few days after the marriage had been agreed, Wilkes came to dine with my father. But later that evening, I heard them arguing."

"You had agreed to marry him, but you did not dine with them?"

"No. I—I had a headache. Our housekeeper, Mrs. Ryder, brought me a tray in my room. She would bring me a tray in my room whenever... *he* stayed to dine. She had never thought him suitable company." She swallowed hard. It was a relief to put the story into words. Yet it was also terrifying to tell the truth.

"And then, for some reason that I cannot understand—I can only supposed that he was drunk—my father set out very early the next morning for Bath. I did not see him leave. On the way there, his carriage overturned and he was killed. I—I had not even had the chance to tell him goodbye."

She broke off and took a breath. She didn't want to cry in front of Keynsham. "And when they came to tell me, I—I—" Despite herself, a sob was rising in her throat. She put her hand over her mouth to hold it in until she could regain some composure. "And now you will hear what a dreadful person I am. My first thought was that I—I no longer had to marry Wilkes."

The sobs broke through. She sat, her chest heaving painfully, her hands over her face. "I *know* that it was wicked of me—but I..." She stopped for a moment and swallowed. "I had prayed that I would not have to marry him. And—and then *that* happened."

Keynsham's voice was kind. "Miss Ryder, I am

certain that you are far too rational to believe that your prayers killed your father. It was his own decision to travel at night. And what he asked of you was cruel and selfish. He knew what Wilkes was. Indeed, it is clear that your housekeeper knew too. Is she the reason that you adopted the name Ryder?"

"Oh." She felt her face warm. "Well, there again, you will see that I am not... I am not a good person."

"That is not at all what I think. Indeed, I think that you are..." He broke off. There was something in his eyes that sent a sudden heat through her body. But he didn't complete his thought, and she forced the feeling away. After all, he was about to hear yet another truth about her character.

She took a shaky breath. "Mrs. Ryder has a daughter—Catherine—who was brought up and educated with her second cousins. Catherine had a position as a lady's companion. Her employer wrote her a character reference. She sent her mother a copy. Mrs. Ryder was so proud of her! Miss Ryder had been about to take another position. But a local landowner offered for her and—well, it was a most eligible situation. She married him."

He looked confused. "But what does Mrs. Ryder's daughter's marriage have to do with you?"

Her face was burning now. "I—I stole it. I stole her character reference. I told myself that she could not need it. I was desperate to escape Wilkes. I took the letter and hid it in my pocketbook. I wrote to the lady who had offered the real Miss Ryder the position and posted my letter. And as soon as it was dark, I walked to an inn on the London road to catch the stagecoach—so that I would be gone before Wilkes returned."

The hurried packing, the fear that he would come... the memory of it still made her hands shake. "I could not tell Mrs. Ryder that I was leaving, though she was as dear to me as a mother. I brought only a few clothes. I was to change coaches in London. And the following day... well, that is when we met. And that is why I had to get my pocketbook back."

"I shall never forget a moment of that night." His words seemed to strike a charge into the air of the room. They were not a declaration. But suddenly she was having trouble collecting her thoughts. Did he mean...? But that was impossible.

"What is your real name?"

She hesitated. "Talbot. Celia Talbot."

"Miss Talbot." He said it as though he were testing it. "I see. Well. There is something about this that does not make sense to me, *Miss Talbot.*"

Her heart skipped a nervous beat. "What is it?"

"You said that your father left for Bath after your marriage had been agreed. Did he intend to skip your wedding? Who was to have given you away?"

"I do not know."

He sat thinking. "It was odd and indelicate of him to leave you at such a time."

"I have never understood it myself. But he could be... impulsive. For a time, I wondered if he had changed his mind. Perhaps he meant for me not to marry Wilkes after all. Perhaps he was going to send for me, so that I might join him in Bath. Perhaps he was a kinder father than I have..." She broke off. "I do not wish to give the impression that he was unkind."

"You do not have to. He was."

Her guilt seemed to prickle her skin. "He simply... he did not think..."

"He did not think of you at all. That is plain. And the result is that you were not merely left unprotected, but that you were thrown to Wilkes—as bait."

"You are being unfair!" She rose, too agitated to sit. "He could not have known that Wilkes would..."

But that was wrong. He *had* known exactly what Wilkes was. It was simply that it had been convenient for him to pretend that he did not. Keynsham was right. Her father hadn't cared what happened to her.

The tears that she'd been fighting overwhelmed her. She turned her face away, half blinded, trying in vain to regain control of herself.

And then his hand was on her arm. "Miss Talbot. Please. I am sorry. I did not mean to... here." He put his handkerchief back into her hand. She buried her face in it and sobbed. His hand was on her back. She turned toward him. He drew her into his arms.

When her tears stopped, she found that her forehead was resting against his shoulder. There was a quiet, regular sound that she realized was the beating of his heart.

It was too late to un-think all the thoughts she'd had about him. She'd imagined being in his arms. She'd imagined kissing him. She'd told herself that it was harmless. After all, thoughts weren't real—and she would never see him again.

Only... now here he was. He wasn't a figment of her imagination. He was a flesh and blood man—warm and surprisingly gentle, considering his brutal fighting ability—and he was holding her as though she were precious.

"Miss Talbot?"

She stepped back, though somehow her hands were still resting upon his chest. "I—I do apologize. I did not mean to... to..."

"It is quite all right. I am certain that my jacket will dry by morning." His voice seemed to travel from her ears, into her spine, and down into her lower belly.

"I am sorry for lying about my name." She wasn't certain why she'd said it—except that she had to say something. It was too awkward not to.

"May I confess something?"

She managed to nod yes.

"I shall miss Miss Ryder."

Her heart was hammering. "Oh."

"Yes." His eyes searched her face. "I thought of her often."

She couldn't think how to answer him. She scarcely knew what she said. And it didn't matter, because words were now beside the point. The real conversation was the racing current of feeling beneath them—the racing current that connected them.

He placed his warm hands gently over hers. Was she leaning toward him—or was he leaning toward her? She couldn't be certain of anything. His mouth was inches from hers. "Did you ever think of me? Of our kiss?"

His voice thrilled through her nerves. She managed another nod. She realized that she was holding her breath. Then his mouth found hers. A shock of pure wanting went through her. She closed her eyes.

This time, there was no inn yard full of shouting men and shoving stagecoach passengers—only the pop and hiss of the fire, already burning low. Stubble teased her lips. His tongue tickled the seam of her mouth until she realized what he wanted and parted her lips. His tongue found hers in another delicious shock. She heard him groan softly, and exhilaration flooded her.

He pulled her closer. She ran her hands down his back, feeling his hard muscles bunch beneath the elegantly tailored jacket. Her palms prickled with longing—a longing to stroke his bare shoulders, to run her hands over his naked skin. She'd never thought of such things before, but her body already seemed to know all about them.

They sank onto the bed as he cradled her. She couldn't remember the last time that she'd felt so safe. And yet the feeling of safety was also blended with elation and anticipation.

She explored his mouth with her own, filled with a yearning to feel his comforting weight and warmth against her... and upon her. Where that desire had come from, she didn't know... but here, in this small room, suspended in the fog, it didn't seem wrong. She wrapped her arms around his neck, luxuriating in his solidity, the masculine scent of his soap, the heat of his mouth on hers.

They sank backward together into the chilly bedding. There was no sound in the room but the intimate whisper of him kissing his way down her neck. With a sigh, she thew her head back, surrendering to pure sensation—and to him.

And then something sharp jabbed into the small of her back. For a moment she tried to ignore it. This was such a beautiful dream. She'd been swept from despair to happiness. Keynsham shared her feelings! She hadn't been going mad. There *was* a connection between them! The bliss of learning that he felt the same felt like more happiness than she could ever deserve.

The sharp thing jabbed her again, more painfully. Something was in the bed. She clapped her hand to the spot, and her fingers met the sharp corner of a little... cube? She pulled it out from under her back and realized that she was holding a small box. "Where did this..."

The words died on her lips as the delicate brass clasp of the box fell open. Inside was a ring—a large, pink stone surrounded by a halo of diamonds.

It was unmistakably a lady's engagement ring. And Keynsham was patting his jacket's breast pocket, a panicked look on his face. He saw the ring in its box. His face fell. "Oh."

He began to reach for it. She held it out of his grasp. "What is this?" She looked from the ring to his face and back again, willing there to be an explanation.

He rolled onto his back and covered his eyes with one hand. "I—I ought not to have... I am sorry. Of course, under any circumstances, I..." He took a breath, avoiding her eyes. "It... it is expected that I will... become engaged to a... a young lady." He seemed to be forcing the words out.

She jerked away from him and off the bed. "*What?*"

"I am not yet..." He stopped and gave his head a quick shake. "That is, the engagement has not been..."

"*No.*" There was a pulse of panic in her stomach. What had she done? She had very nearly... And all this time, he'd been *lying*. She couldn't seem to get a full breath of air. "The simple truth. I am not asking you if the banns have been read or for some—some *technical detail*. I am asking you for the *truth*."

He sat up. "There is no betrothal. There have been..."

"Really?" She cut him off. "And yet you are carrying about her engagement ring."

His shoulders sagged. "The situation is more complicated than..." He stopped. He tried again. "That is, as a gentleman, I cannot discuss..." He stopped again and gave his head a shake. "I can make no excuse for myself. I am sorry."

She'd dropped her guard. She'd told him her story. She'd told him her real name. She was alone with him in a room in an inn.

And she was still holding the ring in its box. She let the lid close upon the gaudy pink bauble and handed it back without looking at him. "I wish to leave."

"No. It is impossible. We cannot travel without the horses. It is not safe. Wilkes may be nearby still, and it is nearly dark."

She glanced around the room as though there might be some escape route she hadn't seen. Oh, if only she were anywhere but here—with him! For a whole year she'd dreamt of Mr. Keynsham. She'd built him up as her image of perfection—a gentleman she could trust, who'd protect her as he'd protected her that night a year ago...

But she was a fool. He wasn't anything like the hero that she'd invented in her mind. He was merely another weak, lying, self-indulgent man. Disappointment was bitter in her mouth.

"Miss Talbot—"

"I am very tired. I should like to sleep now."

For a moment he seemed about to say something else. But then he sighed. "I shall take the floor."

"As you wish."

"Miss… Talbot, I…" There was a pause. She waited for him to say more. "I—I shall turn my back, then."

She unlaced her boots, slipped into the bed, turned her back to him, and shut her eyes, willing all of this not to have happened.

He pulled off his boots and took off his jacket. She tried not to listen. The small sounds created an illusion of domesticity, of intimacy, that she knew wasn't real—and ought to have known could never be real.

He was a viscount. And he was a liar. And he'd just admitted that he was engaged to another lady.

He blew out the candles. A tear trickled out from beneath one tightly shut lid. She let it run silently into the pillow, determined not to sniffle.

"Good night, Miss Talbot."

She didn't answer.

Chapter Nine

He felt a soft hand on his face.

"Miss Ryder?" he whispered.

No. That wasn't right. "Celia." But he wasn't sure he'd managed to say her name aloud. And it didn't matter, because now her mouth was on his.

There was a very good reason why they ought not to be kissing. It was just that he couldn't for the life of him remember exactly what it was. He groaned as her lips played over his. The delicious tickle as she gently urged his mouth open, and her naughty tongue meeting his, had him instantly and almost painfully hard.

He'd drifted off for only a few minutes. And this was the most unexpected awakening of his life. The warmth of her breasts against his chest, her hands sliding down his sides... Part of him longed to seize her, pull her close, and roll her onto her back.

But the other part of him didn't dare move, lest she change her mind. And so, he lay still as her lips found the hollow in front of his ear and her hands moved slowly up his body. She caressed his hair, pushing it back. Her exploring tongue found its way into his ear. A ticklish explosion of sensation and wetness shot through his body, straight to his groin. He groaned again. It was taking all he had to let her control the pace of this slow, wordless firelight seduction.

Her gown was much more low-cut than he'd noticed it being earlier—which struck him as strange. Surely, he would have... but no. He couldn't focus on such a detail now. As she moved over him in the dim, flickering light he knew that everything between them was perfect, and that they returned each other's desire.

Did he dare reach for her? He seemed strangely paralyzed. Things he'd wanted to do with her tumbled through his mind—the possibilities that had tormented him on lonely nights: her bent forward over his desk, whimpering in pleasure... or with her legs around him, up against the wall of his study.

Already he could imagine her shudders of ecstasy, her gasps of surrender. He was more aroused than he'd ever been in his life—yet he couldn't break free of this strange trance.

And then her hand slid down his chest and over the front of his breeches. But the pressure was far too light. "Celia," he pleaded. He could bear it no longer.

He reached for her. His hand flailed in air and closed on... nothing.

What the devil...?

He was on the floor of a room that he didn't recognize. The fire was almost out—and someone was shouting.

Where was he? Was this France?

The light of a lantern glanced off unfamiliar panes. A horse whinnied. He flung himself at the window.

Three men ran past, clutching lanterns that swung wildly. "They must have gone through the stables!" called one.

This wasn't France. It was Kent.

"Stay here." He jerked one arm into his jacket. "Something is happening outside. It may be Wilkes and his men."

There was no answer.

"Miss Talbot?"

It seemed to take far too long to light a candle from the last embers of the fire. He held the guttering new flame high—and saw nothing but sheets.

The bed was empty. She was gone.

He pelted downstairs, nearly skidding on the landing, sick with dread. Had Wilkes's men broken in and taken her? Even in his sleep-fogged state, he didn't see how it was possible. He'd been on the floor between the bed and the door. They would have had to come through him to get to her.

"Your lordship!" The innkeeper's hair was a frizzy halo around his terrified face. His nightshirt billowed around his belly. Every candle in the place was blazing. "Housebreakers! They forced open a window in the kitchen! Jeb seen 'em creeping up the back stairs!"

"Send for the local constabulary." Despite the sick tightness in his throat, he was accustomed to giving orders. "Have you seen my—my wife?"

"Your wife?" His mouth fell open. "Your wife is missing?"

Keynsham forced himself into what he hoped was an appearance of calm. "No—no. Not missing, no. She set out early."

"*This* early? Without you, your lordship?" He

looked confused and disbelieving. "But... where would she go?"

How he wished he knew that. Fortunately, before he could say anything else stupid, one of the inn servants rushed in. "The stable door was open, but they didn't get away with any of the horses!"

Someone pounded on the inn's thick, wooden front door. Keynsham threw open the bolt. Outside were several lantern-carrying men, clearly villagers. One was armed with a sturdy cudgel. "What has happened, Mr. Hart?"

"Jeb saw a man on the back stairs. He ran out across the stable yard. Big fellow."

The big fellow. Of course. "You and you." Keynsham began organizing the men into search parties. "Take the other side of the road. You and you, come with me." He must force himself to focus on the task at hand—and not on a mental picture of Celia kidnaped and terrorized.

Carrying torches, he and the men with him fanned out across the fallow field behind the inn. The lights of the little village—early candles in the windows of alarmed villagers—receded behind them. A few tatters of mist were all that remained of the fog, and the moon was setting.

How could she be gone? She hadn't cried out. There was no sign of a struggle. She couldn't have simply vanished.

Unless... she'd left of her own accord.

That was the answer. Even knowing that Wilkes was out there, hunting for her, she'd decided to slip away—alone, and in the dark. Because of him. Because he hadn't told her about his obligation to Miss Spry.

Because Miss Talbot had learned of it in the worse possible way. Because she no longer trusted him.

Because he'd ruined everything.

Oh, he could make excuses for himself. That he hadn't meant to kiss her. That his attraction to her had momentarily overcome his judgement.

But she'd been under his protection. He'd questioned her about her past, and then—when she'd been vulnerable, he'd kissed her. He'd pulled her down onto the bed with him.

How far would he have let things go? Would he have said anything, if the cursed ring hadn't fallen out of his pocket?

He didn't know. What he did know was that he'd given her every reason to leave. And he, of all people, should know that once Miss Talbot made up her mind to leave—she left.

How long would it be before he saw her again this time? Would he ever see her again? He wasn't even certain that he deserved to.

The sky began to lighten. His footsteps slowed, then stopped. This search was futile. Wilkes and his thugs hadn't dragged Celia out of the inn. She'd left on her own. And he couldn't blame her. He ought to have been by her side, helping her. Instead, he'd made her feel that she must flee from him, too.

As to where she'd gone, he had a very good idea: She would want to get as far away from him as she could, as quickly as possible. And she had a history of taking stagecoaches. She would have made for the coaching inn on the London road—the one that the farrier's apprentice had mentioned.

And meanwhile, Wilkes's gang had returned to

scour the area nearest to where they'd lost them. This village inn would have been an obvious target. All he could do was hope that because his carriage wasn't there, but at the farrier's, they might have been thrown off the trail. And that might buy Celia enough time to escape from Wilkes.

He said a brief prayer to anyone who was listening: *Please, keep her safe.* A light breeze was rising. The sky lightened a degree. He was standing amidst the broken hedgerows and tumbledown sheds of London's relentless expansion. The market gardens were already busy with workers in the chilly pre-dawn.

Smoke rose from some of the sheds that stood amidst the plots of vegetables. The glow of small fires dotted the field, putting him in mind of an army encampment. He realized that people must be so desperate for shelter that they were sleeping in these tiny wooden shacks.

The sun's first rays caught the feathery tops of carrots, making a green haze above this strip of land. A man in a dirt-streaked smock passed him, pushing a wheelbarrow laden with freshly dug new turnips.

Keynsham turned and began making for the inn. The moment the horses were re-shod, he and Young would set out. If Celiahad taken a stagecoach, someone at the inn might remember her. With luck, he and Young could catch up with her.

Because the moment Wilkes worked out that Celia had left on her own—and Keynsham couldn't afford to think that he wouldn't—he'd make the same search. There was only one way to make this right: He must find Celia before Wilkes did.

* * *

She must disappear, and never see him again.

Shame burned deeper into her with every passing minute. Why had she been so... so *stupid?*

She'd always known that she was allowing herself to dream of a man that she couldn't have. But her dreams had seemed harmless. Only look where they'd led her: Very nearly into ruin. When all along, Keynsham had been betrothed to another lady.

She was a fool. *A fool.*

The cold spring night air was a bracing shock as she slipped out of the inn. Just past the end of the tiny village, she found what she wanted: A country lane that led west, in the direction of the main London road.

Only a few wisps of fog were left. Fortunately, the way wasn't muddy, and for the first mile or so, a half moon provided enough light to see by. She hurried along, desperate to put distance between herself and Keynsham.

But now the moon was setting. And she had the sudden, prickling intuition that something was wrong.

Perhaps it was the same sense that made a mouse freeze when an owl was hunting. All she knew was that there was a change in the air. She moved to the edge of the road, where it was overhung by the bare boughs of an old orchard. But the darkness no longer felt protective. Someone was out there... someone who meant her harm.

Wilkes. She didn't know how, but she knew that he was coming. And he wasn't far away. She slipped over the tumbledown remains of an old stone wall and knelt behind it. A moment later, the twin lanterns of a carriage appeared at the bend in the lane.

She ducked lower on the cold ground. The creak of the harnesses and the horses' breathing were loud in the still air. The coachman spoke to the team. Their hoof-beats slowed from a trot to a walk.

She could picture Wilkes as clearly as though she could see into the carriage—his hair slick with pomade, a jeweled stickpin in his neckcloth, lounging against the squabs. Were the curtains open? Was he looking out? Did he sense her presence the way that she sensed his?

The weight of terror on her chest made it hard to breathe. At any moment, she was certain, the carriage would stop. She'd hear the squeak of the springs as the coachman climbed off the box, the click of the door latch, the clunk of the steps being let down... and then Wilkes's boot upon the road.

Then there would come the inevitable moment when the beam of a lantern would find her, huddled behind the pitiful protection of a few stones. Tears of fear slipped silently down her face. Everything was frozen in the instant before something terrible would happen...

But then a barely perceptible breeze passed through the orchard trees. Like the gears of a clock clicking forward, all at once the sky lightened by a degree. She thought that she heard a voice within the carriage—Wilkes's voice.

The coachman clucked to the horses. "Walk on." The carriage rolled forward, picked up speed and disappeared down the lane.

Long after the sounds of it had faded, her knees shook too much to hold her. She sat, shaking, as the rising breeze and stirring birds signaled the approach of dawn. Finally, she rose and, listening for any sound of Wilkes's carriage returning, took to the lane again and hurried onward.

The farrier's boy had said that the nearest coaching inn was the Bullock. When she reached the main road between London and Southampton, there it was—a cluster of lit windows to the left of the crossroads. But it was too soon to relax her vigilance. She hadn't escaped yet.

Only a half hour later, the clatter of a heavy carriage drawn by four horses announced the arrival of a stage. A southbound coach swept into the yard. She hung back in the shadows as dazed-looking passengers made for the coffee room or the conveniences. Fresh horses were already being led out as the team was unhitched. To Celia, each second was bloated into an eternity by her fear that Wilkes would reappear.

She couldn't stay here a moment longer. The coachman exited the inn, wiping his mouth on the back of his cuff. She paid the fare. The rested horses stamped, eager to move. She stumbled blindly up the step into the coach, took her seat, closed her eyes, and prayed that there would be no hailing voice before they started.

The coach jerked into motion. The shadowy arm of the stable block, a low dark shape against the fading stars, disappeared behind them. Then they were on the open road. The four-horse team picked up its pace, and in moments they were thundering south.

She'd done it. Just for the moment, it scarcely mattered where she was going. As long as the coach was in motion, she was nowhere in particular, and she didn't have to think about Keynsham, or her fears, or her heartbreak, until later.

The sky turned orange, then blue. The stage pulled into inn yards and out again. Horses were changed. Passengers got off and new passengers got on. Not long after noon, she got out and lingered in a coffee room until the coach rolled out of the inn yard without her.

If Wilkes managed to trace her—and she was certain that he would—he'd learn that she'd purchased a ticket that would take her all the way to the end of the route, to Southampton. She had to hope that it wouldn't occur to him that she would alight before then, on the outskirts of a nondescript market town. And if her luck held, and she managed everything perfectly from here on out, she could disappear again.

All the coffee rooms she'd been in since this morning's pre-dawn start were beginning to blend together in her mind. This one was notable only for its dirty windows and the greasy rings on the un-wiped tables. Two or three people were conducting a loud argument in the inn's kitchen.

She forced herself not to think of Keynsham. People were always watching and criticizing a lady's behavior. If she did anything slightly out of the ordinary, she'd be memorable. She couldn't afford to be memorable. She couldn't afford to have anyone recall a crying young lady seated by herself in the coffee room.

Instead, she took out the letter that she'd purloined from Mrs. Lewes's desk at the agency and sat reading the few lines over and over. There were few details, and the address written at the top almost made her lose her courage.

Then again, what choice did she have? Indeed, her only hope was that because she'd stolen the letter, there would be no other candidates for this position. And perhaps it made no difference. After all, it was beginning to seem that Wilkes could trace her almost anywhere.

She swallowed hard and stared out the grimy, flyblown window at the chickens scratching in the dirt. A few minutes later, they flew and scrambled away as another stage—this one on its way to Portsmouth—drew into the inn yard. The passengers swarmed into the coffee room. For a quarter hour, the place was near pandemonium. An elderly lady squabbled with a man who seemed to be her son. Two boys helped an older man hoist a trunk onto the coach roof. Another man was loading ducks in wicker crates into a cart.

The call came for departure and the passengers all rushed back into—and onto—the coach, leaving behind tables piled with plates of greasy-looking food. A maid in a stained apron and gown moved sullenly through the room, collecting what remained to take back to the kitchen—where, Celia suspected, it would be reheated and served up to the next passengers.

An hour dragged by. Finally, another coach arrived. She watched as the passengers flooded in, eavesdropping on their conversations to be certain of the stage's destination. She hadn't realized until this moment how terrified she'd been that she might be stuck here overnight—alone—while Wilkes and his men searched for her up and down the road.

The coachman was downing the last of a tankard of ale as she approached him. "Yes?" he said, in the harassed tone she'd come to associate with people who lived in the capital.

"One inside place to London, please."

Chapter Ten

The road curved around a green hillside dotted with sheep and lambs. Wild daffodils danced amidst the new grass, and the air that blew in through the empty hole where the rear window had been was mild.

Keynsham's horses were rested and newly shod, and his bruises hurt less than they had the day before. They were making good speed, racing the shadows of clouds across the south downs, traveling on a well-maintained side road.

One of the servants at the Bullock had been almost certain that he'd seen a young lady matching Celia's description board a southbound stage very early in the morning.

Why was she going south? He wouldn't know until he could ask her. It felt as though his life wouldn't start again until he could see her face. He'd slipped the man a pound not to talk to anyone else. Of course, he had no way to know if his bribe would keep him man silent—

but he had to do something. Doing something felt better than doing nothing.

This route would allow them to cut a wide curve of the main road out of their journey. With any luck, they could catch up to the stage at the next inn.

There was only one problem: He still hadn't the slightest idea how he could explain himself. He couldn't tell Celia the truth—that he didn't wish to marry Miss Spry. That would be ungentlemanly. That would mean explaining how his obligation to Miss Spry had come about in the first place.

There was no way to explain the situation without casting Miss Spry in a bad light. That was what had kept him silent the previous night. Under the circumstances, there was nothing that he could say to explain his engagement—or, well, his near-engagement.

And besides, Miss Spry wasn't the real problem. The real problem was his own dishonest behavior. Celia had depended on him to help her. He'd taken advantage of the situation. He'd taken advantage of *her*. And he'd done so despite knowing that he wasn't free to marry her.

Misgivings flickered through his consciousness like the shadows of the March clouds racing over the hill-side. He leaned forward, his elbows on his knees. If only there were a way that he could go back in time and not kiss Celia!

But that was impossible. So he must do the next best thing. He must rescue her.

Yes. He stared out the window. Perhaps, once he was back in London, he'd once again feel foggy-headed, beset by complexities, and depressed in spirits. But for now, out in the open countryside, his objective was clear: Find Celia—and keep her safe from Wilkes.

The road wound down the side of the hill and into a wood. The carriage slowed. "Your lordship!" Young pulled the horses to a stop. "There is a tree down on the road ahead."

That was odd. Keynsham pushed the carriage window down and leaned out. The trunk that lay across the road was just big enough that it would take both him and Young to move it. Well, it would add a few minutes to their time—but they would still have minutes to spare and every hope of catching the stage. He opened the door and was about to spring down when some sixth sense made him hesitate.

They were in the midst of a beechwood. Thickly growing trees stretched up and down the hillside. But instead of the birdsong that he would have expected, there was a curious silence. He had just time to note the prickling sensation of being watched when he heard the unmistakable sound of a gunshot.

He dropped to the floor of the carriage. A moment later there was a second shot. The carriage window burst, showering glass over him.

"Young!" he called.

There was no answer. Had the coachman been shot? The report of a pistol just outside answered that question: Young was returning fire. "Sir!" he called back, his voice hoarse.

Wilkes. It couldn't be anyone else. He must have cut across country and ambushed the carriage, like some highwayman of the previous century.

Still on the carriage floor, Keynsham was already feeling for a hidden latch under the rear-facing seat. His father had faced many sticky situations of his own making—including enraged husbands and bill collectors. When he'd ordered this carriage, he'd had it built with a secret compartment in which to stow guns.

The latch clicked and the compartment opened to reveal two rifles and a brace of pistols. He checked the pistols and stowed the double-barreled revolver in his breast pocket, and a pistol in his tailcoat pocket. His mind had gone unnaturally calm. He loaded the rifles with the speed born of years of practice and slid out, long guns in hand, just as another bullet hit the side of the carriage with a *thunk*.

Young was flattened against the side of the carriage, his face strained and his forehead beaded with sweat. "They're up there." He motioned up the hill.

Keynsham edged past him and peeked past the nervous horses. Between the trees, not far up the hill, were a few stones that might once have been a hut.

Whoever was hiding behind the stones also saw him. A bullet whined past. He threw himself flat against the side of the carriage again. "How many?"

"Two, maybe. Didn't get enough of a look."

Keynsham took a deep breath and ducked around the corner just long enough to aim and fire. He heard the ball ricochet off stone. He'd aimed too low.

A moment later an answering shot passed through the carriage. Shards of glass sprayed his coat and stung his cheek. The horses whinnied in fright and began to sidle backwards. Much more of this and they'd be lucky if the bastards didn't kill one of them.

He reloaded and handed Young both rifles. "Take these. I shall work my way up the hill to get a clear shot at them."

Young's face was gray. "Work your way... But your lordship! If you go out there, they'll blow your head clean off!"

"If I do not, they will keep us pinned down and kill us where we stand. I am counting on you to provide covering fire."

Young seized his arm. "I'm no marksman!"

"You do not need to be. You simply need to make them keep their heads down for a few moments, until I am across the road."

Young swallowed. "Yes, sir."

Keynsham ducked past the shattered windows. He paused. "Oh, and Young?"

"Yes, your lordship?"

"Don't get shot."

Young fired twice. Crouching as low as he could, Keynsham ran for the edge of the woods, where he'd seen the start of a narrow trail. He dropped to his belly and, on his elbows, began to crawl along what seemed to be an ancient, slightly sunken woodcutter's track that led uphill from the road. After the war had ended, he'd hoped that he'd never have to do anything like this again.

Young fired twice in quick succession again. For the moment there were no answering shots. Good. That meant that the men who'd ambushed them were staying down. He hoped that the sparse underbrush would provide him enough cover as he tried to work his way level with the tumbled heap of stones where they were hiding.

A puff of smoke rose just ahead and to his left as the

bastards got off another couple of shots. But Young must be quick at reloading, for there were answering shots from below. Keynsham rolled onto his back and pulled out the revolver. It felt solid in his hand. He could say one thing for his father: The fifth viscount had always bought quality guns.

He rolled over again, took a steadying breath and raised his head above the level of the ivy that twisted over the ground.

He was scarcely forty feet from the pile of stones. There were two men crouched behind it. And one of them must have heard something, for he turned and looked directly at Keynsham.

Keynsham didn't have time to think. He barely had time to sight. The man was raising his gun and shouting something. Keynsham squeezed the trigger. The man reeled backward, dropping his rifle.

He'd hit him. He must have. But there was no time to be certain, because the other man was charging him. He was the same massive thug that Keynsham had fought in Grosvenor Square.

Scrambling to his feet, Keynsham fired again. He missed. Now the double-barreled pistol was empty, and something glinted in the man's hand. A knife. *Nothing like a London thug for a knife fight*, he thought grimly.

The man lunged. Hours of training in boxing and fencing meant that Keynsham's body dodged the first few strikes almost effortlessly. But the big man had done plenty of fighting too. He was powerful—and his arms were long.

He held the knife flat in a practiced grip in his huge hand as he lunged, the blade poised to slash and thrust upward into Keynsham's ribs.

Again and again, he tried to close. Keynsham took a step backward, eyes on the blade. His foot landed on a loose stone. He almost went down as the thug lunged again. He barely managed to stumble aside in time, and brought the butt of the now-empty pistol down where the man's skull met the back of his neck.

The blow had no effect. The ruffian righted himself and came straight back at Keynsham. He was disconcertingly fast. The knife flashed toward Keynsham again and again. He hadn't a split second or an inch of space in which to grab the second pistol from his tailcoat pocket.

The thug's enraged breathing filled Keynsham's ears, and his sour body odor filled his nose. Dodging the man's knife strikes he was forced back and back—until his shoulders met something solid.

He was cornered against a massive tree trunk.

A smirk of triumph broke across the thug's dirty face. He'd planned this. He struck; the knife angled toward Keynsham's gut. Keynsham twisted away just in time. The knife went through his jacket, pinning him to the tree.

Keynsham made a desperate plunge forward. Something tore, and he found himself with just room enough to swing.

The enormous man was caught off guard. Keynsham's empty pistol connected with his temple with the full force of a trained punch behind it.

The thug collapsed.

Footsteps pounded toward Keynsham. He had just enough time to tear the other revolver out of the jacket, his shaking finger on the trigger.

George Young skidded to a stop, a rifle in his hand.

"Your lordship! You got them! You got them!" He was beaming.

Keynsham stared at him, panting. He had to force himself to point the pistol at the ground. Good God. He'd almost shot Young.

The coachman clapped him on the back. "You got them both!"

Keynsham's hands were shaking. Would the man get up and attack? No. He was lying still, face down. He might be dead.

He knelt and felt for a pulse in his neck. "He is merely unconscious. Find something to tie his hands." His voice sounded oddly normal.

Young hurried back to the carriage for rope. Keynsham looked over at the pile of rocks. The man he'd shot lay in a heap, blood visible on his coat. He could tell even from this distance that whoever he was, he wasn't well-dressed enough to be Wilkes.

A pair of horses were picketed behind a tree. They'd have to free them—they could likely wander home on their own—but he didn't fancy seeing the body any closer. He'd shot enough men in the war. He'd never thought he'd have to shoot another. The air under the low canopy of the trees seemed suffocating. He felt sick.

He pulled out the knife that pinned his jacket to the tree trunk. The blade was four inches long and deadly sharp. He set it on the ground, shook out his ruined jacket almost mechanically, brushed it off, and put it back on. One sleeve hung by a few threads, and he'd narrowly missed being gutted, but it wouldn't do to appear in public half dressed.

"Your lordship." Young rushed back with a length of rope. He seemed to be full of something that was very nearly hero worship. Keynsham could have told him that there was nothing heroic about what he'd done. He'd killed a man before he could kill him. That was all it was. That was all it ever was.

Keynsham bound the big thug's hands behind him. "Help me roll him over." They heaved him onto his back. His mouth hung slackly open as Keynsham searched his pockets. A few coins amounting to perhaps a pound, a tinderbox—nothing that identified him.

The man groaned. It wouldn't be long before he regained consciousness. Keynsham straightened. "Let us not linger. Wilkes may be nearby."

They worked together to roll the tree trunk off the road. Any optimism he'd had was gone. The sky had clouded over, and the grimness of death lingered in the place. And the carriage—all of its windows shattered, its sides splintered by bullet holes—wouldn't offer any comfort for Celia. But there was nothing that he could do about that now.

He reloaded and stowed the rest of the guns under an old blanket on the box. Then he put on his greatcoat, climbed up next to Young and sat with a loaded rifle across his lap, concealed by the coat. If there were any more of Wilkes's thugs lying in wait, they'd be the ones who got an unpleasant surprise.

Young whipped up the horses. They left the eaves of the wood behind for more rolling pastureland dotted with sheep. Keynsham pulled out his watch. Miraculously, it wasn't smashed. Each moment of the fight had seemed to stretch on for eternity. In reality, they'd lost only three quarters of an hour.

It began to rain. Soon a heavy, silvery curtain shut out the distant line of the sea to the east. He rearranged the rifle to be certain that his greatcoat protected it. The gun battle had made him even more fearful for Celia's safety. Wilkes would stop at nothing. If he harmed her... He'd never forgive himself for having driven Celia away.

When they reached the inn, they found the rain-swept yard empty. The ostler's boy ran out, pulling his jacket collar up against the downpour. Yes, the early Southampton-bound stage had already departed. No, he hadn't seen a young lady answering Miss Talbot's description.

Keynsham's heart sank. What could this mean? Had Wilkes intercepted the coach first? The thought made him feel sick.

Well, no matter what, before they could continue, he had to hire a fresh pair of horses. After miles of the pace they'd set, his team was done for.

"Well, well, well—this won't do!" The ostler, unharnessing the horses on the slick cobbles of the inn yard, stuck a finger in one of the splintered holes in the side of the carriage and whistled. "This won't do at all! Why, you'd as well drive yourselves about in a cheese grater, your lordship!"

Keynsham was too tired and sore to be amused. And he certainly wasn't about to discuss how his carriage had got riddled with bullet holes. There would be enough talk as it was. "Indeed," he said curtly, and stowed the guns back in their compartment.

Now that he had a chance to look at it, he realized that the once-elegant carriage had taken so much damage that it might not be worth repairing. Its expensively lacquered body was a splintered wreck, and the rain had soaked the fine leather upholstery through its shattered windows. Like everything on which his father had spent money, it had been but a fleeting luxury.

He and Young sat at a quiet table in the low-ceilinged snug to wait while the horses were changed out. It was now obvious that Wilkes and his men were following Celia south. So it all came back to the same refrain that had been going through his mind since before dawn: He must find her before they did.

The rain lashed the window. He swallowed some ale. The once-promising day had turned bleak. He'd shot a man. Celia wasn't on the coach. And there were still twenty miles of increasingly muddy road between them and Southampton.

And when he reached into the pocket of his ruined jacket for money to settle the bill, his fingers met a folded piece of paper that hadn't been there before. He withdrew it. It was a note. His eyes went first to the signature. It was from Celia.

Though it had been written hastily in pencil, the message was plain enough. He read it. He read it again. He slumped back in the seat and put his hand over his eyes.

He'd failed.

Young put down his ale. "What is it, your lordship?"

He took a deep breath. "We shall return to London."

"Your lordship?"

"I do not believe that Miss Talbot has gone to Southampton."

Young looked puzzled. "Then... where has she gone?"

"To London. But where she has gone beyond that, I do not know."

Chapter Eleven

"It has been a fortnight. How is it possible that you have not yet found her?"

The smallpox-scarred man who'd been waiting across from his desk shuffled nervously. "I—I can't say, boss. We searched every inn in Southampton. Nobody seen 'er."

"*Cannot say.* I see. How interesting." He straightened a stack of papers. "Well. I sent you to intercept Miss Talbot and bring her to me. That was not a difficult task—was it?"

"I—no, boss."

"No. It was not. She is one young woman, alone in the world. She has no money, no family, and no friends. And yet, somehow, she has been able to evade three grown men." Wilkes sighed. "Imagine that, Gooley! Imagine it! Why, the man who employs those men must be a fool indeed."

Gooley stared at the floor.

"What do you say to that, Gooley? Am I a fool?"

"No, sir."

“Eh? What’s that?”

“No, boss. You ain’t a fool.”

“Ah.” Wilkes rose slowly from his chair. The air of menace seemed to congeal around him. “Well. It is kind of you to say so.”

Gooley’s scarred face was greyish and shiny with sweat. He kept silent.

“Shall I continue?” Wilkes paced across the thick pile of the luxurious Turkey carpet. “Or—no. Let us, instead, start at the beginning—when Miss Talbot first arrived in London, and managed to slip past you. And then, when you picked up her trail and followed her, you were clumsy. She saw you, and gave you the slip. In Grosvenor Square! Marvel for a moment at the incompetence required, Gooley! *Grosvenor Square.*” He tutted. “It would be almost amusing, were it not so pitiful.”

“But boss, the young lord—"

“Oh, spare me your *sniveling* about the viscount!” Wilkes’ voice was a hiss.

Gooley was silenced. Wilkes straightened his cuffs. “Well. And so you lost Miss Talbot.” He ticked his index finger to the left. “You found her again.” He ticked his index finger to the right. “Lost her again.” Left. “Found her, lost her, found her, lost her.” Right, left, right, left. “Dear me, Gooley! Is it any wonder that —when I ask myself what it is that I pay you for—I find myself all-a-mort?”

Gooley stared fixedly into the carpet.

Wilkes studied him. He was beginning to think that the little man had reached the limit of his usefulness. His neckcloth was a wrinkled and grimy strip of yellowed cotton. He was unshaven. His hat was battered. His neck bore an ancient and blurry tattoo. In short, he was instantly recognizable as what he was: A small-time criminal.

Wilkes needed cleaner men. Cleverer men. Men who used their brains as well as their fists. He sighed again. "So. Now we come to Fenton. Refresh my memory, Gooley. What was it that you were to have done about Fenton?"

"Found 'im?"

"Correct. And did you find him?"

"No, boss. 'E scarpered."

"Ah." He nodded. "I see. Most interesting. And these failures were caused by... what, Gooley?"

Gooley thought for a while. "Dunno, boss. Ill luck?"

"Wrong. They were caused by you."

Wilkes strolled to the fireplace. At one time, he'd enjoyed bullying his underlings. Now it had lost its luster. After all, he already knew that nothing he said would make them any more competent.

He considered himself in the glass over the mantel. He was cut out for bigger things than this. Already, his hair was cut every fortnight by William Truefitt himself, in the style known as the Titus, and swept forward and arranged in artful waves with the help of pomade. His neckcloth was fastened with a sapphire stick pin of perfect clarity—from Rundell, Bridge and Rundell, of course. His jacket was of dark blue superfine, in the understated fashion approved by Beau Brummel. In every detail of outward appearance, he was a gentleman—from the crown of his freshly barbered head to the soles of his glossy top boots.

But what good was it to *appear* to be a gentleman,

unless he could actually *live* as a gentleman? And how could he live as a gentleman when he was surrounded by these incompetents?

He sighed. "Well. Humor me, Gooley. Where do you think Fenton and Mowcher might be, if you had to guess?"

"I—I couldn't say, boss."

"So it has not occurred to you that they might simply be drunk somewhere between here and Southampton?"

"I—I dunno, boss."

Wilkes leaned against the mantel. Was Gooley really this stupid? Or was he lying? Or were he and Fenton conspiring together—against him?

On the day that Miss Talbot had vanished, he'd sent Fenton and Mowcher to search the road southwards, while he and Gooley had checked all the inns northward into London. And then Fenton and Mowcher simply hadn't returned.

Fenton, in particular, was a worry. He'd been with Wilkes a long time. He knew too much... and he drank too much to keep it to himself. If Fenton were to tell anyone what had really happened to Squire Talbot... A chill passed through Wilkes—a chill that no gold cuff-links or sapphire stickpin could alleviate.

"Boss?"

He came back to the present to find Gooley gaping at him. He had to get a grip on himself.

"Boss? You want me to look for Fenton—or the lady?"

His grating London accent rendered the word as "lie-dee." Wilkes's patience was slipping. "I do not want you to *look* for either of them."

"Boss?"

"I want you to *find* them." He folded his arms. "Do I make myself plain?"

"Yes, boss. Where… where should I start? To look for the lie-dee, that is."

Wilkes stared down at him. "I am the one who is paying *you*, Gooley. Where do *you* think you might find a lady?"

Gooley thought. "Dunno, boss. A… a brothel?"

Wilkes had the little man pinned up against the wall before he could breathe again. "*What* did you say?"

"Sorry, boss! Sorry!" Gooley held up his hands, his panicked breathing loud. "I don't mean nuffink by it, I swear!"

Wilkes gave him a couple more hard shoves into the wall. "*Miss Talbot* is not in a brothel. Miss Talbot is a *lady*. Do you understand me?"

"I—no, boss. No. I—I understand."

"Good." Wilkes shoved him again, banging the back of his head into the paneling, and let him go. "Now. Get out of my sight."

Gooley fled, his rotting boots loud on the stairs to the street before the armed guard, who stood on the landing at all times, could even shut the door behind him.

A *brothel!* Why, that sniveling, useless little… Wilkes slammed his hand down onto the mantel.

To his relief, his enquiries hadn't uncovered the slightest connection between Celia and Lord Alford. This tallied with what he already knew. Squire Talbot had had a wide acquaintance, but his daughter was a sheltered girl who for eighteen years had never been farther from home than Chichester. She knew nobody and nothing. Indeed, he'd never detected in her the slightest hint of spirit—which was one of the things that he liked about her.

No. It was simply impossible that she should ever have met the viscount before.

Wilkes began to think that the situation was as he'd surmised: The young lord had simply been drunk and looking for a fight that first evening. Apparently, he was known to frequent Jackson's boxing saloon. And his interference the next day could be explained by the unfortunate coincidence that he'd seen Fenton on the Strand—Fenton was hard to miss—and had stopped to confront him.

Yet the fact remained that the viscount ought to have stayed out of Wilkes's affairs in the first place. He'd caused a great deal of trouble and inconvenience. People could not be allowed to cross Wilkes, so the viscount's interference would have to be punished. The only question was how.

Fortunately, Wilkes's informants had provided some interesting and useful information. Lord Alford's father had been a notorious gambler and womanizer. And, while the details weren't public knowledge, the late fifth viscount was said to have mortgaged many of the estate's income-producing properties. Rumor had it that his son's financial position now hung by a thread.

Well, as it happened, Wilkes was just the man to snip that thread. Men all over London owed him favors. The next time the young lord needed to renegotiate a mortgage or borrow money, he'd get a nasty surprise.

But Wilkes couldn't shake a feeling of unease. From the very moment that Celia Talbot had reappeared, nothing—*nothing*—had gone according to plan. It was as though she'd brought with her a statement of accounts for what Wilkes had done... and payment was overdue.

But that was impossible. She was just a girl. She'd do as she was told—or at least, she *would*—as soon as he got her back.

And yet the fact remained that two of his formerly most reliable men were missing. And Celia—powerless and unworldly as she was—had managed to vanish yet again.

* * *

"Has Miss Ryder gone yet?" Mrs. Ellesmere's querulous voice floated down the stairs.

"Not *yet*, madam." Mr. Tate, the middle-aged and solemn butler, gave Celia a reproachful look.

Mr. Tate didn't approve of her. His view seemed to be that lady's companions were somehow unreliable—though why he thought that, she didn't know.

"Tell her that I shall want the second volume of *The Children of the Abbey*!"

"Yes, madam."

"Tell her that under no circumstances is she to accept any more excuses from that clerk!"

"Yes, madam."

"Tell her that she is not to come back without it!"

"Yes, madam."

"But..." began Celia in a whisper.

Mr. Tate held his finger back to his lips and shook his head.

Celia finished collecting the letters from the tray on the hall table, placed them in her reticule and arranged her veil. The dim illumination provided by the fanlight over the door made it difficult to see through the fabric.

But then, that was the point: Even if her ruse hadn't made Wilkes believe that she'd gone to Southampton, her face was so well concealed by the dowdy brown veil that she almost felt safe.

Almost.

She took up her armload of parcels and books. Mr. Tate opened the door and stood on the top step, frowning at the spring morning as though it wasn't up to his standards. He folded his arms and glared at the house next door, where two tradesmen were unloading a large, rolled rug from a delivery wagon. "They are at it again, I see."

Mr. Tate was a barrel-chested man with salt and pepper hair and fierce dark eyebrows. In his starched neckcloth and black superfine jacket, he was an intimidating figure. Or, at least, he would have been, if the tradesmen had paid him the slightest notice at all.

"Good morning, Mr. Tate." Celia hurried past him and into the square. She had a great many errands to run, as she did almost every morning.

Mrs. Ellesmere was a demanding woman. As soon as Celia returned, she would be expected to answer her correspondence, play the pianoforte, read aloud, pour tea, and agree with her employer's observations on politics, bad servants, and other things that annoyed her—especially her next-door neighbor, a widow named Lady Morton.

In fact, from the time Celia rose in the morning to whenever she could finally lie down again at night, she was almost too busy to think. But then, not thinking was preferable to thinking—especially when thinking meant going over and over the episode with Lord Alford.

She hurried east toward the City, the thick veil tickling her nose. For obvious reasons, she'd been afraid to take a position in London. But it had been her only option—and she was beginning to think that a crowded, bustling city of over a million people wasn't a bad place in which to hide in plain sight.

She stopped just in time for a massive dray cart drawn by a team of draft horses to roll past only inches from her face. She was still becoming accustomed to the traffic in the capital, and had to keep her wits about her. But she was beginning to learn her way around—and even the past two weeks had seen spring advance enough that the lengthy errands Mrs. Ellesmere made her run were becoming more tolerable.

At present she was on her way to Leadenhall Street, in the heart of the City. Mrs. Ellesmere subscribed to the Thetis Library, and every two or three days she sent Celia there to borrow another volume—and to add her name to the waiting list for whichever sensational new novel she wished to read next.

Celia pushed open the polished wood door and joined the line of smartly dressed ladies waiting for the clerks at the counter. The library was always crowded with fashionable people from all over London. The Thetis Press—which was upstairs—published many of the most popular titles itself, and they were available here before anywhere else.

Today the queue moved quickly. Fortunately, the volume of *The Children of the Abbey* that Mrs. Ellesmere had demanded was finally available. The clerk wrapped it in brown paper and handed it to Celia.

And now came the test.

She glanced around. She ought not to do it. She ought to leave this very instant and walk straight back! After all, each time she gave in, the compulsion to look again the next time only grew stronger.

But it was too late. Her heart was already thudding with guilty dread as her feet carried her into the reading room, where arched windows overlooked the street and a crowd of well-dressed gentlemen lounged about gossiping and eyeing the stylish ladies queued at the counter. Others stood at the tall, angled reading desks, perusing newspapers and magazines and consulting their expensive pocket watches.

Celia crept toward the desk where *The Times* lay, nearly sick with apprehension. The gentleman who had been reading closed it and turned away. Before another gentleman could move in, she darted forward and scanned the first page.

Nothing. *Nothing*.

She turned the pages, her hands shaking and the ink smudging the fingertips of her gloves. Nothing at all... not even a small notice on the back page.

She checked the *Morning Call* as well. There was no mention there, either. Her heart began to slow. The sick tightness in her stomach eased slightly.

But... what could it mean? Viscount Alford was a peer. His marriage would be reported in the newspapers. Yet she had seen nothing here—or in the print shop windows.

She came out of her daze to realize that a gentleman was scowling at her through his quizzing glass. She scowled back. She knew quite well that she looked as though she didn't belong here. Her gown was drab, and her bonnet had seen better days. By contrast, the fashionable ladies crowding the front room were like a colorful flock of exotic birds in their smart walking costumes, swansdown muffs, and plumed and beribboned bonnets.

Still, his stare reminded her to rearrange her veil to conceal her face before she left the library. She hefted the parcel containing *The Children of the Abbey* and struggled through the throng to the door. At least she would be too busy reading from it to be able to think of Keynsham this afternoon.

* * *

But when she finally reached Red Lion Square, Mr. Tate opened the door and held his finger to his lips. Annie, one of the housemaids, tiptoed past toward the stairs, carrying an armload of linens and looking terrified.

Celia was alarmed. "What is wrong? Is someone ill?"

"Mrs. Ellesmere has been *agitated*," Tate whispered, as he shut the door. "There has been a *disturbance*."

"A disturbance?"

"Keep your voice down!" Tate made a frantic shushing gesture. "Mrs. Ellesmere's nerves are *at their breaking point*!"

The house was unusually silent. Celia lowered her own voice to a whisper. "I do not understand. What has happened?"

"It has been *most* shocking. Most shocking indeed!" He looked nervously from side to side. "For almost the whole of the time that you were gone, Miss Ryder, there was… *an odor of paint.*"

She blinked. It seemed best to treat this seriously. "I see."

"Mrs. Ellesmere called me into the sitting room to ask my opinion, and I opened a window to check." His brow was furrowed. "After some efforts at detection, we were *quite* certain that the smell was emanating from Lady Morton's residence."

Celia's arms were aching. She set the parcels down. "How dreadful."

Mr. Tate shot another nervous glance about the hall. "You must be *perfectly quiet*. She must have absolute rest."

"I shall do my best." She unpinned her veil and began to take off her bonnet.

"Poor Mrs. Ellesmere has been *singularly* unlucky in her neighbors." Tate seemed to be in a mood to confide in her. "The previous tenant of the house was an artist who hosted the most disgraceful entertainments."

"Oh dear."

"Oh, that is not the worst of it. Can you guess where that artist is now?"

"I—I am afraid that I cannot."

"Well, of course you cannot. No reasonable person could. So I shall tell you: He is in the House of Lords."

Celia wasn't sure what to say. "How, er… surprising."

"*Surprising*!" He recollected himself and lowered his voice again. "Poor Mrs. Ellesmere has never fully recovered from the shock! 'Tate,' she will say, 'That man is the very last man who ought to be anywhere near His

Majesty's government. No wonder the country is in such a state.' You see, he inherited the title from his uncle, the late Earl of Foxborough. Poor Mrs. Ellesmere! She took to her bed for several days when the news reached us. She had prayed that God would strike him down—so you may imagine her sufferings upon learning that he had, instead, been elevated to the peerage. And now we have Lady Morton, and her endless refurbishment of the house!"

Celia folded her gloves and took up her bonnet. "Well, if you do not think that she will wish me to read aloud today, I had better go to my room."

"*Quietly*, I entreat you, Miss Ryder. *Quietly*!"

She tiptoed upstairs.

Chapter Twelve

"But my lord, I am afraid that you do not have security for this loan." The banker folded his manicured hands on his desk. His small smile was smug. "We cannot risk an amount such as this. It is, er, *known* that many of your properties are already mortgaged. There is nothing that I can do for you." He coughed delicately. "My hands are tied, your lordship—quite tied."

Though he was a young man—shiny-faced and self-satisfied and sporting a pale blue silk neckcloth held by a large garnet stickpin—he spoke as though he were explaining facts to a child.

Keynsham frowned. He'd come prepared for questions about his proposal, of course. What he hadn't prepared for was a dismissal without being heard at all.

But it wasn't just that. There was something underlying the banker's condescending manner that didn't seem to fit. The man seemed...*frightened*.

But why?

Since the ambush in the woods, Keynsham had

trusted his instincts when they told him that a situation wasn't as it seemed. And now they were warning him that, even though he was in a well-known bank, something was wrong. He hesitated only a moment before gathering his papers and rising. "Well, then. I shall take up no more of your time. Good day."

The banker's face registered shock. He seemed to have expected Keynsham to plead his case—and to show him the contents of the folio under his arm. He cleared his throat. He had gone pale, and as he stood, Keynsham saw beads of sweat on his forehead. "I, er... see. Well. You must please yourself, your lordship. Of course. Of course." He made Keynsham an obsequious bow—but saw him only as far as the door of his office.

Downstairs, on the main floor of the bank, clerks at large mahogany desks conversed with customers under a vaulted ceiling. The whole place emitted a low hum of money. Keynsham strode across the airy room's red marble floor—half bemused and half irritated.

No one understood better than him that his father's imprudence had left him in a bad position. Yet the proposal that he'd prepared was meticulously calculated. If the banker had bothered to look at it, he would have seen that the risk was lower than it might first appear, and the potential for profit much greater... and moreover, that Keynsham had security for the loan.

There were other banks and other bankers, of course. But as he stepped onto the pavement he was frowning. Something wasn't right. The only question was whether he would meet the same treatment at his next appointment.

* * *

When he was satisfied that the viscount had left the building, the young banker pulled out a sheet of paper and a quill and wrote a note. He blotted the ink, folded the paper, sealed it, and hurried down to the crowded City street himself.

"Here! You!" He'd used the boy before when he had letters he wanted delivered—letters that dealt with matters that fell outside the bank's official business. "Take this to Bell's Buildings. Be quick about it and there's a sixpence in it for you."

"Yes, sir!" The urchin ran off.

The banker wiped the nervous sweat off his hands on the sides of his trousers and went back to his desk. He supposed that he ought to have drawn out the conversation and seen why the viscount had wanted the money. But he didn't want to know. All he wanted was for this to be over.

The man to whom the note was addressed looked like a gentleman, dressed like a gentleman, and spoke like a gentleman. But there was something in his eyes—something reptilian, ruthless, and cruel—that made the young banker shudder. And then there was his reputation... a reputation about which he seemed to hear more every day.

Yes, he'd needed money to pay some unexpectedly large gaming debts... but he wished to God that he'd borrowed it from anyone else. He wanted only to forget that he'd ever met the man.

Indeed, if he never saw him again, it would be too soon.

* * *

There was a knock on the door. The man guarding the landing announced, "Message for you, boss."

A grubby boy darted into the luxuriously furnished office. Wilkes barely glanced at him as he tossed him a sixpence. He tore open the note and scanned it. "No reply." The boy ran out again. The guard shut the door.

Wilkes dropped the note onto his desk. Suddenly, he felt as though he could take a deep breath again. His fears had been foolish. Everything was unfolding exactly as he'd foreseen: The viscount was trying to borrow money. He wouldn't get it. The walls were closing in on Lord Alford even more quickly than Wilkes could have hoped.

He leaned back in his chair and put his hands behind his head. Well, the young lord had brought this upon himself. And if there was one thing that Wilkes had learned the hard way, it was that there was no room for leniency.

It was time to teach everyone—from Viscount Alford to the lowest cutpurse in St. Giles—a lesson about what happened to those who meddled in his affairs.

* * *

The rest of Keynsham's morning went the same way. He'd made appointments at all the foremost banks. But at each of them he received the same strange treatment.

He could have understood it if the bankers had looked over his projections and found flaws or raised other objections. But just like the first man, they seemed to wish to rush him out of their offices as quickly as possible—as though even having him on the premises was a risk. Indeed, it was almost as though they were terrified to be known to have spoken to him at all.

He drove home, his mind at work. What had just happened? He hadn't missed so much as a single mortgage payment on a single farm. So why had he become persona non grata in the City? And how was he to borrow the money that he needed? Without it, his bold plans would remain just that: plans.

In the two weeks since he'd last seen Celia—that was how he thought of time now—he'd driven back to Grange Grove several times to meet with Downey. They'd walked the site together. They'd costed the materials needed to finish the first two streets of houses, and discussed the plans not only for the remaining streets, but even for the second and third phases of the development.

Keynsham had met Downey's wife. He was beginning to think of him as a friend. He didn't want to let Downey down.

His mind was busy with these worries as he walked into his dressing room and straight into a stack of chairs that hadn't been there when he'd left.

"Your lordship!" His valet, Rogers, came at a sprint at the sound of furniture crashing to the floor. At the sight of the viscount sprawled amidst the chairs, he stopped dead in the doorway. "Can you speak? Are you injured?"

Keynsham winced, sat up, and assessed the damage to himself and the furniture. One of the chairs was now missing a leg. He clambered ruefully to his feet, rubbing his ribs. "Really, Rogers. I cannot imagine why you have booby-trapped my dressing room."

Rogers—who'd been with him at Quatre-Bras and

Waterloo—was indignant. "I assure you, your lordship, that I did nothing of the sort! I shall demand an explanation of Mr. Brock!"

He rang the bell. Martin, the first footman, appeared. "His lordship has been *injured*, Martin. Fetch Mr. Brock."

Martin turned pale. "Your lordship! I... I... that is... her ladyship..." He hurried out. A few moments later he returned with Mr. Brock, the butler.

"Your lordship!" Mr. Brock was aghast. "I beg your pardon! Her ladyship instructed us to remove the chairs from the Blue Drawing Room and place them in your dressing room."

Rogers, who didn't get along with Brock, glared at the butler. "The scene speaks for itself. His lordship could have been killed!"

Keynsham dusted off his palms. "Oh, I hope not. It would be a hard thing to survive the war only to be cut down by a side chair. But what I should like to know is why the furniture is being moved at all."

Brock and Martin exchanged a look. Brock cleared his throat. "Her ladyship is... preparing for the ball."

Ball? It was apparent that Keynsham needed to have a conversation with his mother. "I see. That still does not answer my question."

The butler and the footman exchanged another look.

Keynsham sighed. Now that he thought of it, he realized that he hadn't seen much of his mother for at least a fortnight. This was often a sign that she was up to something, and wished to avoid questions until she'd got her way and it was too late for anyone to do anything about it.

But before he could go downstairs to see for himself what she was doing, his mother appeared. "Brock! What on earth was that noise? I told you to... Oh. Good morning. I... I did not expect you back so soon."

"Ma'am." He made her a bow.

Lady Alford had been considered a great beauty in her youth, which was why the fifth viscount had married her. She was beautiful still, though hard lines of ill-temper now ran down from the corners of her mouth. "Well. I shall not disturb you."

"Oh, you are not disturbing me at all. Indeed, I was about to come and find you, in order to discuss the preparations for this, er... *ball.*"

Martin and Brock appeared to be backing slowly toward the door. "You may take these chairs somewhere else," he said to them.

"Very good, your lordship." Brock looked relieved. They withdrew.

Lady Alford's golden hair was twisted up into a high knot, with fashionable ringlets before her ears. She wore a cream silk morning gown, a fashionable figured Kashmir shawl, and an expression of exasperation. "But the chairs must go *somewhere*. We must have space for the *dancing*!"

"Space for dancing?" Had she gone mad? "As you undoubtedly recall, ma'am, Alford House is equipped with a ballroom."

"I suppose you may call it that." She waved an irritable hand. "Of course, when the place was built a century ago, people were happy to have any sort of simple little space in which to jig about."

"Simple little..." He took a breath. "Ma'am. The

ballroom is nearly one hundred feet long. It was remodeled by Henry Holland himself not twenty years ago."

His mother emitted a puff of exasperation. "Well, *precisely*! Twenty *years*! People have *seen* it! Something *new* is wanted! Something... something *surprising*!"

"*Ma'am.*" He rubbed his forehead. "This is a house —not a balloon ascent at Vauxhall. No one can reasonably expect to be *surprised*. Now, I have not troubled you with the details, of course, but you are perfectly aware that my late father left us with considerable debts. So let me be clear: We cannot afford an expensive entertainment."

"But Pomona must have"—

"What Pomona must have is a simple yet elegant evening party which will allow her to appear to advantage. And let us also remember that this will be the first entertainment that we have given since my father's death, and that a large and boisterous gathering would be in poor taste."

She narrowed her eyes. "What do you mean, *large*?"

"Let us say fifty or sixty guests at most. Of course, if you feel that is too many" —

"*Fifty*!" She clapped a hand to her breastbone as though she'd been stabbed. "*Fifty guests*! You cannot possibly be *serious*! Why, at Colonel and Mrs. Beaumont's ball for Miss Beaumont's come-out there were *over four hundred*!"

"*Ma'am.*" He held up a hand. "We are not in competition with a family that owns half of Yorkshire. And besides, the Beaumont's ball was not considered elegant. Indeed, it was so overcrowded that many ladies found it unpleasant—not to mention that it was infiltrated by pickpockets. We cannot wish criminals to attend Pomona's ball."

"*Criminals!* How perfectly ridiculous! Of course there will be no *criminals* at my ball. You need not patronize *me*!" She tossed her head.

"Sixty guests. No more. Do I make myself clear?"

She ignored this. "Criminals indeed! Why, I am almost certain that the prince regent himself will attend! After all, he always attended Lady Sophronia's balls."

"Ma'am. Please do not change the subject. Are we in agreement?"

"But I do not *understand*!" She clasped her hands tightly. "What about the *money*?"

"What money?"

"Miss Spry's thirty thousand pounds! Surely you realize that the ball cannot be a *stingy* affair! Not when it is also to serve as the announcement of your marriage to an *heiress*."

"Ah." He should have seen this coming. "Well, as to that, there has been a..." He cleared his throat. "I regret to say that Miss Spry has not yet had leisure to hear my proposal."

She stared. She gasped. "Not yet had... What can you mean? No! *No*! It is not possible! It was all to have been settled! Why has it not been *settled*?"

He wished that he knew the answer to that himself. "Miss Spry has been unwell. It has not been possible to make a private appointment with her ever since the unfortunate episode in which she, er... fainted."

His mother gave an unladylike snort. "I have never believed that for a minute. Why, it must have been a most particular fit of the vapors indeed—if she could not be brought round again by the sight of a ring box from Rundell and Bridge!"

"*Ma'am.*"

She lifted her hands in a pantomime of bewilderment. "But it has been a *month*! I cannot recall a *single* instance in which a young lady has cried compromise and then dragged her feet afterwards. Not a single one! It is simply *not done*!"

"Be that as it may, as a gentleman, I must defer to the lady's wishes."

"But everyone knows that you ought to have been married immediately!" She sank into the remaining unbroken drawing room chair, clutching her temples. "This will cause *talk*. Everyone will say that there has been some serious objection to the match. They will dredge up all the rumors about the estate. They will say that it must be the money!"

Well... as far as he knew, it *was* the money. That, at least, had been obvious, based on what Mr. Spry had said about him having been "left in a fix."

Lady Alford flung an elegant hand over her eyes. "This is ruination! Just when it seemed that we were to be saved! I am the unluckiest woman alive!"

Keynsham glanced at the clock. There was something that he wished to check in his study. "Ma'am, please. We need not imagine the circumstances to be worse than they are. If there is any gossip, it is best if we do not dignify it with our notice. The less we say, the better."

"Now we see what the young ladies of today are come to! Willful! Spoiled! Lady Deverel tells me that Miss Spry has been driving herself about in her own phaeton! She was in the park only yesterday. With a pink dog beside her!"

This was news to Keynsham. Every day he'd called at the Spry mansion, and every day he'd been told that Miss Spry was still indisposed. Still, there was nothing that he could do about the situation.

A painful stab of hope shot through him. He ordered himself not to entertain it. Even if, by some miracle, he were freed from his obligation, he couldn't dare to hope that Celia would ever speak to him again.

He bowed to his mother. "Please excuse me. I have business to which I must attend."

* * *

"This is most interesting." The elderly banker took off his gold-rimmed spectacles and squinted at Keynsham. "Most interesting indeed. The fourth viscount—your grandfather, of course—was involved in a similar scheme. It proved most profitable. Although, of course, you would be taking a more active role."

Keynsham was so surprised at not being dismissed that it took him a moment to recover. "I am prepared to do it, sir. You may see my documents." He pushed them across the wide desk.

Because Keynsham had spent so many hours with the estate records, he'd remembered that this man's information appeared amongst his grandfather's tidy ledgers. After his conversation with his mother, he'd hurried to his study and looked up his direction—though until he'd arrived at the door, he'd been unsure whether the man was even still in business. But this discreet private bank in Knightsbridge was his last hope.

The banker put his spectacles back on and opened the portfolio. He ran his finger down the columns of numbers in silence. "Yes. Yes. I see." He turned the page and examined those numbers too. He jotted some figures on a piece of his own paper and studied them. The clock on the mantel behind his desk ticked.

Finally, he looked up at Keynsham again. "Did you put these figures together yourself?"

"Yes." Keynsham cleared his throat. "It seemed to me that it is not much different from managing an estate. One's tenants require housing, and so do other workers. I—I happened to be in the area and saw the houses myself. I spoke to one of the men who'd been building them."

"Yes." The banker drew the word out, running his finger slowly down the column of numbers, as though for the pleasure of reading them again. He looked at the plan of streets yet to be built. "Quite so. Quite so. London is expanding rapidly. And I see that there is an option to purchase these two additional tracts, too."

He tapped the papers with his forefinger. "I must counsel you that it is unconventional. What is more often seen is the building up of new sections of the city —Mayfair, of course, and now Belgravia—on land already owned by some wealthy family—like the Grosvenors or the Portmans. And thus are great fortunes multiplied." He looked back at the plans. "Your scheme is more risky."

Keynsham took a breath. "Two full terraces of houses are almost complete. With the remaining materials—and the men's wages—my foreman estimates that one of them can be ready in a fortnight. Twenty eight families will thus be housed. Over sixty more houses can be complete by next quarter day. And I am certain that there is demand."

"I see." The ghost of a smile seemed to flicker about his mouth. "Well, you certainly have a head for figures. And if appearances are anything to go by, your lordship, you, er… have the necessary tolerance for risk."

It took Keynsham a moment to realize that the banker was making a joke about the lingering bruises on his face. "Ah. Yes. A mere accident."

The banker raised his eyebrows. "Of course, your lordship. Of course."

Keynsham took the deed out of his breast pocket. "I have security for the initial loan: A house in Grafton Street."

"Oh? Grafton Street?" The banker frowned and unfolded the paper. "Interesting. Interesting. I was not aware that your family owned property there."

"Nor were most people." Keynsham cleared his throat. "My late father bought it, er… *sub rosa*, only a few years ago."

"Ah." The banker raised his eyebrows even higher. "Well, well. I see. I shall have to value it, of course." He studied the deed, then refolded it. "However, I am certain that it will be sufficient." He closed the portfolio. "I see no reason to decline."

Keynsham waited for him to say more. But the banker merely took off his glasses and began polishing them. "I beg your pardon," he said, finally. "Did… you just agree to loan me the money?"

The man inclined his head. "I did indeed, your lordship."

Keynsham had to force himself not to leap up in triumph. “I see. Thank you.”

“Oh, there can be no need to thank me, your lordship.” The old banker rose. “No, no, do not thank me. You will, after all, be paying interest.”

Chapter Thirteen

He pulled her into his arms, pinning her against the wall. Slowly, he bent his head. His mouth brushed over hers and along her jawline. She couldn't breathe. His grip was fierce, but the caress of his lips was feather light.

His voice tickled her ear. "Celia. My darling. Nothing and no one can come between us ever again. Say that you are mine."

"I am yours," she whispered.

He closed his eyes and groaned deep in his throat. "And I am yours." His mouth found hers. The kiss began as the lightest of touches—a caress of hot skin on hot skin. But as she pulled him closer, his kiss grew more demanding. Shivers of sensation traveled through her. Past and present mixed into a pulse-pounding longing....

"Miss Ryder. *Miss Ryder!*"

Celia jumped. "Yes, ma'am."

Mrs. Ellesmere was glaring at her. "I begin to think,

Miss Ryder, that you are queer in the attic—or that you simply do not care about your employment. I do not pay you to skulk on the landing, hugging your elbows and daydreaming!"

"No, ma'am."

"Come at once! I require you to read to me!"

"Yes, ma'am." Celia's face was burning. She followed her employer into the sitting room. Why had she slipped into a daydream about Keynsham? After all, he was a liar and a seducer—and his marriage to another lady would be announced any day now.

Every Sunday Celia accompanied Mrs. Ellesmere to church in the morning, ensuring that she had her extra shawl, mitts, peppermints, prayer book, reading spectacles and any letters that she wished to show to her acquaintances after the service.

Afterwards, if Mrs. Ellesmere had no callers, Celia read aloud. Her employer's chief pleasures in life were gothic romances and newspaper accounts of murders, fires, violent crimes and fatal accidents. Neither were suitable reading material for a Sunday... but there was certainly nobody who would dare to tell Mrs. Ellesmere that.

She placed a screen between Mrs. Ellesmere and the fire and took up the book that she was reading aloud. Anyone would have thought that her employer was an elderly invalid. In fact, she was in her fifties and perfectly healthy—apart from a knee that troubled her occasionally, which gave her a reason to carry a cane.

As Celia read, Mrs. Ellesmere clicked her tongue. She was annoyed with the book—*The Sorceress of*

Sarteano. But then, she was *always* annoyed by the books. "Dreadful," she would mutter under her breath, getting louder each time she said it. "Dreadful! *Dreadful!* Shameful! Disgraceful! *Trash!*"

She'd said the same of *The Confessional of Valombre, The Grotto of San Lorenzo, The Pirate of Naples, The Crypt of Crispiano* and *Sicilian Mysteries*—all of which she'd chosen herself. Celia had never been farther away than Lincoln, but thanks to these sensationalistic novels she was beginning to feel that she'd visited Italy herself... or at least, the parts of it that were most heavily beset by forbidden love, murderous ghosts, abducted heiresses, secret babies and icy tombs.

Finally, Mrs. Ellesmere thumped her cane on the floor. "That is quite enough humbug for one day. You may play now."

"Yes, ma'am." Celia settled herself at the pianoforte and began a sonata. Playing rested her throat, which was tired after almost two hours of reading. But unfortunately, it also allowed her mind to wandered to painful thoughts. Somewhere in London—only two or three miles away, though he might as well be on the far side of the moon—was Keynsham.

She ought not to care what he thought. But... did he ever regret how he'd behaved? Probably not. He was probably with his fiancée... perhaps in an open carriage in the park... no doubt admired by the entire *ton*. She would be wearing an elegant carriage gown, and Keynsham...

But no. She must stop thinking of him. She must forget the determined set of his jaw as he'd held out a protective arm behind his carriage... the fire in his eyes when he'd told her that he'd never forgot her... the feel of his lips on her earlobe...

"Miss Ryder! *Miss Ryder!*"

She came back to the present with a jolt. "Stop!" Mrs. Ellesmere's face was red with rage. "*Stop!* This is intolerable! Your playing is dreadful! Dreadful! Never have I heard so many mistakes and wrong notes!" She thumped on the floor again for emphasis. "You are making no effort. No effort whatsoever! If there is one thing that I cannot and will not tolerate, it is a young lady who makes no effort!'

"I—I am sorry, ma'am." Celia was so stunned by this outburst that she wasn't certain what to say. Had she missed notes? She hadn't thought so, but perhaps she was wrong. "I apologize. I believe that I may be somewhat fatigued."

"Fatigued? Did you say *fatigued*, Miss Ryder?" Mrs. Ellesmere rose. "Fatigued indeed! What a hum! How can *you* be *fatigued*? Why, you have done nothing at all all day!"

She pounded her cane on the floor. "All the young ladies nowadays are pale and weak and vaporish. I suppose that it is the green sickness. Well, I tell you to your head that I will not stand for it! I will not stand for sickliness in my household! Miss Goodman was precisely the same. Indeed, you may be *worse* than her!"

Miss Goodman had been Mrs. Ellesmere's previous lady's companion. Celia still hadn't learned the exact circumstance of her departure... "I beg your pardon, ma'am. I do not suffer from the green sickness."

"Do you dare to contradict me?" Mrs. Ellesmere's eyes snapped with fury.

"No, ma'am." Too late, Celia realized that she ought

to have said nothing. She'd thought herself immune to her employer's irrational fits of temper. Now she realized that Mrs. Ellesmere had, until now, been on what passed as good behavior with her.

Mrs. Ellesmere stamped across the room. "First that woman at the employment agency told me that she would send me no more companions. And then she foisted *you* on me—with no notice whatsoever! I suppose she thought that she would leave me no choice but to hire you! Well, I shall write to her and tell her *exactly* what I think of her petty stratagems."

She rang the bell. "You are unsatisfactory—just as unsatisfactory as Miss Goodman, Miss Black, Miss Fremont and Mrs. Bristol all were. And you may be certain that I shall replace you, too."

Celia's stomach did a sick lurch. "Please, ma'am...."

"Silence! You have given me the headache. I shall have to go lie down. Tomorrow morning I shall write the letter, and you will take it to the employment agency yourself—so that Mrs. High and Mighty may see the shabby way that you are dressed, too. It depresses my spirits to see you in that drab gown. I should have expected better of"—

The sitting room door opened. Tate walked in, bearing a tray with the tea things. Mrs. Ellesmere frowned. "I did not order tea."

Tate raised his eyebrows. "I beg your pardon, madam. You requested it earlier."

Mrs. Ellesmere paused, thrown off her tirade. The delicious odor of baked goods rose from the tray. "Is that *lemon* cake?"

"Yes, madam. And Cook's chocolate tarts."

"Oh, very well—since you have brought them

anyway." She scowled. "What is this?" There was also a folded newspaper on the tray.

"Ah. It is the Sunday *Observer*. I thought that you would be interested to know that there is a notice about the murder committed by the butcher's apprentice in South Lambeth. You were quite correct, madam. The body has been discovered."

"*Indeed!*" Mrs. Ellesmere's face lit up. "And was it cut up—as I predicted?"

"Yes, madam."

"How dreadful!" She snatched up the newspaper and began to read. "Exactly as I said! And the head! Chopped off with a cleaver and pickled in a barrel with the corned beef!" She took a large bite of a chocolate tart. "Is that not precisely what I predicted? Did I not say that he had hid the head in the shop?"

"Indeed you did, madam. Perhaps Miss Ryder might pour the tea."

Mrs. Ellesmere, still engrossed by the newspaper, merely grunted. "It says here that a man was knocked unconscious on Westminster Bridge after being run down by a young lady driving a phaeton—with a pink dog beside her! Humph! I disapprove of ladies driving. I shall pray that they catch her—and that she is whipped." She gestured at Celia. "Fetch me my paper scissors, Miss Ryder—and my folio. I shall want to add this article to it."

"The folio" was a large collection of newspaper clippings of stories of gruesome murders and deaths. Until now, Celia hadn't been allowed to touch it.

In the corridor she took a shaky breath. Would Mrs. Ellesmere put her out on the street? She wouldn't last long without a roof over her head—not with Wilkes hunting for her! If only she hadn't allowed herself to daydream of Keynsham. If she'd missed notes as she played, she had no one to blame but herself.

She hurried up the stairs to Mrs. Ellesmere's dressing room, where a large writing desk contained her employer's letters and papers. The cherished clipping collection was in its top righthand drawer.

But as she lifted the heavy, untidy pile, papers slid out of it in all directions. Her heart pounding, she struggled to retrieve them without dropping others. Would Mrs. Ellesmere notice if she they were in the wrong order?

A name, printed on one of the escaped clippings, caught her eye: *Mr. Julian Talbot.*

She blinked. Julian Talbot?

No. It could not be.

But it was.

Mr. Julian Talbot. Her father.

She sank to the floor, everything else forgotten.

Inquisition Held in Surrey

An Inquisition was taken at Guildford, Sy., before His Majesty's Coroner Mr. Inchbald, on view of the body of Mr. Julian Talbot, Esq., of Oldbourne, Hants.

Mr. Talbot's carriage was discovered at sunrise Thursday morning, overturned on the London road some four miles from Guildford. Mr. Talbot's right forearm was broke, as were several ribs. His head had received such grievous injuries as to render identifica-

tion of the corpse difficult. The coachman had fled the scene.

On Friday the Coroner's Inquest sat on the body at the Queen's Head, a public house in Guildford, where the jury brought in a verdict of Accidental Death.

She clapped her hand over her mouth. No. *No.* This was a mistake. Her father had not been on the London road. *His head had received such grievous injuries...*

She closed her eyes to block out the mental picture, but that only made it more vivid.

"Miss Ryder! Miss Ryder! *Miss Ryder!*"

Her hands were shaking. She couldn't manage to put the stack of papers back together. She couldn't manage anything.

"*Miss Ryder!*"

She stood and tottered, puppet-like, downstairs to the sitting room.

"Well?" Mrs. Ellesmere glared at her. "Where is it?"

Where was what? *The newspaper collection.* "I... I could not find it."

"Really, Miss Ryder! You are utterly incapable!"

"I—I beg your pardon, ma'am." Her voice was a near-whisper.

Tate shot Celia a strange look. "Miss Ryder, perhaps, did not know where to look. It will take me but a moment, madam." And before Mrs. Ellesmere could stop him, he hurried out of the room.

Mrs. Ellesmere glowered at Celia. "Now you see? You are putting Tate to a great deal of trouble. He should not have to do your work!"

"I am sorry, ma'am. I do not think that I...." Her head was pounding. "That is, I do not feel at all well."

"Do not *feel* well? Miss Ryder, you are *sickly*. I have told you specifically, several times, that I do not tolerate sickly young ladies."

"I—I beg your pardon." She turned, almost blindly, and left the room.

"Is it your throat?" Mrs. Ellesmere shouted after her. "I will not have a putrid throat in this house!"

#

Celia lay on her narrow bed, shivering as though a fever were wracking her with chills. She longed to cry, but tears wouldn't come. Horrifying images appeared when she closed her eyes.

Nothing made sense. Her father had been traveling to Bath. Hadn't he? All his talk had been of Bath: the friends that he would see, the titled and fashionable people he was expecting would be there. Besides, Wilkes had told her that the wreck had been found on the Bath road.

Wilkes. Pulling strings... wheedling her to obey her dead father's wishes... He seemed to know everything. So why had he been mistaken about the road?

She turned over, but the unanswered questions wouldn't stop plaguing her. She knew in her heart that there was something wrong with the whole story.

There was a knock. It was Annie with a tray. "Oh,

Miss Ryder!" Her freckled face was ashen. "All of us feared that it would come to this."

Celia's thoughts were in such a whirl that they seemed to be consuming all her energy. "I beg your pardon?"

Annie lowered her voice. "This is how the nervous complaint took Miss Goodman. She went to bed and couldn't get up." She set the tray on the dresser. "Look, I am pouring you some tea! Do have it while it is hot."

Celia forced herself to sit up. "I do not mean to worry you."

"She wears you out!" Annie handed her the tea. "It isn't right that you go out on your own, carrying her parcels in all weathers. You ought at least to have one of us with you."

Celia took a sip of tea. "I was used to walking long distances alone in the country."

"And this ain't the country!" Her young face was serious. "Ladies in London ought not to go about by themselves, is what I'm saying! There's bad men out in the streets."

Didn't Celia know it... Yet her errands allowed her to escape the house for a few hours. If nothing else, she was free to choose which streets she walked on, without someone scolding her every step of the way.

Which streets....

"Miss Ryder!" Annie pounded her on the back. "Is the tea too hot? Did it go down the wrong way?"

Celia, coughing, shook her head. "No. No. I am fine."

She was not fine. She was not fine at all.

But she did have a plan.

. . .

#

At best there might be an hour of time that she could steal from her errands—and even that would need to be explained away somehow. Well, she would think of something.

She followed a passageway into a hushed and damp courtyard surrounded by a rambling half-timbered building that seemed to have no door. When she found one, it led her to a long empty corridor where her footsteps echoed on an ancient flagstone floor.

She'd never been to the Inns of Court before. She followed the corridor until she came to an open door that revealed an office where three men were hunched over wooden desks stacked with papers, writing furiously. One glanced up and frowned at her.

She forced herself to step forward. "Good morning. I am looking for Mr. Maddox. Do you know where in these buildings I might find his chambers?"

The young man was handsome, ginger-haired and foppishly dressed in an aubergine colored jacket with a sharp collar. He did not rise. Indeed, he stared at her for so long that her face began to warm.

"I *beg* your pardon," she forced herself to say.

"And who might you be?"

She drew herself up—as much as it was possible to draw herself up in her shabby ensemble. "My business is not with you."

"Godfrey!" An inner door flew open and banged

against the wall. Celia jumped, her hand to her throat. "What is the meaning of this?"

"This young... *lady*"—the clerk said this in a sneering tone, as though he doubted that she were a lady at all—"says that she is looking for *Mr. Maddox*."

The man who'd flung open the door advanced. He was red-faced and grey-haired, and his silk waistcoat strained over his belly as he scooped an armload of papers off Godfrey's desk. He scarcely bothered to glance Celia's way. "I am Mr. Maddox."

"Then... then it is you I have come to see, sir."

"Do you have an appointment?"

"Oh... no."

"Then you shall have to make one." He turned to go back into the inner office. "I am afraid that I am very busy."

"Please. I have only one question. It is about my father. I believe that you were his solicitor?"

He scarcely paused. "Who is your father?"

"Mr. Julian Talbot. Of Hampshire."

He froze mid-step.

The office went silent. Mr. Maddox turned. The florid color drained patchily from his face. "Miss—Miss Talbot?"

Godfrey and the other two clerks put down their quills and stared.

Mr. Maddox recovered and bowed low. "Miss Talbot. There are important matters that must be discussed. *Privately*." He glared at his clerk, who was watching the exchange as avidly as though they were actors in a play. "Godfrey! You are idle as usual!"

Godfrey picked up his quill without taking his eyes off Celia. He seemed determined not to miss a moment of the drama.

"Miss Talbot." Mr. Maddox stepped back and gestured at the door to his office. She walked past Godfrey, who was fragrant with scent and now seemed to be trying to wink at her.

The lawyer shut the door and pulled out one of the leather upholstered chairs that faced his desk. She sat down. The windows faced north, over the hushed courtyard, and the only sound was the ticking of a clock on the mantel.

His steps as he returned to his own chair were heavy. "I have been searching for you for over a year, Miss Talbot. To have you simply appear here is…." He shook his head. "Are you… Are you… safe? Well?"

"Quite well, thank you," she lied. "I did not mean to cause a disruption. My question is only a small one. It may seem silly, but I…" She broke off and swallowed hard. "I wondered whether my father had had an appointment with you. When he was… killed."

Mr. Maddox frowned. "Had an appointment? No. He did not. It would have been in my calendar."

"Are you certain? He was to have gone to Bath, but I thought perhaps that he might have been coming here first to discuss my… my marriage settlements."

"Marriage settlements? I must beg your pardon. I was unaware that you are married."

"I—I am not."

There was a brief silence. The lawyer's frown deepened. "Miss Talbot, forgive me, but… are you in some sort of trouble?"

"No! Not at all!" She rose, her face heating. "Thank you very much for your time. I am sorry to have caused trouble. Please excuse me."

"Miss Talbot, please!" Mr. Maddox rose as well. "You must not leave without—that is, there are papers that you must sign—papers regarding the property in Oldbourne."

Her face heated. This respectable man with his three clerks and damask waistcoat would recoil if she explained the bargain that her father had struck. "There is no property. My father… mortgaged it." She didn't dare speak Wilkes's name.

Mr. Maddox was still frowning. "I am afraid that that is quite impossible."

"He… he was in a great deal of debt." There was a long silence. She couldn't bring herself to look at Mr. Maddox. Now that he understood her situation, he must see that she was poor, and unimportant, and not worthy of so much courteous treatment.

He cleared his throat. "Miss Talbot, you seem to be confused."

To her mortification, tears began to prickle her eyes. She blinked them back.

"Has no-one explained your position to you? Please—sit down."

What could he mean? She had no position. She hesitated, and she sat down again.

Mr. Maddox sat down again and folded his hands upon his desk. "Well. At risk of telling you facts with which you are already familiar, my father was your grandfather's solicitor. I took over his practice some years ago."

She hadn't known this. In fact, she'd only been able to recall Mr. Maddox's name because she'd had to write some of her father's business correspondence for him.

"And you know, of course, that your grandfather—

Sir Ramsey—settled Talbot Hall on your father when he married. He had hoped that your father—who had been a rather wild young man—would settle down to the responsibilities of land ownership. But..."

He broke off and shook his head. "Well. A few months after your mother's death, your father went to Sir Ramsey. He wished to purchase a commission in the army and make a new start in life, he said. But he needed money to settle some debts first. And he proposed that you be sent away to live with his older brother."

"Sent away?"

"Yes. He proposed that Sir Ramsey buy Talbot Hall back from him—but also allow him to live there and hunt on the lands whenever he wished to. Well, Sir Ramsey did not care for this rather... lopsided plan. He did not believe that your aunt and uncle would be kind to you. He also did not believe that your father would follow through with purchasing a commission in the army. In fact, he suspected that without the responsibility of managing the estate, your father would, instead, spend all of his time traveling to, er... race meetings, and watering holes, and so forth."

He sighed. "And so he insisted, instead, upon his own proposal. In exchange for advancing a generous sum of money—which was to relieve all your father's embarrassments and make him easy for the future—he made arrangements regarding Talbot Hall that were meant to protect your interests."

"Mine?"

"Yes. I suppose that you do not remember him well, but he was fond of you. At any rate, despite the money, your father—who was not used to not getting his own way—was angry. But of course, he could not afford to turn it down."

Mr. Maddox cleared his throat. "Miss Talbot? have now laid out the facts of your position. Do you have any questions?"

The facts of her position? "I beg your pardon, but... what position?"

Mr. Maddox's eyebrows went up. "I have just been explaining that Sir Ramsey made the estate over to you, in trust, with a life interest to your father. Talbot Hall is yours—although I am the trustee until you are twenty eight, or until you are married."

"I beg your pardon." He must not have understood. " My father ran out of money again. He mortgaged the property to—to... a moneylender. The estate is his now."

The lawyer's eyebrows climbed even higher. "That is impossible."

"I believe that he had... gaming losses."

"No, Miss Talbot. What I mean is that the estate could not be touched. Indeed, I told your father so—several times. He ordered me to draw up papers for you to sign. I had to tell him repeatedly that it was quite impossible, as you were not yet of age."

She couldn't reconcile this with what her father had said, the day that he'd told her that she must marry Wilkes. "But... if the estate was in my name, how did he continue to borrow money against it?"

There was an awkward silence. "Miss Talbot, without all the facts before me I cannot... but what you have described to me is... well, in a word... fraud."

She found herself on her feet. *Fraud*? Her mind was in a state of blank panic.

"Miss Talbot." The solicitor rose as well. "Please. I

did not mean to offend you. You must sign"—

"Thank you, good day."

She flung open the door to the outer office, bumped blindly into the corner of Godfrey's desk, and rushed down the corridor, rubbing her smarting thigh.

She must not cry. She must not cry. And yet, as she made her way through the jostling crowds of High Holborn, she found herself gulping back sobs and dabbing her eyes with her handkerchief. Just when she'd thought that she could sink no lower, she'd learned that her own father had tried to rob her—and had committed fraud.

She was too preoccupied to remember to put her veil down. And she was too preoccupied to notice the big man with the bruised face lounging against a wall.

And she was also too preoccupied to notice when he began to follow her as she made her way east—toward the lending library.

Chapter Fourteen

As it did every day, Spry's enormous house presented an indifferent face of pale cream stone to Grosvenor Square. Keynsham climbed the steps to the large front door. In the center of the door was a heavy brass knocker in the shape of a lion's head. He rapped it and waited.

He could have sworn that each day he came here, he was made to wait a little longer. He rapped again. Still no answer. He leaned against the iron railing and turned to face the square. The weather had been chilly and unsettled all spring, but today the air was warm and honey-scented. Meltingly golden afternoon sunlight streamed through the leaves of the trees, and the purple rhododendrons were in bloom. The street was swept and not a leaf was out of place. Birdsong rang from boughs hanging over the street and echoed from thickets deep within the square.

The peak of the season was approaching and London—or at least its wealthiest neighborhoods—was busier by the week as families continued to arrive in town. Several luxurious open carriages rolled past, doubtless on their way to the park.

Keynsham rubbed the back of his neck. To outward appearances, he too was a gentleman of leisure. But the reality was very different. He rose every day at dawn and spent the day at the building site. He and his men were racing to finish the second terrace of houses, and he couldn't afford to have the work slowed down by problems. He had to be on the spot, heading them off before they cost time—and money.

This morning he'd arrived to find Downey inspecting a pile of wood that had just been delivered by dray cart. "Well, well. Mr. Neate has sent us inferior timber, it seems." He slapped the pile with a large hand. "Look at the knots in these boards. And these ones here are warped."

Keynsham frowned. "I shall pay him a call, and clarify that we are perfectly happy to take our business elsewhere."

He got back into his old gig and drove himself north again to the river, where ships delivered wood from all over the world directly to the docks of the timber yards that lined the Southwark riverfront. If they couldn't get the boards today, the framers' work would be delayed... which would mean that the roofers' work would be delayed... which would mean that the glaziers' work would be delayed... and so on, and so on.

As he drew up in the yard at Neate's sprawling and busy establishment, he was greeted by the sharp, sweet scent of freshly cut boards. "Good morning, sir!" Mr. Neate puffed out from his office, bowing. He turned to shout into the open doors of the warehouse. "Davis! Lord Something is here."

That was Keynsham's nickname. Downey had started it, of course. The other men at the building site had picked it up, and now Lord Something was just what everyone called him. He was quite certain that Mr. Neate didn't realize that he was actually a peer. "Mr. Neate. Good morning. The timber that you have sent us is entirely unsatisfactory."

Neate turned red under his bushy side-whiskers. "My apologies, sir! I 'ave no idea which of the men loaded that order. I'll make sure it don't 'appen again."

"Please ensure that it does not. And in the meantime, I shall personally select the timbers for a replacement order—with your warehouse to cover the cost of immediate delivery, of course. We require the wood today."

"Of course." Mr. Neate winced, but went off to shout at his staff. "Davis! Where 'ave you got to? 'Oo loaded the Grange Grove order? Lord Something's 'ad to drive all the way 'ere on account of it!"

The nickname was useful. After all, if it became known in the *ton* that Viscount Alford was spending his days haggling over terms for orders of glass and bricks, people would talk.

Yet his long hours and attention to detail were beginning to pay off. The first terrace of houses was complete. Families were moving in as the rest of the development took shape. Smoke rose from chimneys and washing hung on lines—and the first quarter rents had covered the second loan payment.

How he longed for Celia to see the place, now that the empty shells of buildings had become real houses! If he could spend just a single day with her...

But of course, he couldn't. He'd ruined everything. And he was still bound to Miss Spry.

Which brought him back... here.

Freshly bathed and dressed in clothes that suggested that he'd done nothing strenuous all day, Lord Something had become Lord Alford again, just in time for the fashionable calling hour of five o'clock.

He rapped on the door again. Finally, it opened. "Ah. Good afternoon, Job. How are you this fine spring day? I have come to call upon Miss Spry."

Job couldn't quite meet his eyes. "I—I... Unfortunately, Miss Spry is... er... not at home."

"Thank you, Job. Please give her my card. Good afternoon."

"Very good, your lordship." The door closed.

This little pantomime complete, Keynsham had fulfilled his obligation. Now all he had to do was find some way to keep his mind off Celia for the rest of the day, until it was time to go to bed so that he could get up early in the morning and do it all again.

He glanced at the sky and checked his watch. "Young! I believe that I shall go to Jackson's. You may take the horses home."

Young touched the brim of his hat. "Very good, your lordship."

* * *

"Well, well, Alford! Something wrong? You are mightily Friday-faced! Shall we have a turn up?"

Keynsham looked up, surprised. He'd been steadily pounding a bag in one corner of the boxing saloon, practicing his jabs, for over an hour. With its dark blue papered walls hung with framed engravings of famous bouts of decades past, and its incongruously academic air, Jackson's had always been his refuge. So long as he was here the world outside faded away, and people left him alone. That was the unspoken etiquette of the place.

"Well? What d'you say, viscount?"

Now he recognized the fellow who was addressing him so familiarly: Mr. Bartlett, a loud-voiced young man he knew only to speak to at his club.

He nodded, concealing his irritation. "How do you do, sir? I should be happy to, but I am leaving presently."

"Oh, come now, Alford! It will do you good. I think that we can all guess why you look so glum! Thirty thousand pounds!"

Keynsham was so surprised that he stopped hitting the bag. "I beg your pardon?"

Bartlett sucked air through his teeth and shook his head. "Damme, but fate is cruel! To think of all that money being swallowed up by the Cheshire coffers! Why, they are already so rich that they will not even notice it! Whereas everyone knows what a difference it would have made to *you*."

"I am afraid that I do not know what you mean."

Bartlett laid a roguish finger next to his nose. "Oh-ho-ho-*ho*! You *are* a deep one! I was told that you keep your cards very close to your vest, sir—and now I see that my informants were correct!" He winked. "Well, you need not fear. I am the very soul of discretion! I know all about Miss Spry and the marquess, and I have told scarce four people." He thought a moment. "Or, well—six. Or seven. At most."

Miss Spry and the marquess...? The Cheshire coffers? Was Bartlett referring to the Duke of Cheshire's son—the Marquess of Ladbrooke?

Bartlett appeared to take his silence as confirmation. "Ah, well. Now, you see, a bout will do you good. Left! Right! Another left!" He raised his hands and jabbed at the air. "You will be over her soon enough—take it from me. But damme, the loss of the money is a plump in the old breadbasket, eh? Particularly as your father lived on the top ropes and left *you* under the hatches!"

"I beg your pardon," said Keynsham in his frostiest tone.

"Oh, no shame accrues to *you*, your lordship! Everyone knows that *you* are an out and outer! But damme, a bit of the Spanish would have come in handy, eh? Always does. Always does." He sighed heavily and shook his head. "*We* all know how it is these days. *Lud*! And whatever the talk about her, no one can deny that Miss Spry is a pretty girl."

He hadn't realized that there was gossip about his financial position... or that Miss Spry had so much as met the Marquess of Ladbrooke. This conversation was filling in gaps in his information that he hadn't known that he had.

"Then there is Townley!" Bartlett shook his head again. "Damme, but this business of setting the young marquess at odds with him over her—for they have quite fallen out now—is not at all the thing. No, sir—not the thing at all! You know Townley?"

At odds? "I cannot say that I do."

"Not surprised." Bartlett snorted. "Nothing to recommend him but twelve thousand a year. And as for the talk that I am jealous of him... well, that little minx may be many things—but she is certainly not worth dueling over. The daughter of a cit, and no better than she should be, as anyone…"

He broke off. The blood drained from his face. "That is, I… I beg your pardon, your lordship. I mean no… I had assumed that your, er… your engagement to the young lady was not…"

Keynsham could bear it no longer. "Miss Spry and I have no understanding."

"*Indeed*, sir?" Bartlett let out a breath. "Well. *Well!*" He produced a modishly spotted handkerchief and swiped it across his brow. "I am vastly relieved! For a moment I thought that I was about to get a thrashing! Your face was what I should call thunderous! And of course, you are a legendary giver, sir! *Legendary*!" He mopped his brow again. "Damme, but I do put my foot in it! Everyone is always saying so. 'Bartlett, you do put your foot in it,' they say—but then I go and do it again!"

Keynsham regretted saying anything. He could be certain that Bartlett would spread his denial all over Brooks's, White's, and Boodle's by midnight… and that it would be all over Mayfair by noon tomorrow.

On the other hand, if even half of what Bartlett said was true, Miss Spry had been playing him for a fool.

"Well, she is the young marquess's problem now, *I* should say!" Bartlett clapped him familiarly on the shoulder. "Of course, the duke is up in the boughs! Says it was a bad day's work when his son went to Twickenham, and that he hopes that he will not live to see the day when an underbred chit like Miss Spry is addressed as the Duchess of Cheshire. Which, when you think on it, he will not!"

He laughed. "Am I not droll? Won't live to see the day…! Yes, I should think not! Because you see, if she *were* the duchess, the present duke would be dead, of course! That is my joke. Rather good, is it not? Every so often I do hit upon a good bit of banter."

He rattled on, but Keynsham wasn't listening. Instead, he was recalling the number of times that he'd gone to the house in Grosvenor Square, only to be met by the barely opened door and Job, the awkward footman—who must have been under orders to lie to him. "I beg your pardon. All of this happened at Twickenham?"

"Why, yes, of course!" Bartlett was still laughing at his own witticisms. "Spry has a house on the river. You have not seen it? After Miss Spry had that driving incident on the bridge… well, her dear papa thought it best to remove to the country until the upset died down. They have been there near a fortnight. Poor Townley! He actually believed that he had made an impression on Miss Spry! But then along came the marquess, and no doubt the girl began to imagine what it would be like to be addressed as 'your grace.'"

Nearly a fortnight. Keynsham blotted his face with a Turkish towel and pulled out his watch. "Please excuse me."

"We are not going to spar?" Bartlett's face fell. "Dear me! I hope that I have not offended you."

"Not at all." With effort, Keynsham kept his face smooth. "I am afraid that I simply did not realize the time. I have an appointment."

* * *

"Well, Gooley. It is good of you to join me. What tidings of our missing colleague?"

The little man looked blank.

"I am asking you if you have found Fenton."

"Oh. That. No. No one's seen 'im."

"What's that, Gooley? You are mumbling again."

"We 'aven't found 'im, boss."

"And no doubt you are leaving no stone unturned."

Gooley didn't seem to recognize this as sarcasm.

Wilkes folded his arms. Something was wrong. People he'd once cowed into obedience had become defiant. His men couldn't seem to accomplish anything at all. Every bit of luck seemed to break in someone else's favor.

He stared out the window at the dirty brick wall a few feet away. The view depressed him. But then, so did all of it. Oh, these rooms were luxuriously decorated enough. Indeed, many of the furnishings—including the carpets—had been seized in lieu of cash from various wealthy creditors. But the place overlooked a narrow alley where sunlight only penetrated at midday, and the neighborhood was noisy—and frequently stank.

Perhaps Fenton was dead. If he'd taken everything he knew about Wilkes's history to the grave... well, Wilkes would shed no tears.

"Well. Let us move on to our final item: Miss Talbot."

"What about 'er, boss?"

"What *about* her?" He had to hold himself back. "You were to *trace* her."

"Oh. That. No. No sign of 'er."

"Let me clarify something for you, Gooley. From now on, finding Miss Talbot is your first objective."

The little man nodded. "Yes, boss."

Wilkes considered. If Fenton was dead—and if he had Celia—he wouldn't have to lie awake at night worrying. And then, once he got rid of Gooley and the rest of these useless men, a move to the country and a new life as a gentleman of leisure might suit him. Yes, it might suit him very well indeed.

"Boss?"

He glanced up. "Why are you still here, Gooley?"

"I—I might 'ave some information."

"Well?"

Gooley shuffled nervously. "Prob'ly it ain't nuffink important."

"I am the judge of that."

The little man cleared his throat. "The young lord is giving a ball. At 'is 'ouse. I 'ad it from a lady 'oo knows a friend of one of the 'ousemaids. She says as they spend all day every day moving furniture back and forth and suchlike."

Wilkes narrowed his eyes. "Did you say a *ball*?"

"A party, like."

"Yes, Gooley. I am aware of the meaning of the word *ball*."

He steepled the tips of his fingers together and sat back. *Well, well, well.* For once, Gooley had brought him something useful.

And now it all began to make sense: The reason the viscount had been trying to borrow money was to pay for a ball.

He ought to have realized that it would come down to something as inconsequential as this. They were all the same, the gentry—putting on fronts of wealth, when in reality half of them were living on credit. Not that he could complain. After all, the desperate financial straits of the gentry had made him rich.

A rare smile—lopsided from disuse—twisted his face. Gooley's eyes widened in alarm.

Wilkes didn't notice. His streak of bad luck had just ended. He could feel it. Oh, Lord Alford delayed his plans for Celia. But now Wilkes could see that he wasn't faultless, or invincible. Indeed, he was just as much of a fool as all the other swells.

And more importantly, on the night of the ball his seemingly impregnable house would be open.

Chapter Fifteen

Keynsham stood on the drive for a moment, collecting his thoughts. This was almost the last place he wished to be. But the elusive Miss Spry had strung him along long enough.

Spry's country house was a fanciful brick pile with a decorative tower on each corner, mullioned windows, and a row of crenelations across the front of the roof like a castle—though as far as Keynsham knew, it had actually been built some time in the last ten years.

He'd driven himself. The day was oppressively warm and overcast. As his boots crunched across the gravel, a rising wind turned the leaves of the poplar trees along the riverbank inside out, showing their silvery undersides. Unless he was mistaken, it would soon rain.

He knocked. The footman opened the door almost instantly—and froze at the sight of him, his mouth agape. "Ah. Good day, Job. What a pleasant surprise it is to find you here! We are old friends now—are we not? I am here, of course, to call upon Miss Spry."

For a moment, Job seemed unable to speak. "I...

your lordship." He gave a strangled cough. "I—I... will see if Miss Spry is at home."

He hurried away, leaving Keynsham in the soaring entrance hall, and returned a few minutes later with the information that Miss Spry was, in fact, at home.

"Well, well. That makes a change. You must have beat me down here, Job. Are you enjoying Twickenham?"

"I—yes, your lordship." He turned bright red.

Keynsham followed him down a long corridor with a gleaming oak floor and violently emerald walls. At last they reached a sitting room with a wall of windows overlooking a broad lawn. Outside, servants were carrying trays to a marquee just below the terrace. Evidently the family was about to hold an entertainment.

"Thank you, Job."

Job bowed, still scarlet. "Your lordship."

A few minutes later, Miss Spry tripped into the room. "Lord Alford!" She held her fingertips to her half-open lips and widened her blue eyes. Her impression of being shocked wasn't much more convincing than her fainting spell had been. "What an unlooked-for pleasure! Why, I have not seen you this age! Whatever can have brought you to Twickenham?"

He bowed. "I came to see you, Miss Spry."

"*Me?*" Now her delicate, be-ringed hand was laid upon her breast. "But... to what do I owe this honor?"

He'd planned a speech. He'd been going to say that he was conscious of the distress that she must have felt after the *misunderstanding* at the ball. He'd also planned to say that if circumstances had caused her feelings for him to change, he would, as a gentleman, accept her dismissal.

But her display of surprise was so overdone that his mind went blank. He honestly didn't know what he could say to her. Was she going to pretend that they had never been on the brink of engagement?

Or... had he gone mad? After all, he'd been under a great deal of strain this past year. Perhaps he'd imagined the entire episode.

But he'd just received a large bill from the solicitors who'd spent many expensive hours trying to thrash out a marriage settlement. No doubt it was possible to hallucinate many things, but unfortunately, he didn't think that a solicitor's bill was one of them.

He took a deep breath. "I apologize, Miss Spry. I believed that you were aware that, er... negotiations were underway, and that we were to reach a formal understanding at our next appointment—the one at which you unfortunately fainted. Your behavior now, however, suggests that you were not aware that this was the case."

"My *behavior...*?" She held her eyes wide and blinked at him in apparent astonishment. "I hope, my lord, that I have not offended you in some way? I greatly value your good opinion."

He felt an almost irresistible urge to shake his head to clear it. "I... Miss Spry, you do recall the events that occurred at the Mainwarings' rout—do you not?"

"The Mainwarings..." She frowned. "Dear me, I am afraid that I cannot be certain which event you mean! I am invited to so very many entertainments! The London season is so very fatiguing!"

Well, this was simply insulting. "I do not wish to be indelicate. But I must refer to the, er... incident in the

Mainwarings' library. Your chaperone and one of your friends made a serious accusation against me. As a result, your father's solicitors and my solicitors were in the process of negotiating our marriage settlements."

Was that a faint blush on her face? "Heavens, Lord Alford! I am afraid that you will have to ask papa about his solicitors. Dull fellows! I am certain that *I* have never spoken to them in my life."

"Miss Spry!" He found himself rubbing his forehead. "I did not come to discuss solicitors. I came to say that..." How was she able to confuse the conversation so much? He cleared his throat. "I will, of course, accept your dismissal. But as matters were all but settled between us, let us at least be frank with one other now."

"*Matters?*" Her head tipped back as she trilled a laugh. "Oh, Lord Alford! You are always so very droll! *Matters*, indeed! What can you mean? Dear me! Why, I hope that you do not feel that you must refer to our *friendship* in such a very formal way! I shall always be very glad to meet you, I am sure—as long as you do not use the word *matters*! Why, I am quite frightened now!"

"I beg your pardon." He made a slight, ironic bow.

She must be aware that unless she released him from his obligation, he couldn't consider himself to be free. But if she wouldn't acknowledge that any obligation had existed in the first place, how could he be released?

A silence fell. "Well!" She smiled brightly. "You certainly have chosen the weather for your visit, it seems! Have you friends staying at Twickenham?"

"Miss Spry, as I have told you, I came only to speak with you."

Once again, her delicate hand flew to her breast.

"Heavens! And the roads are so hot and dusty! I scarcely know what to say!"

Her dark ringlets and china doll prettiness were set off by a ruffled pink muslin gown with deep lace trim. She was a lovely girl. But nothing about her touched him. It never had. And then, as she gazed at him with those wide, innocent blue eyes, he saw that she was wearing the very pair of pink coral ear bobs that he'd given her during their brief, enforced courtship.

The sight of them made it all real. It *had* happened. He'd paid those awkward calls. He'd endured the stilted conversation and the horror of knowing that he was trapped.

How much more of this humiliation must he endure? All he wanted was his freedom—freedom to find Celia and make her the promises that he'd longed to make her months ago.

Outside, the parade of servants carrying trays out to the marquee continued. The party must a large one. He tried one last time. "Miss Spry, I have no wish to, er, distress either of us. If you do not wish this interview to continue, please tell me. I merely wish to understand what your feelings are now."

"My *feelings*?" She paused, blinking, apparently racking her brain to try to imagine what he could possibly expect her to say. "Of course, I hold you in great esteem, Lord Alford." She gave him another bright, vacant-seeming smile. "I do hope that we shall always be friends."

He folded his arms. "Friends."

"Why, of course, Lord Alford! I shall *always* be glad to consider you my friend."

Well, it wasn't a direct dismissal. But it seemed to be

the closest that she would come to it. And besides—he'd reached the limit of his patience. He bowed. "Miss Spry."

And then, before he could say anything that a gentleman would regret, he found himself leaving the room, striding down the long corridor and through the entry hall. Job darted after him and opened the door just in time.

He took a breath as he stepped back onto the gravel drive. What a relief it was to be away from Miss Spry's lash-batting and titters and talk of "friendship."

He sprang up onto the gig's seat. A winding gravel drive led back to the road through a lawn dotted with enormous cedars of Lebanon. He was free. He didn't see how any sane person could consider him obligated to Miss Spry after that insulting interview.

As he reached the gates, a high-perch phaeton with enormous glossy wheels rolled through them—and Keynsham found himself locking eyes with the Marquess of Ladbrooke himself. The marquess's weak chin dropped.

Keynsham pulled up. "Ah! Good day, Ladbrooke!"

"Alford." The marquess's tone was suspicious. His eyes narrowed, which increased his resemblance to a weasel. "Were you, er, calling upon Miss Spry?"

"Indeed I was!"

"I see." His eyes narrowed still more.

The young fool! The Marquess of Ladbrooke was all of nineteen, and said to be hot-heated and prone to jealousy. But surely he couldn't be jealous of *Keynsham*! Or... could he?

In an instant Keynsham saw it all. He almost had to admire Miss Spry's ingenuity. She'd come perilously close to settling for a penniless viscount—him. Yet only a few short weeks later, she'd managed to leverage the rumors of their engagement to provoke a rich and jealous marquess into declaring himself.

"Not staying for the party, then?" Ladbrooke was still eyeing him suspiciously.

"No indeed. I have an appointment in town."

"Ah." Ladbrooke's expression relaxed into a condescending smirk. "Well, I shall not keep you. No doubt you have many... *pressing* matters to discuss."

Evidently he was referring to the gossip about Keynsham's finances. Keynsham forced himself to look grave. "Indeed. Well, enjoy the, er... *jollification.* It looks like rain." Before the marquess could reply, he clucked to his horses. A moment later, he'd cleared the gates and was turning onto the road for London.

To know that he didn't have to marry that scheming, lying... He took another deep breath. For once, his selfish, spendthrift father had done him a favor. If the fifth viscount hadn't left the estate in near ruin, Keynsham would have been accounted one of the wealthier peers in England.

And if that had been the case, Miss Spry most certainly wouldn't have thrown him over.

And Celia would have been lost to him forever.

* * *

"Let me in." There was the sound of a scuffle outside the door, followed by a thud. "*Let me in*!"

Wilkes rose and straightened his cuffs. The door burst open. A large man stumbled into his office, followed by the guard. The guard raised and cocked the pistol he held.

Without taking his eyes off Wilkes, the large man raised his hands.

Wilkes met his scowling gaze. "Ah. Fenton. I wondered if you might turn up."

The big man's scowl deepened. "I ain't saying nothing 'til he takes the gun off me."

Wilkes glanced at the man holding the pistol and nodded. "Shut the door, Comstock."

The man lowered the pistol, gave Fenton one final glare, and left the office, jerking the door shut behind him.

For a moment all was silent but for the big man's breathing. Wilkes studied him dispassionately. So. He wasn't dead. That was unfortunate.

He had a badly healed cut across the bridge of his nose and two fading black eyes. It seemed to cost him visible effort to unclench his fists.

"Well. What brings you here today, Fenton? Sentimentality?"

Fenton's eyes narrowed. "Not happy to see me then, eh, Wilkes?"

"Oh, I don't know, Fenton. Let me see. I sent you and Mowcher to follow Miss Talbot and bring her back. And instead, both of you disappeared for over a month."

"Mowcher's dead."

"Dead? How's that?"

"The young lord shot him in the throat."

The young lord. If Wilkes never heard that phrase again it would be too soon. "I see." He stared hard into Fenton's face, wondering whether he was lying and had killed Mowcher himself. "And where exactly have you been?"

"The young lord knocked me out and left me tied up."

"And yet here you are."

"A woodcutter untied me."

"Convenient. And what then?"

"I killed him."

"Who? The woodcutter?"

"I had to. He'd seen Mowcher's body and was raising a fuss. He was all for taking me in and fetching the local constabulary."

"I see." Wilkes stared out the sunless window of his luxurious office. So. Fenton had left a trail of destruction. As usual.

"I had to walk all the way here—at night, in case they was searching for me. I hadn't even the blunt for a stagecoach fare."

Wilkes refocused his eyes on Fenton. He hadn't got any better looking—or cleaner—in the time that he'd been missing. "Then you have been back in London for some time, I take it. It does not take six weeks to walk here from Hampshire."

Fenton, who usually slouched, drew himself up. "I just told you what happened. And I ain't eaten in more'n' a day now. And you ain't paid me, neither."

Wilkes said nothing.

Fenton's ordinarily blank and slab-like face flushed. "Oh. I see how it is. And after I helped you with the... the matter, too. When me own brother was hanged for less!"

"Your 'help' created a whole new problem, Fenton

—so I wouldn't be so hasty to bring that up, if I were you."

"Is that so." Fenton folded his huge arms. "Well, you was the one who said where I was to leave it."

That was true. But Wilkes didn't appreciate being reminded of it. And more importantly, Fenton's words were a veiled threat. He knew what Wilkes had done.

Fenton folded his arms and rocked back on his heels. "The reason I come to see you is that I happen to have information. Information that I know you want. But mayhap I'll keep it to myself—seeing as how you ain't even going to pay me."

Wilkes didn't look at Fenton. He tidied a stack of papers on his desk. Seconds ticked by.

"Ain't you going to ask me what it is?"

"No."

"Suit yourself."

Fenton turned and headed for the door.

Wilkes could tell Comstock to shoot him and he'd be dead on the landing before his foot was on the first step.

But Fenton wouldn't have come back at all unless he thought that his information was valuable... valuable enough to get him back into Wilkes's good graces.

"Very well." He would make Fenton pay for this insolence later. "I shall advance you two pounds, and you will tell me whatever it is. And if you are wasting my time, it will be the last time that you do so."

Fenton turned and studied him. "Two whole pound, eh? Oh, I want more than that. I want *all* the pay I'm owed—and something else, besides."

There was a long silent moment. Wilkes was suddenly uncomfortable. He'd always thought of

Fenton as stupid. But what was he really thinking? It was impossible to read his expressionless face. "Five pounds, and that is all. Now, what is it?"

Fenton studied him. He folded his arms. "I seen her."

"Seen—saw—who?"

"Squire Talbot's daughter—as was."

Wilkes felt as though the air had been knocked out of his lungs. If Fenton were lying... "Where? When?"

Fenton gave a little chuckle. "Now then, Andrew Wilkes. We need to come to a *proper* agreement afore I tell you that."

Wilkes's heart was thudding painfully. He realized that he'd feared that he'd never see Celia again. He forced a conciliatory tone into his voice. "Surely there is no need for this suspicion, Fenton. There has merely been a... temporary loss of trust. On both our parts."

"Aye. Seemingly so."

"Where did you see her?"

The big man shrugged. "Now, now. I'm coming to that. See, I knows you, Wilkes. I knows how you get jumpy. I'd wager ten yellow boys that you was thinking to have Comstock out there shoot me dead."

Wilkes took a long breath. "I do not know where you got such a notion, Fenton. I should say that you are the one who is 'jumpy.'"

"Is that so?" Fenton continued to stare at him. "Well. Then I'll tell you a little story. After the young lord left me tied up out there in the woods, I had a few days to think things through—as a man will do, when he's wondering if he's going to die of thirst. And do you know what I thought? I thought to myself, 'What have you been doing with your life, Fenton?'"

Wilkes spoke through clenched teeth. "Stop your jawing, Fenton, and tell me what you want."

"I'm coming to that. See, I ain't happy. And what I want is to get out of the game. Can't nobody trust you, Wilkes. And I don't want to be nowhere near you when certain things as you've done catch up with you. Like that nasty business with Squire Talbot."

Wilkes spoke through clenched teeth. "The man *cheated* me."

Fenton's expression didn't change. "Aye—and so you've said, many a time. But if you'd kept your head, you'd have had Miss Talbot to wife a year ago. Best revenge is money—but now you don't got that, neither."

His insolence was so provoking that it was all Wilkes could do not to reach into his desk drawer for his pistol and shoot him himself. He forced himself to speak calmly. "Very well, Fenton. Thank you for your... observations." He opened his other desk drawer—the one where he kept his ready money—took out a leather purse and began counting out coins. "And now you will tell me where you saw Miss Talbot, and how you will help me to get her back."

Fenton would have to die. But for now, Wilkes had no choice but to play along.

Fenton's eyes were on the gold coins. He seemed to be calculating something. Wilkes held his breath. Fortunately, Fenton's stupidity—or perhaps his greed—won out.

"Where I saw Miss Talbot. *Where I saw Miss Talbot.*" He blew out a breath. "Oh, I can do better than that, Andrew Wilkes. I can tell you where she'll *be.*"

Chapter Sixteen

As she hurried along the crowded pavements of Cheapside, Celia felt as though everyone could see straight through her veil to the disgrace of what her father had been. She was filled with shame. How had she not suspected that her whole life had been a lie?

Oh, by the time she was fifteen or sixteen, she'd seen her father for what he was—or so she'd thought, anyway. His London shopping trips, his rings and stick-pins and snuff boxes, his travel, his horses... all his interests were expensive and frivolous, and always seemed to leave him with little time to be at home—let alone to manage the estate.

But she'd excused all of this. After all, everyone in Oldbourne knew that Mr. Julian Talbot wasn't just *anyone*. He was the third son of Sir Ramsey Talbot. He was the owner of Talbot Hall! And he was tall and handsome, with easy manners that gave him a natural consequence everywhere he went. He received countless invitations and spent months traveling from country house party to country house party, his valet and hunters in tow.

He didn't remarry. As the years passed, his vanity continued to be gratified by his belief that various ladies were secretly infatuated with him—but he snickered at all of them behind their backs. He could discern faults in the loveliest ladies, and hints of barely repressed desire for him in the most banal conversations.

Still, he was unfailingly charming, and everyone began to say that the reason that poor Mr. Talbot hadn't married again was that he'd loved his wife so much that he couldn't bear to think of it.

But Celia knew him better. And finally, she'd begun to admit to herself that the father she'd once idolized wasn't what he ought to be. And when he'd told her that she must marry Wilkes, she'd asked herself whether he cared about her happiness at all.

Well, now she had no choice but to face the truth: Her father hadn't been a careless gentleman who'd kept poor records of his expenditures. He'd known exactly what he was doing. He'd even tried to rob her—his only child—of the legacy that her grandfather had left for her.

Meanwhile, Wilkes had continued to advance him money—likely on no more security than a handshake and a night of drinking. No doubt the gangster had thought had that he was taking advantage of her father's lack of business sense. But all along, her father had been the one cheating him.

At least now she knew why Wilkes was still hunting her.

He wanted what was owed to him. He wanted Talbot Hall.

* * *

"It is at number thirty-three, Leadenhall Street. The offices are upstairs." Pomona was all but wringing her hands. "You are certain that you do not mind? It is dreadfully fashionable. If you are anxious that you may run into Miss Spry or some of her friends, I should understand completely."

"Why should I be anxious? I have nothing to hide. Any connection between me and Miss Spry is at an end."

"Is it, though?" She looked at him. "I, for one, shall not feel secure of that until she has actually married the marquess!"

"*Pomona*. Now, you have told me the direction three times. I promise you that the fact that Mr. Wynde's offices are above his lending library is burned into my memory. And I am certain that I am quite capable of locating the door."

"He has ever so many, you know. Libraries, I mean. In Brighton, and Tunbridge Wells, and Bath, and... well, all the fashionable places." She turned pale and swallowed. "Oh no! What if he publishes it and no one likes it? Then I shall be the laughingstock of the entire country!"

He laid a hand on her shoulder. "Pomona. Take a deep breath. In thirty seconds you have gone from imagining that Mr. Wynde will not like your book to imagining that all of England will not like it."

She gulped. "I would feel so much better if I could speak to Mr. Wynde myself. Do tell him that if he wishes me to make any changes—anything, the slightest changes at all!—I shall make them without hesitation!"

She clutched the brown paper-wrapped parcel tighter. "Oh, if only mama had not arranged this last-minute dress fitting!"

"I shall tell him that only if he brings it up himself first. You need not volunteer until then."

A housemaid knocked on the open dressing room door. "Miss Keynsham? Begging your pardon, but Lady Alford says that you must leave now."

Keynsham nodded. "Thank you, Sally. You may tell her ladyship that Miss Keynsham will be with her in a moment."

Sally winced, curtseyed, and hurried off on the unenviable errand of giving this message to their mother.

Pomona—who was dressed in a dowdy lavender bonnet and pelisse that made her look jaundiced—gave her brother a pleading look. "Promise me that you will remember every word that he says! And you must not reveal your identity."

Keynsham was dressed for the building site, where he was going later. "I promise. And I shall tell him that I am the imaginary Mrs. Elizabeth Brown's... brother-in-law? Cousin? Uncle?"

"Brother will do." She bit her lip. "Oh dear! What if something goes wrong?"

"Thirty-three, Leadenhall Street. Upstairs. Give manuscript to publisher. I cannot imagine that there is much to go wrong—even in the hands of a blockhead like me."

"Pomon-*a*!" Lady Alford's voice echoed through the house in a most unladylike fashion.

"Oh no! She is on the stair! Here!" She thrust the heavy parcel into his hands. "Be certain that she does not see it! She threatened to burn it if she saw me working on it again."

"*Pomona*!"

"Go!" He squeezed her shoulder. "And please stop making yourself ill."

With a final anxious glance, his sister hurried away.

* * *

"Well, well, well." The grubby little man leaned back against the wall with a smirk. "Seems a lending library is the place where all the ladies is nowadays, eh? Wonder what's in them books. All kinds of filth and smut, I shouldn't warrant —for all these gentry morts look so innocent and clean in their lace and their frills!" He spat into the gutter. "What do all the ladies want to be reading for, anyways?"

Fenton folded his arms. "Mayhap you'd have a better notion of that if you'd ever learned your letters."

Gooley squinted up at the threatening sky. "Waste of time, if you ask me."

"I *didn't* ask you."

"And as to that Miss Talbot, you got no way to know she's going to be 'ere."

"I seen her at this library before."

"Is that so?" Gooley snorted. "That don't mean she's coming back."

Fenton stared down at him. "Thought you was supposed to be clever, Gooley. Thought you was the boss's big man in London. Don't you know how a lending library works?"

Gooley spat again. "No. And I ain't interested."

They were standing in the mouth of an alley off

Leadenhall Street. Further down the alley, a carriage waited, its shades already pulled down. This little operation ought to be easy enough.

But the racket of the City was making Fenton's head ache. He'd got his bell rung when Lord Alford had pistol-whipped him, and no mistake. Not only that, but there was still a sharp pain in his side whenever he took a deep breath. Curse the young lord. He hit harder than a gorger like him should have any business hitting.

Gooley elbowed him. "Boss weren't too 'appy when you didn't come back, eh?"

His elbow caught Fenton in his sore ribs. He swore loudly. "Keep your mitts off."

Gooley held up his hands in exaggerated innocence. "Didn't lay a finger on you."

Fenton stared down at him until Gooley looked away. "Prime pair of stinkers you 'ave there," he said finally, by way of a conciliatory remark. "The young lord pulled your cork, eh?"

Fenton didn't bother answering.

"Don't see what we're doing this for, anyway." Gooley spat again. "Why this particular bit of skirt? Plenty of London ladies prettier than her."

"It's because her father..." Fenton broke off. He still got the shivers when he thought of that night. It was Wilkes who'd done it. But Fenton had helped him get rid of the evidence. He'd seen plenty in his time, but...

Gooley was staring at him expectantly. "Her father what?"

"Nothing. Her father were the village squire."

"Oo-*er*!" Gooley began to snicker. "Well, why didn't you say so? Dearie me! The daughter of the village squire, is she? Very grand, very grand. What village was it, again? Nothington, Nothingtonshire?"

Fenton's naturally blank and slab-like face betrayed none of his inner rage. He wished now that he hadn't come back to London at all. He shouldn't have told Wilkes that he'd seen Miss Talbot. It would be a bad day's work turning the poor girl over to him.

In his opinion, Wilkes had gone a little queer in the attic. On the terrible night when he'd tried to call in his loans and the squire had told him that the deed to the property was no longer his—well... the memory of Squire Talbot's bloody, battered body out there in the stables still turned Fenton's stomach.

He shook his head to try to clear it. At least he could be certain that the young lord wouldn't interfere again today. Fenton'd had more than enough of him swooping down out of nowhere, all gleaming hair and righteous blows, like a stained glass window of the Archangel Michael come to life.

Fortunately, there wasn't the slightest reason that the viscount would be visiting a lending library in the City on a showery Tuesday morning. Besides, Fenton would have spotted him. With his liveried coachman and his matched grays and his silk top hat, Lord Alford was hard to miss.

Gooley spat again. "How long we going to stand out 'ere, then? Why, any one of these London girls is twice as smart and pretty as that whey-faced Miss Talbot. Look at that frigate!" He jerked his chin towards a young lady in a bonnet bedecked with blue silk flowers. "Fetching thing, ain't she, with them pink cheeks and that yellow hair? And that's if the boss wants a lady. Me, I wouldn't bother. Since the war, the brothels is full of the prettiest French whores you ever seen. Clean, too. Or mostly clean. Boss could 'ave 'is pick. 'E's made a success of 'imself 'ere in London."

Fenton snorted. "Oh aye. He's a regular Dick Whittington, Wilkes is."

Gooley narrowed his eyes. No doubt he planned to report this disloyal remark to Wilkes.

A downpour began. The chattering girls on the pavement shrieked as they scattered to waiting carriages. Within a minute or two, the street was nearly deserted.

At that moment, a veiled lady appeared and darted into the library. If you hadn't been watching for her, you'd never have known she was Miss Talbot.

Fenton straightened. Poor girl. She'd never done him any harm.

But then, business was business.

* * *

The clerk who showed Keynsham upstairs eyed his broad-brimmed hat and loose hopsack jacket with a raised eyebrow. "Mr. Wynde will be with you momentarily." He gave a little cough. "*Sir.*"

Keynsham took off his hat and suppressed a smile as he made himself comfortable on the elegant settee. He'd driven himself in his gig—as he did every morning—and was dressed to walk through a muddy building site with Downey later. No doubt he'd have had a different reception dressed as Lord Alford... rather than Lord Something.

The antechamber was remarkably stylish. Evidently the Thetis Press took its status in the fashionable world seriously. The walls were papered in arsenic green set off by glossy white woodwork, and a polished ebony table displayed stacks of what must be the latest titles from the publisher, smartly bound in gold-embossed blue and red morocco.

At length the inner door opened. "Mrs... ah... *Mr.* Brown?" The harried-seeming man who spoke bounced a pair of gold-framed spectacles in one hand as he studied Keynsham. "I confess, sir, that you are not at all what I expected! Although it is fair to say that your prose does have a certain, er... *muscular* quality to it."

Keynsham stood and bowed. "Oh, I am not the author. That is my sister—Mrs. Brown. I am come merely to deliver her manuscript to your hand."

"Indeed, sir!" Mr. Wynde bowed as well. "Because we do have a considerable number of male authors who use ladies' names. I assure you that we at Thetis Press are notably discrete."

"And I assure you that I have never had a literary bone in my body." He handed the manuscript to Wynde.

Wynde put on his spectacles. "Ah. Thank you." He hefted the parcel as though he were assessing its weight. "Well, please tell your, er, *sister* how favorably impressed I was by the sample chapters that she sent me. The opening scene of the heroine's escape down the icy mountainside in the Alps was positively harrowing. *Harrowing*! I could not put it down! I must tell you, Mr. Brown, that unless I am very much mistaken, *The Tomb of Valdarno* will be amongst our most successful debuts of the year."

The Tomb of Valdarno? Keynsham blinked at the tightly wrapped parcel. "I... see."

"Of course, the story is thrilling, but you—er, *she*, I

mean—could not possibly have chosen a more fashionable setting than Italy. There is unquenchable demand for Italian stories amongst our readers. *Unquenchable*!"

"I... had no idea."

"Oh yes! It is, perhaps, due to the association with Lord Byron, lending a *frisson* of forbidden passion and romance." He waved a hand. "And with the scenery and the ancient ruins... well, the whole country is simply irresistible to our patrons. It is a stroke of genius, sir, that you—er, *she*, of course!—set your tale there."

Keynsham didn't know what he'd expected, but it wasn't this. Alps? Tombs? *Harrowing scenes*? Pomona had never even been to Italy!

"You seem surprised, Mr. Brown. Is it possible that you were unaware of Italy's popularity?"

"I, er... had never considered it."

"Ah!" Wynde's face took on a look of satisfaction. "Then the book proceeded from a purely artistic motivation. I thought as much! It has the unmistakable ring of sincerity."

"How gratifying it is to hear you say that." Keynsham was beginning to enjoy this.

"Now, assuming that the manuscript is accepted, you... er, the *author*, of course... will then be asked to sign a contract. Though I have little doubt that it will be. Accepted, that is." He gave the wrapped pages a possessive pat. "Would *the author* be available tomorrow? Or the next day? We shall wish to finalize matters and get it onto our presses as soon as possible."

Tomorrow was the ball—which would go on until six the following morning. "I am afraid that I must confirm that with my sister. She finds herself with social obligations this week."

"Certainly! Certainly! Your *sister*. Yes. *Social obligations*." He eyed Keynsham. "Of course, I would like to be certain that you—er, *she,* of course—is not entertaining offers from rival publishers."

Keynsham bowed. "I cannot doubt that you would. I shall pass along your message to *Mrs. Brown*. Good morning, sir."

Downstairs, the library seemed twice as busy as it had been only a half hour earlier. The outer door to the street was temporarily obstructed by a group of laughing, chattering young ladies who'd darted in from the rain. As he stopped to avoid walking into them, someone bumped into him from behind.

"I beg your pardon." The lady had a large wrapped book in her arms, which she was endeavoring to stuff into her reticule, and her face was obscured by a heavy veil. Both of these facts perhaps explained why she hadn't been quick enough to avoid colliding with him.

He stepped out of her way with a slight bow. She looked up at him... and froze.

The veil was heavy, but when he saw her face in the light coming through the large windows, he couldn't fail to recognize her even through its obscuring folds.

Celia.

He would have that his heart stopped beating. He would have sworn that the busy library went utterly silent. He would have sworn that everyone around them vanished. He would have sworn that time ceased to run, and that nothing existed but her.

He reached toward her. "Miss Talbot."

She glanced to one side of him, as though calculating whether she could make a dash for the street.

"Please. I must speak with you. It is important."

She shook her head, stepped past the chattering ladies, and was gone out the door.

What the...?

To have seen her, after all this time, only to have her dismiss him without a word?

He took a step to follow her. But one of the chattering girls turned at the same instant and collided with him. In the ensuing giggling, and hat straightening, and batting of lashes, he lost sight of Miss Talbot's bonnet. "I *beg* your pardon!" he said, a little too forcefully.

"Well!" The young ladies fell silent and glared at him as he strode past them and out the door.

He looked right and left. It was raining harder now. There she was, making for Cornhill, one hand to her bonnet, her head bent as though to shield her face from the rain. She was walking so quickly that she was very nearly running.

And because she had her head down, she didn't what see he saw: Two of Wilkes's thugs were moving toward her from the mouth of the alley in which they'd been lurking.

"Miss Talbot!" he shouted. "Look out!"

Chapter Seventeen

She heard him shout. "Miss Talbot!"

She couldn't face him. As she'd stared up at him in the library vestibule, not a single word had come to her mind. All she knew was that she had to get away.

He'd already made a fool of her once. And now she'd discovered that her situation was even worse than she'd known. The only way that she could think to avoid more damage to her heart was to leave as quickly as possible.

As she rushed along the wet pavement, the heavy novel that she'd fetched for Mrs. Ellesmere made her large reticule bounce painfully against her hip. Surely a gentleman wouldn't chase a lady down a public street!

"Miss Talbot!" He was shouting her name.

She hurried onward through the downpour, the puddles on the pavement splashing the hem of her gown and beginning to soak through her worn boots. Her heavy veil flapped wetly against her face, half obscuring her vision. She kept her head down.

"*Miss Talbot*!" Keynsham shouted again. "*Look out*!"

Look out?

She glanced up.

Two men were coming straight at her. The larger was Dick Fenton. He had two fading black eyes and wore an almost apologetic expression.

The smaller man's hand was already outstretched to grab her arm.

She didn't pause to think. She swung her reticule at the small man with all her might. The heavy novel inside connected with the side of his skull with an audible *thunk*. He staggered backwards, clutching his ear and howling curses.

A blur flew past her. One moment Keynsham wasn't there. The next he was—and he was dealing out blows. Fenton swung at him, but Keynsham wove out of reach. His fist caught the big man under the chin. Fenton staggered backward. A knife appeared in his hand.

A scream froze on Celia's lips as Fenton slashed at Keynsham. Keynsham dodged again and smashed his fist down on Fenton's forearm. The weapon clattered to the pavement, spinning into the torrent of filthy water that filled the gutter. Fenton backed away, shaking his hand as though it had gone numb.

Though they'd lost the advantage of surprise, the smaller man tried to grab Celia again. But as his hand clamped onto Celia's wrist, Keynsham's fist caught him square in the face. He let go and crumpled to the wet pavement.

"Come with me!" Keynsham's hand closed around hers. She couldn't speak. Everything seemed to have happened in a single instant. There was no sign that anyone else had even noticed the fight.

"Quickly!" He un-looped the reins of a gig from a hitching post and jumped in after her. She back fell against the seat as the horses sprang forward.

They passed the motionless heap that was the small man—scarcely more than a bundle of dirty clothes. Fenton had vanished. Her mind didn't seem to be working properly. All she knew was that they were racing westward through streets half emptied by the sudden, violent downpour. Rain and spray blew into her face.

Fenton... Wilkes's thugs... They'd known where she would be. But somehow, so had Keynsham. How... why...?

She risked a glance at him. His jaw was set as he guided the horses through the slick streets. She opened her mouth to say something, realized that he was grimly focused on driving, and closed it again.

They passed Chancery Lane, where she usually turned on her walk home. She was expected back in Red Lion Square! But they were going so fast that the turn was behind them before she could speak, and she was too shaken to know what to do or say.

What seemed only moments later they drew up before an imposing house. He sprang out of the gig, handed her down, escorted her to the door, and unlocked it. The rain dripped off the broad brim of his hat. "I must go around to the stables and unhitch the horses. I did not bring my tiger, and I cannot leave them standing in this rain."

It seemed an oddly commonplace thing to say after

their wild flight. Numbly, she nodded. He showed her inside, shut the door and disappeared.

Now she recognized the place: His father's mistress's former establishment. It seemed larger by daylight—a hushed hideaway of heavy gilt furniture and tasteless art.

She tried to avoid her own pink-nosed reflection in the enormous looking glass as she removed her soaked and battered bonnet. She looked dreadful. Her hands were shaking with nerves and cold. She tried to unbutton her sodden pelisse, which was dripping onto the white marble floor.

A door from the back hallway opened. "Miss Talbot." Keynsham paused long enough for a curt bow and then strode toward her. He wore a country-style jacket, a check waistcoat and a blue-spotted neckcloth. His expression was stern. "It has been some time since we saw each other."

She'd forgot the dimple that appeared and disappeared at one side of his mouth when he spoke and the narrow scar that ran through one eyebrow. His face was lightly tanned now, as though he'd been spending time outdoors. He took off his soaked hat, leaving his damp hair sticking up at odd angles. She tried to force herself to look away, to stop staring, to stop drinking in the sight of him, but she couldn't make herself obey.

"Please assure me that you have suffered no harm. I have suffered the greatest anxiety on that score."

"Oh. Yes." She was trying not to let her teeth chatter. "They... they did not hurt me."

"No. I mean, have you been safe, these past two months?"

She had a wild vision of Keynsham meeting Mrs. Ellesmere. "I—I have been—safe."

His face relaxed, but only slightly. "You cannot know how relieved I am to hear that."

She managed to strip off one of her wet gloves, but her cold, stiff fingers weren't fully obeying her.

He blinked. "What are you doing?"

"I cannot... I cannot..." Her teeth began to chatter uncontrollably.

"Why, you are half frozen! Why did you not..." And then he was unbuttoning her pelisse for her, his big fingers hurrying over the many small fasteners, his face full of concern. His warm hands brushed hers. "You are shaking!" He slipped the sodden garment from her shoulders. "You will catch cold."

She would have protested, but shivers wracked her in a way that scarcely seemed possible for this time of year. Some small, unfrozen part of her brain was able to reason that she was reacting as much to the shock of the attack as to the unseasonable weather.

Keynsham disappeared again through the back hallway door. She ventured a peek at herself in the glass. Loose strands of wet hair hung lankly about her pallid face. Lovely.

A moment later, he strode back into the entry hall, this time carrying a blanket. "My mother is giving a ball tomorrow night, and I have had to send the servants there to help." He wrapped the blanket around her shoulders. Though his hands didn't touch her through the thick fabric, a thrill ran down her back and arms. "There is only a man of all work to look after this house until they return. I have put water on to heat for a bath."

She took a step back. "Do you mean to say that we are *alone* here?"

He folded his arms. "Miss Talbot. However justifiably low your opinion of me may be, it must be plain that I did not plan these circumstances in order to take advantage of you."

Despite her chill she felt her face heat. "No, I..."

"I was running an errand for my sister. The next thing I knew, I was fighting to save you from being snatched off the streets of London. For the *third time*, I might add."

It was then that she registered the red mark on the left side of his jaw. "Oh!" Her hands flew involuntarily to her mouth. "I—I am sorry!"

"For what?" He leaned toward the hall mirror. "Ah. I see. Scarcely has one bruise healed than I find myself with another." He straightened. "Do you know, I have never been a poetic sort of fellow, but I am certain that there must be a metaphor in here somewhere. The whole of our... I do not know what to call it." He thought a moment. "*Association*. The whole of our *association* has amounted to moments of recklessness—interspersed with longer intervals of pain."

Their eyes met. His were dark with emotion. "Miss Talbot, certain... circumstances have changed in my life. I hope that you will hear me out. But before anything else, I must apologize for my behavior at the inn. I have regretted it every moment since then. When I saw that you had gone, and realized that I was to blame..." He broke off for a moment. "I then knew that if you came to any harm because of my selfish actions I—I should never be able to live with myself."

She opened her mouth to answer.

And what came out instead was a sneeze.

* * *

It was, of course, inappropriate to let him prepare a bath for her. She wouldn't even have thought that a viscount would know how to do such a humble task. But as she let the hot water ease the cold and some of the fear from her body, Celia knew that she had no choice but to depend on Keynsham—at least, for now.

She hugged her knees, dreading the conversation that she'd have to have with him. When he'd told her that his circumstances had changed, he must mean that he was married. As much as she'd tried to brace herself for the moment when she'd learn that his wedding had taken place, now that the moment had arrived she wanted to run away rather than hear the words from his mouth.

But she was only making it worse by delaying. She got out of the bath, dried herself, dressed in her chemise and began drying her hair. The expensive soap had left a fragrance of jasmine behind, and just for a moment she closed her eyes, imagining what it would be like to return to a time when she could take hot, scented baths for granted... a time when she hadn't had to try to keep one step ahead of Wilkes.

She pinned up her damp hair and put her gown back on. The hem was still wet, but she smoothed the bodice down and made herself look as presentable as possible. She would have to leave London again. That was all that was clear to her. How to find another position, how to retrieve her meager belongings from Mrs.

Ellesmere... somehow she would have to solve these problems, too.

She found Keynsham in seated at the window of the bedroom across the hall, his booted heels upon the sill. He'd set a tea tray on a low table before the fireplace. "I am keeping watch on the street."

"Oh." She hung back in the doorway, almost afraid to come closer. What was it about him that was so attractive? Was it the alert yet relaxed manner in which he sat? Was it that his hair was still tousled in a way that suited him? "Do you—do you think that we might have been followed? Or traced here?"

"I cannot know. I doubt it. But I have learned that it does not pay to underestimate Wilkes." He looked at her, and she would have sworn that his eyes softened. "I have made a fire, as you see. You must not become chilled again. The tea may be rather strong by now, but there was plum cake and gingerbread in the pantry—and there is a wrap there for you as well, if you would like."

"I... thank you." She perched on the edge of the chair. Rain lashed the windows. The fire began to warm her.

Keynsham cleared his throat. "As I began to say, in the past few days my situation has changed. I wish to explain that..."

"You cannot owe me any explanations, your lordship," she said, too quickly. Her heart was thudding with dread.

He studied her. "I see. Well, perhaps you will humor me by listening anyway."

"Are—are you not expected elsewhere?"

"My time is quite my own, Miss Talbot. I shall spend the rest of the day guarding you."

"But..." She pulled the shawl tighter around her. "Could you not simply drive me to where I have been staying? Then you would not be... inconvenienced."

"That would be most unwise. We must assume that you were followed to the library. Indeed, Wilkes may already know where you have been living."

"Oh. Yes. Of course." She felt foolish for not thinking of this herself. Still, the rage that Mrs. Ellesmere would fly into, when Celia didn't return, was almost impossible to imagine. Mrs. Ellesmere would hate her more than she hated Lady Morton and her niece combined!

"Miss Talbot, forgive me—perhaps it is none of my business—but where *have* you been living?"

She hesitated. But he might as well know her real position in life. "I am employed. As a lady's companion."

"I see." She couldn't tell what he thought. She risked another glance at him. His jacket was hanging over a chair by the fire and his shirtsleeves were rolled up to the elbow. She dragged her eyes away from his tanned forearms.

"Well." He seemed to be having difficulty looking at her, too. "We have a chance to speak now. So let us be honest. You may think that I do not deserve to be heard, but I wish to apologize. I ought not to have... well, forced my attentions upon you."

"You did not force..." She stopped. "I was as much to blame as you were for... for..." Her face heated. Already they were on dangerous ground. They were discussing—without actually saying the words—the fact that they'd kissed each other.

Was it her imagination, or did he flush slightly? "Well, I am the one who took advantage of the situation. And as to the—well, the circumstances of my... the engagement." He cleared his throat. "At the time, I believed that any explanations would have been ungentlemanly. Unfair to the, er, lady involved." He frowned down at the street.

"But surely our spending time together *now* is equally as unfair to her!" She thought quickly. "Perhaps you might drive me to a coaching inn? Perhaps one outside of London—so as not to alert Wilkes? I do not wish to create complications in your life."

"A coaching inn outside of London!" He swiveled to face her. "Miss Talbot, why is it that your solution to every problem in life seems to be to catch a stagecoach?"

"I... well..." But sometimes leaving *was* the solution. After all, leaving Talbot Hall and its bitter history behind had saved her from Wilkes. She rose, agitated, and moved closer to the fire.

Keynsham was frowning. "Do you still resent me so much that you refuse to listen to my explanation at all?"

"What possible good can an explanation be when you are married?"

"Married? I am not married!" Once again, he suddenly found something very interesting to look at out the window.

He wasn't married? *He wasn't married!* At least... not yet. "But your... your fiancée—would no doubt object."

"No doubt she would. But I have no fiancée. In fact, I never did." He turned to face her again. "Miss

Talbot, it will take less time and be less confusing if you will let me tell you what happened. I was accused of compromising a young lady. And, of course, the remedy for that is always the same: immediate marriage."

"*Compromise!*" That hadn't even crossed her mind.

His tanned cheekbones reddened again. "Yes. Well. No doubt you believe me capable of it. However, I did not touch her, or... Well. I wish to be clear on that point. I *was* caught alone with her—in someone else's library, at a ball. I do not need to explain how the *ton* views such a situation. And I was prepared to do my duty, and marry her. But before the marriage settlements could be agreed, she... er, cried off."

"*Cried off*? But... how is that possible?"

"Well, er... I myself am not certain how it is possible. But she has managed it."

"Oh." She tried not to imagine Keynsham infatuated with some other lady... someone young, and beautiful, and rich... "Well, I—I hope that in time you will recover from your disappointment."

"*Disappointment*?" He rose from the chair and leaned on the window frame, apparently intent on the street below. "No."

"I do not understand. How could you not be disappointed, if you were... in love?"

"*In love*? No! I scarcely knew the young lady at all."

"Oh. *Oh*." An odd noise came out of her throat—but whether it was a suppressed laugh or a sob, she couldn't say.

"Miss Talbot?" In three strides he'd crossed the room. "Was that a cough?"

She turned away, unwilling to let him see her emotion. "I thought... I thought..."

"Miss Talbot?" He put his hands gently on her shoulders and turned her back to face him, ducking his head to gaze searchingly into her eyes.

She could only shake her head. If she opened her mouth to speak, she might begin to cry.

"I apologize for my manner of telling the story. I am not... well, you must know by now that I am not the most eloquent of fellows."

But that didn't matter—because once again, the magical silent conversation had begun between them. Each glance and each touch made every awkward pause and half-formed sentence unimportant.

She ought to say something. She ought to break the spell. But her throat was too thick. Perhaps she had caught cold after all. Perhaps that was the reason that shivers seemed to be flying over her skin.

His hands slid from her shoulders to her upper arms. A current of warmth spread from them—down to her elbows, across her back, up her neck. They were so warm, and his touch made her feel so safe and yet so alive at the same time. He held her gently, his thumbs stroking her arms. "The fact is, Miss Talbot, that I... well, I had no interest to spare for another lady."

She dared to look up. Their eyes met, and she was startled by the bolt of heat that went through her, warming her from the inside. He took a breath. "Miss Talbot, we met over a year ago. And my feelings and wishes have not changed since—well, since shortly after we met."

Surely he could not be... Her heart seemed to be beating too quickly. She felt almost as though she might faint.

"I have no choice but to speak now. After all, you

are already planning your next disappearance via stagecoach."

His hands were on her shoulders. She didn't know what he was about to say—only that whatever it was, it might change her life.

"And I must be honest: If history is any guide, as soon as you leave I will suffer pangs of remorse and despair. And then at some point in the future you will reappear—which will be wonderful, until I find myself in another fistfight." For a moment, the corners of his mouth twitched. "So. I shall speak now. Because I must confess that I am growing rather tired of being punched in the face."

His words were light… but there was a look in his eyes that made her think that he wasn't joking. He picked up both her hands in his. "Miss Talbot—will you marry me?"

Chapter Eighteen

She couldn't seem to breathe properly. "*Marry* you?"

"Yes. Marry me."

"But…" She tried to think. "But how would we…?"

"In St. James's Church. Before a clergyman. I am told that it is a simple procedure. Would Monday suit?"

His hands were still warm on her arms. Her eyes searched his. The fire caught the gold sparks in the hazel blue, and a slight smile was still playing about his lips.

"*Monday? This* Monday?"

"Yes. Monday. By special license. I know you too well, Miss Talbot. I am not so foolish as to risk having banns read. That would give you three entire weeks in which to change your mind and run off again—to St. Ives, or Inverness, or—well, who knows where."

She closed her eyes and allowed herself to imagine it. To see Keynsham every day… to know that he was hers… that they belonged to each other. To speak with him, to make plans together and share private jokes, to be able to kiss him—and… well, more…

And then the sick feelings of fear and shame came back. All of that was a foolish daydream. Her life was poisoned. Nothing good could happen for her as long as Wilkes was pursuing her, bent on vengeance. And he would never stop pursuing her. He was the violent legacy of her father's fraud.

"Miss Talbot? Celia?" His voice was gentle. "What is wrong?"

She opened her eyes, but kept them fixed on the floor, unable to look him in the face. "I—I cannot."

"Cannot what?"

"I cannot marry you. Or anyone." She stared into the carpet—cream, with pink and green pattern of leaves.

"I see." His tone was neutral. "Well, perhaps it is ungentlemanly of me to ask, but... why?"

She shook her head.

"If this is about Wilkes..." He stopped. "Surely you cannot imagine that I am frightened of a gangster and his hired thugs. And surely you are far too sensible to have any notions of sacrificing yourself on his account."

"But you do not know what my father..." She broke off. "I am entirely unsuitable. And you do not know how dangerous Wilkes is."

"Really? I think that I have enough experience now to have a fairly good idea. I do not underestimate Wilkes. I simply do not believe that he ought to control our lives."

She took a shaky breath. "But I—I have learned the reason that Wilkes is pursuing me."

"What do you mean?"

"I went to see my father's solicitor. I had wondered whether..." She stopped and swallowed. "Well, it does not matter. What matters is that my father cheated Wilkes out of a great deal of money. Deliberately. Which means that he was just as much a thief as Wilkes is. That is why Wilkes is so angry. He wants it back."

Keynsham half-turned toward the fireplace. "I see."

His expression—what she could see of it—was serious. He must be disgusted. Anyone would be.

"And you were right when you said that my father had—well, schemed to—to sell me to Wilkes. Indeed, it was worse than..." She broke off. She couldn't bear to tell Keynsham that her father had even tried to get the title of the estate away from her. "So now you know the truth. My father was a fraudster."

She felt sick. But Keynsham would see why he had to allow her to slip out of London... and out of his life. "Any connection between us must be out of the question. My family name is tainted. And Wilkes is a danger to anyone that I should... well, anyone with whom I associate."

"What?" He turned back to her, his dark brows drawn into a frown. "Well, that is simply nonsense."

Despite everything she bristled. "It is not *nonsense*."

"It *is* nonsense. Tainted family name! Good heavens! What utter... flummery! You are not your father any more than I am *my* father. And Wilkes will not dare threaten you when you are married to me."

He reached for her hand. Part of her—most of her—wanted to believe him. But he hadn't listened to her. Not really. "Yes, he will. He will never stop. There can be no doubt that influential people are in his pocket already. Politicians. Peers. I saw him insinuate himself into my father's life. He has access anywhere that he wishes to go. Anyone who is close to me is at risk."

He snorted. "Miss Talbot, if you have not noticed, not only am I a peer of the realm, but I have bested Wilkes every time that I have met him *or* his thugs."

"For heaven's sake! Now is not the time to be... to be arrogant!" She stopped herself. "I do not doubt your fighting abilities. But Wilkes would have shot you dead in Grosvenor Square, had your coachman not arrived at the moment that he did."

Keynsham opened his mouth to reply, glared at her, and shut it again. Then he was silent, frowning. "Well, I suppose that in that particular case, you are right."

She was caught off guard. "I... I beg your pardon?"

"I take your point. If Young had not run him down, Wilkes would have fired upon me." His frown deepened. "But it does not follow that I agree with the rest of what you have said."

"At least admit that I know him better than you do, and do me the courtesy of respecting my judgment."

He was still frowning. "It goes without saying that I respect your judgment, Miss Talbot. It is your *plans* that I question. You are telling me to accept that the only solution to this situation is for you to vanish on a stagecoach to some distant town where neither Wilkes nor I will ever find you. And that is pure nonsense if I have ever heard it."

"I wish that you would stop using that word!"

"Well, in this case it is apt. You have developed a certain expertise at running away. And that has preserved you. But sometimes one must take a stand. And I am taking a stand against Wilkes. Because he is a bully, and because..." He stood in silence. "Well, because I cannot bear to let you go."

Her heart was beating wildly. She wished that he

wouldn't say such things. Already, she wasn't sure that she would be able to make herself leave.

"I understand if your feelings are not... if they do not yet match my feelings. My proposal is sudden. But I hope that you will consider it. I know that my own feelings and wishes will not change. Because they have not —not since the night that we met, on the outskirts of Whitechapel—where I first saw the bravest lady I have ever known."

"But I am not..."

"Let me finish confessing to you. After that, you may dispute everything that I say—as I have no doubt that you will." For a moment, a smile flickered around the corners of his mouth again.

"From that moment, I felt something for you. But I told myself any number of stupid things—that it could not be appropriate to follow my feelings, that I did not know you well enough, and that I must simply be infatuated—perhaps because you were so different from the other young ladies to whom I had been introduced.

"And—well, you were clearly in some sort of trouble—which I reminded myself was not a quality that ought to recommend you to me, the heir to a viscountcy—let alone to my family. In fact, the arguments that I invented for why I should forget you might be nearly as good as any that you can muster yourself."

She felt her face warm.

"Well." He took a breath. "And they may be perfectly valid arguments, in the eyes of many. But— well, in the night that we spent together, I saw more of your character than most couples see of each other in the accepted week or month of chaperoned dances and formal calls. And no one in the *ton* raises an eyebrow at *those* courtships.

"I saw your bravery, and your resourcefulness—and your dignity in the face of cruel treatment. I saw that—whatever you may say now—you are a lady through and through. And after you got on that stagecoach, I realized that none of the arguments that I had invented to persuade myself to let you go could change those feelings. When you left, you took my heart with you. And I realized that I ought to have done something to stop you from leaving."

She pulled her hands away. "You could not have stopped me. I had made up my own mind."

"I could have offered you enough money to live on."

"We both know that it would not have been proper of me to accept it."

"Well, I could have insisted upon intervening in the troubles that you so clearly faced. Something. Anything! Because within a very short time after you'd gone, the thought of never seeing you again was..." He broke off.

"I planned to follow you north, while it might still be possible to learn where you had gone. But when I got home I discovered that there was a crisis within my family—a crisis with which I had to—well, help."

Her mind went back to his grandmother's ball, when his mother had told him that she must talk with him about his sister.

Keynsham looked into the fire, silent for a moment. "Less than a week later, my father—who was only two and fifty—died. He had, as I told you, concealed the estate's financial position. By the time I had even begun to come to grips with it—and settled the most pressing demands from creditors—many weeks had passed. I knew that there was no longer any chance that I could trace you."

There was a flush on his cheekbones. "And that is when… well, I used to pretend that I was having conversations with you. I am not mad," he added quickly. "I was aware that these conversations were imaginary, and that you, yourself, were not…" He rubbed his forehead. "Oh, God. I do sound mad."

"No." She had to force the words out. "No. You do not. I—I thought of you, too." Confessing her own feelings was the most frightening thing that she'd ever done. Compared to this, running away from home, taking a public stagecoach and lying her way into a job were nothing. "I felt something too. But I—I told myself that I was imagining it." She felt as though she'd run a mile. It seemed hard to catch her breath, and she was lightheaded.

"Celia!" A blazing smile broke across his face. He seized her hands again and held them to his chest. "Celia! That is, Miss Talbot! I feared that I had frightened you!" He lifted one of her hands to his mouth. He kissed her knuckles. He kissed her folded fingers. He turned it over and kissed the inside of her wrist. Each kiss sent a fresh shiver up her arm and into her already perfectly useless brain, making it even more useless. She didn't want to think anymore. She wanted to melt against him.

"Tell me that you will not talk of leaving again." He uncurled her fingers and kissed her palm. "And say that you will at least consider my proposal. You need not decide right away, if it is too sudden. But if you wish to marry me, you need only say yes."

His hot, tickling kisses on her palm were making it impossible to think. She'd admitted that she shared his feelings. It was already too late to simply leave London and pretend that none of this had happened. She closed her eyes. There was a roaring in her ears that she realized was her own pulse.

"I know that you are brave enough to defy Wilkes." He kissed her fingertips, one by one. "And I will be with you. I will be at your side—always." He kissed the inside of her wrist. "Nothing that either of our fathers have done can matter. What matters is the future, and what we do together—you and I."

Her knees were weak. Even her skin felt weak. The moment that she'd confessed her feelings, she'd become vulnerable.

He ducked his head again, trying to meet her eyes. "Miss Talbot, we may both be mad—but we are meant to be together. "

She tugged her hands away again. "I—I do not know!" She hid her clenched fists in the folds of her skirt so that he couldn't see that she was shaking.

"I beg your pardon." His face was suddenly serious. "I did not mean to... It appears that I have pressed you once again, despite assuring you that I would not." He turned away to the fire and studiously rearranged the coals with a poker.

He hadn't pressed her. She wanted to tell him that. But her throat was too tight. Her father... Wilkes... her own mistrust of the future...

If only she could allow herself to *want* something and believe that she could have it. If only she could believe... that she was worthy of happiness. But though she'd daydreamed of Keynsham, she'd never dared to dream that they would have a real future together.

Only... his proposal was real. *He* was real. At last they were together. Perhaps that was all that she needed to know. She couldn't be expected to see into the future —so perhaps all that she needed to do was take the first step toward it.

She took a shaky breath. "Yes."

He glanced up the fire. "I beg your pardon?"

She didn't think that she could repeat herself.

He understood. His face lit with joy. He straightened and took her hands. "If you need more time..."

She shook her head wordlessly.

"Then you are certain that it is what you want?"

For now, she would not fear what might be. She swallowed hard. "Yes."

He kissed her knuckles. "Then I know what it is to be the happiest man in London." He kissed them again. "In the country." He kissed them again. "On earth."

He pulled her closer and dropped a kiss on her temple. The brush of his lips upon the fine hairs sent a flare of heat through every pore of her skin. His voice was a vibration against her ear. "Fate has brought us back together again and again. And so, as to the wedding—well, the sooner we bow to Fate and marry, the sooner Fate will stop playing tricks on us."

"No!" She drew back. "I mean, I—I do not like talk of fate. It is not at all amusing."

The laughter faded from his eyes. "No. I suppose that you are right. After everything that has happened... Well, I ought not to joke about it." He slipped a caressing finger under her chin. "Celia. Celia?"

She forced her eyes upward to meet his. And when

they did, she wondered how she'd ever been able to look away again. She'd never imagined that the mix of tenderness and heat that she saw in his gaze could exist. So perhaps, although she hadn't been able to imagine happiness, it might still be granted to her…

He caressed her cheek. "Until we are married, you shall stay with Lady Sophronia. You will be safe there. And as you have no relations in London, she is by far the most appropriate person."

"Oh." All of this was moving so quickly. She felt dazed. "I… but… who is Lady Sophronia?"

"My grandmother—a rather formidable lady, but also very kind."

"But will she mind? And will she… will she remember me?"

"Mind! No. She will be pleased. She did not… Well." He looked awkward for a moment. "I do not think that she will remember you, under such different circumstances. And she will act as your chaperone for the ball tomorrow night."

A grand London ball! But she had nothing to wear but the clothes on her back. And how could she possibly mingle with wealthy and titled people when she knew no one at all? "Must I… go?"

"To the ball? Of course! Do not worry. It will not be a large, noisy affair. It is in honor of my sister's come-out. She dislikes crowds. There will be—well, eighty people, at most. We will announce our engagement then as well."

She thought almost longingly of her tiny, plain bedroom in Red Lion Square, and the small, predictable cast of characters in the house there. In the space of only a few hours, her entire life had begun to change beyond all recognition.

Mrs. Ellesmere's book! She clapped a hand to her mouth, panicked. What had she done with it? Oh—it was still in her reticule, downstairs. But there was no way to get it to Mrs. Ellesmere! She would be furious!

Keynsham put his hands on her shoulders and drew her closer. "Celia?" A smile was flickering around his mouth. "Celia, I do not know what you are thinking of, but every detail that is worrying you now will be resolved. I promise it."

He kissed her temple again. She closed her eyes and wished that she could absorb his optimism. There was but a tiny shift—perhaps a degree or two—wanted in her thinking... All she had to do was replace the constant fear of looming disaster that underlay all her thoughts with the belief that she was allowed to be happy.

For now, it was enough to be in his arms. Gently, he lifted her chin. His lips touched hers. A bolt of heat and light shot through her body. Even the skin of the insides of her arms came alive with exquisite sensitivity as she wrapped her arms around his neck.

She brushed her lips against his, exactly as she'd imagined doing so many times. But none of her fantasies could compare with this reality. The faint prickle around his mouth, the smoothness of his lips, the scent of his shaving soap... the totality of his masculinity, and the growing, intoxicating certainty that he was hers... all hers...

His mouth claimed hers more firmly, exploring the contours of her lips and urging them apart. His tongue brushed hers. She found herself slipping into a world of sensation—a world in which her fears of the uncertain future were replaced by a perfect present. Who might object to their marriage, or what Wilkes might do next, no longer seemed to matter.

Her hands explored the hard, flat muscles of his shoulders, and then lower, down the line of his spine. Without his jacket, his skin was hot through the linen of his shirt and the fine wool of his waistcoat.

He drew reluctantly back. "I suppose that we ought to leave."

"Leave?" She laid her head against his chest. She could hear his heartbeat. It was faster than his steady tone would have hinted.

"So that I may drive you to Lady Sophronia's house."

"Oh. Yes. Of course." She gazed at him and then glanced at the windows. "Only..."

"What is it, darling?"

"Well... it rains very hard."

Chapter Nineteen

As if in confirmation, a rumble of thunder rattled the roof. A moment later, the noise of the downpour redoubled.

The corners of Keynsham's mouth turned upward. "You are quite correct, Miss Talbot. It is a perfectly dreadful afternoon. And as you know, my gig is open. And you have already been soaked through and chilled once today. I agree that it might not be wise to venture out until the rain stops."

She felt as though she couldn't breathe. "No."

"After all, I must consider your health." His hands were on her upper arms. He pulled her closer. "Indeed, you are still rather chilled. It will not do for the future Lady Alford to have a hacking cough on her wedding day." He bent and placed a gentle kiss on the corner of her lips. "It will not do at all."

She turned her head a bare half an inch and their lips met properly. He deepened the kiss. She heard herself gasp. Her hands found the back of his neck again, pulling him down to her. He kissed the hollow under the corner of her jaw.

Shivers of flame skittered over her skin, and any lingering chill seemed to disappear as her body melted against his, molding into his warmth. His fingers moved to the back of her head. "Dear me, Miss Talbot," he said, into her ear. "Your hair is still wet. There is no quicker way to catch cold than to go about with wet hair." Deftly, he began pulling out hair pins.

She hadn't realized that such a small thing could send sparks of pleasure flew from her scalp through her body. The damp lengths of her hair tumbled down onto her shoulders. He lifted them away from her skin so that he could kiss down her neck, and every sense ignited. His neckcloth smelled sweetly of ironed linen. Heat uncoiled at the base of her spine, spiraling upward and through her body, like a curl of smoke from a burning ember.

They were to be married in only a few days. If this were wrong... surely it was only a *little* wrong.

His warm lips moved along her collarbone, teasing half inch by teasing half inch, and her breath caught as the desire in her lower belly burst into open flame. She longed to feel his heat all over her. But there was too much fabric between his skin and hers. She tugged his shirt loose from the waist of his trousers and ran delicate exploratory fingertips over the smooth, hot skin of his stomach.

"Celia." He caught her mouth again with his. The room was silent in the stormy spring twilight as he rained kisses down her neck, her shoulders and the upper slopes of her breasts. Her hands slipped higher under his shirt, and she felt his intake of breath rush past her own lips. She could feel the unfamiliar hardness of him, pressing against her hip.

He moved back. "There is a line that we must not cross—yet. Because there is, of course, a risk."

"Yes, I... understand."

"But we may..." He pulled her closer again. "That is..."

All she knew was that she wanted more and more of him. She reached for him and found his mouth with hers. His fingers were behind her back, loosening her gown. The fabric slid off first one shoulder and then the other. His hands were shaking slightly. When she saw that, she knew that this was just as important to him, too. The lingering doubts in her heart began to melt.

They sank into the luxurious depths of the featherbed, and for a long blissful moment they simply held each other close. She buried her face in the crook of his shoulder. He stroked her hair. "I feared that this would never happen." He kissed the top of her head. She raised her face to meet his, and the heat of the kiss caught her off guard.

She pulled him closer, filled with a longing that she couldn't name, tugging again at the hem of his shirt. Gently, he pushed her chemise up, and at last, she felt his skin against hers, like two fires joining together. His head dipped, his mouth found the sensitive peak of her breast, and she gasped. She hadn't imagined that her body was made for such pleasure. He sucked at the puckering skin, his intake of breath a shock over the heat of her flesh.

At the light touch of his fingertips on the soft skin of her inner thigh she moved involuntarily toward him. But he took his time, tracing a random lazy path up one thigh and down the other, never touching the place in her core that had begun to tighten and heat and ache for him.

She reached again for his waistband—wanting to feel every inch of his skin against her own—but he pushed her hand gently away as his fingers continued their leisurely exploration. Soon her breath was coming in shaky pants, and she could do nothing but cling to him, waiting for him to give her what she wanted.

There. Her body jerked as he brushed over her molten core and the tight bud of desire above it. *That* was what she'd wanted, without knowing it. But his fingers skated away again and she whimpered aloud in frustration.

She felt him smile against her skin. It was as unexpected and intimate and new as all the rest of this. She was still marveling at being able to feel a smile when his fingers dipped lower, found a slick heat, and dragged it back up over that secret nub.

Her mind went blank with pleasure as his fingers circled exactly where she wanted them. Her hips pushed towards his hand, seeking something more... a relief from the ever-increasing tightness inside her. Everything in her seemed to focus. She couldn't think. She couldn't do anything but feel. Every sense in her body seemed concentrated in that one place.

He sucked the tip of her breast back into his mouth, and the two sparks joined into a fire that raced over her skin and set her alight. She writhed beneath him, begging wordlessly without knowing what she was begging for.

His thumb found that aching nub again and worked it slowly. But this time, his finger slipped inside her. She gasped as it began a slow plundering of her slick channel. Shivers and flame raced over her skin. She bucked against his hand, fearing that the pleasure itself would tear her apart. It felt as though she were struggling against an onslaught of sensation, her body overwhelmed by something that she couldn't name.

And then his teeth scraped her taut nipple, and she came undone. The earth itself was gone, and she seemed to go flying into a vast starry sky full of ecstasy. Her muscles spasmed tight while her nerves let go, and she was helpless in the grip of pleasure.

When she came back from wherever she had gone, he was still stroking the already throbbing bud between her legs. "I... I..." She had no words to describe what had just happened to her.

"Celia." He nuzzled her neck as his hand kept up its gentle torture. She heard herself whimpering. Her core seemed to wind even tighter. She was moaning aloud. Another merciless wave of pleasure bore down upon her. Heat rolled up her and she flew out of her body again.

Afterwards, he held her close, kissing her hair and her face as she drifted back into herself. "We cannot do —well, the rest of it—until we are married."

"Oh. I see." He must mean... "No. I—I suppose not." She was light-headed and heavy-limbed, a warm bundle of satiation in his arms. She could have gone to sleep... but she didn't want to waste a moment with him.

"You sound as though you are disappointed."

"Well, I..." *Married*. It still seemed impossible that she was to have any sort of future that was not merely survival. "You really do wish to be married on Monday? You were not... joking?"

"*Joking*?" He chuckled into her hair. "I grant you that I am not always serious, but that is not at all the sort of thing about which I would joke. No. Monday is to be the day—as early the morning as possible. Do you suppose that they would do it directly after matins? Perhaps at dawn? Although, of course, we will have the wedding breakfast as well."

"Oh. Yes. Of course." Her heart sank. "The wedding breakfast."

He laughed and rolled onto his back. "Try not to sound quite so dismayed! You will have met my sister by then—and Lady Sophronia, of course. And I am certain that you will like my friend Captain Grenville and his wife. He has been with his ship for several months, but is due back in London in a day or two."

He thought a moment. "I do not think that you will meet my second cousin, Harry—Viscount Montfort, however. He was meant to have returned to London last week but was unavoidably detained—or so he writes. I suspect that he is staying away out of a wish to avoid my mother's hysterics over the ball. At any rate, I have a small circle, but I believe that you will like my friends."

A nervous knot was forming again in her stomach. "But your mother..."

"My mother will have to adjust her thinking—or not, as suits her."

"But... will she not believe that I am marrying you out of... well, self-interest? After all, I have nothing. Or at least—nothing besides the house. And I cannot even claim that."

He propped himself up on his elbow and frowned at her, puzzled. "Wait a minute. What house?"

"Talbot Hall."

"Talbot Hall?"

"My grandfather bought it for my father when he married. But he made the title over to me—in trust, the solicitor said. That is the reason why my father could not use it as security for the money he borrowed. I was too shocked by all of it to ask the solicitor any sensible questions."

She pulled a pillow to her chest and clutched it tight. The knot in her stomach was getting worse.

"It sounds to me as though you did ask sensible questions." Keynsham was frowning. "And you had never been told of this before? Why not?"

"I suppose that my father did not wish it."

He frowned. "Your father was more like my father than I realized. Both of them kept ruinous secrets, and gave no thought to their children."

"I went to see the solicitor because I learned that my father had been killed on a different road than the one thatWilkes had told me he died on. He had been going to London, and I wondered whether I was the reason for his journey." She turned onto her side and stared at the window. She ought to be happy. Why couldn't the ghosts of the past—discontented, dishonest, and malicious—leave her alone?

"Celia. You are not the reason that your father died." He touched her shoulder. "There is something strange about this story. I do not understand why Wilkes was the one who gave you the information."

"He said that I ought to go through with the marriage—to honor my father's wishes."

Keynsham was silent a moment. "I shall write to my solicitor and ask him to communicate with your father's solicitor. It will be a simple enough matter to resolve any outstanding matters about the house. Even a poor viscount has advisers who can sort out legal papers." He was silent a moment. "In fact, it may be best to come to an understanding with Wilkes."

"An *understanding*?" She jerked around to face him.

"He is a businessman—well, after a fashion. He has a price."

She frowned. "What do you mean?"

"I mean that there is some amount of money that will make him go away. All we have to do is learn what it is."

"Money!" She was shocked. "But he would have murdered you! He has tried to kidnap me!"

Keynsham ran a fingertip along her jawline. "And I would pay any price to know that you will be safe. It appears that he is pursuing you because your father owed him money. Very well; I shall look upon this as repaying the debt. After that, he will sink away into whatever hole he inhabits, and we need never think of him again."

But Wilkes didn't forgive anything: not a bad business deal, not a broken promise… and certainly not the daughter of the man who'd cheated him, and who'd injured his pride by running away rather than marry him.

"You do not agree?"

"I… I think that there is more to it." She struggled to put it into words. "I believe that the reason he spent so much time with my father is that he—he wished to *become* him. He emulated his clothes, his speech, his mannerisms. Wilkes wanted to be the village squire himself. It is not simply the money."

"People always say that it is not the money—but nine times out of ten, it is the money. In fact, I would wager that it is more like ten times out of ten." His eyes glinted. "If there is one thing that I have learned from dealing with my late father's creditors, it is that."

"And you have trouble enough already, with the debts that your father left!"

"Ensuring that you are safe and happy is not *trouble*." He leaned closer and kissed her. "It is what I wish to do. Besides, you must remember the half-built houses that we found the day that Wilkes chased us out of London. Well, I invested in the project. I cannot wait to show you the changes that we have wrought in the place. And there are rents coming in already—enough that I have applied to discharge the mortgage on one of the estate's farms."

His grin reappeared. "And now that Fate has succeeded in bringing us together, I believe that she will shower rewards upon us." He rolled onto his back and addressed the ceiling. "Do you hear that, Fate? We are to be married! You may cease to plague us with separations, misunderstandings, gun fights, thugs, and everything else in between! It stops now!"

"No!" She clutched his arm. "Do not say it aloud! If there *is* such a thing as fate, you are tempting it."

"Shh!" He kissed her. "You are superstitious. You have had to spend too much of your life worrying. But from this moment on, we shall lead the most blissful life that any two people have ever led." He pulled her closer. "Indeed, I have an idea—several ideas, in fact—about how to make a start on that bliss immediately."

His talk of fate had stirred up old fears... fears that she was not destined for happiness, and that if she dared to want anything, it would be snatched away. The doubts that she'd tried to banish were back and swirling in her mind.

But then his hand began to slide up her thigh. His mouth found hers, and everything else disappeared in a haze of desire.

Chapter Twenty

"You say that it was here?" The carriage drew to a halt. Holding his glossy black top hat, Wilkes pushed down the window and leaned out to take a long look at the street.

The two men who'd been standing on the back of the carriage leaped down, crossed the pavement, and vanished into the narrow mouth of the alley.

The rain had paused at the end of the day. A watery yellow sunset lit a strip of sky above the western horizon and reflected in the puddles standing in the road so that, for a brief moment, the streets of London really were paved in gold.

"Well, well. And so this is the very street corner where Miss Talbot *hit* you. Miss Talbot! A chit of a girl. She hit you, with all the strength in her... mighty arms? Is that what I am to believe?" He gave a mirthless chuckle and turned back to face the man on the seat opposite. "Cat got your tongue, eh, Gooley?"

The little man's eyes bulged with terror. His mouth was stuffed with dirty rags—one of which was his own neckcloth—and his hands were bound together. Wilkes studied him with distaste. "Do you know, Gooley, I always thought that of the two of you, I would rid myself of Fenton first." He sighed. "But here we are, I suppose."

The men returned to the carriage. "Leads to Lime Street and through to Fenchurch. Any number of places where 'e could 'ave gone from here, boss."

"Ah." Wilkes pushed the window up again. The carriage springs bounced as his bodyguards resumed their places standing on the rear platform. He gazed meditatively at Gooley for a long moment before thumping on the roof. The clip clop of the horses' hooves rang out on the cobbles and the carriage moved on.

"Well, it is a remarkable tale, Gooley, I will concede that." He sighed. "Oh, Gooley. Gooley, Gooley. Did you really think that I would believe such a pack of lies? I must say that I am disappointed."

Gooley made muffled, frantic noises. Wilkes tut-tutted. "Oh, stop fussing. You have given me a headache already."

The carriage turned south. After a few minutes, it turned east. They passed the grey bulk of the Tower. The little man seemed to become more confident. Obviously, he thought that he knew where they were going. But they did not stop. They continued east, and then wound south again through the bleak streets that led down toward the river. When he realized that they were not going back to Wilkes's rooms, his eyes grew first worried and then panicked. Muffled cries came from behind the gag.

A damp breeze was blowing as the carriage finally

stopped before a cluster of sagging wooden buildings that hung over the river, supported by pilings. Wilkes got out of the carriage and took a deep breath. The tide was going out, and the iodine and sewage stench of the muddy riverbank was the smell of easy money.

They were in the forecourt of a warehouse. At the moment, the warehouse was stacked with casks of French brandy—casks that, as it happened, didn't bear the stamps and seals of His Majesty's excise men. Smuggling wasn't a large part of Wilkes's business, but it was a nice little sideline.

And this old warehouse was useful. Goods—and other things—could be loaded directly up a ladder from small boats bobbing in the Thames beneath its floorboards, well concealed from prying eyes. If anyone asked, Wilkes would have described the man who owned the warehouse as a "business associate"—though to be strictly accurate, he was someone whom Wilkes was blackmailing.

He poked his head back into the carriage. "Come along, Gooley."

The little man shrank back against the squabs, shaking his head wildly. Wilkes stood back and folded his arms. "Then I will have to have you dragged." He nodded to the men who'd been on the back of the carriage. They opened both doors, seized Gooley, and pulled him out. He was already bound hand and foot, so his struggles were useless as they dragged him across the small courtyard and into the warehouse.

At another nod from Wilkes, his henchman pulled the gag from Gooley's mouth and let go of him. Gooley collapsed onto the floor. Tears streamed from his eyes, leaving streaks on his dirty face. "Please, boss," he croaked, gasping. "Please. I didn't do nothing. I didn't cross you—I swear! Give me another chance."

"Oh, Gooley. Stop embarrassing yourself. Another chance? I am not doing this because you failed. I am doing this because you believe that I am stupid. Because you lied to me." The floorboards squeaked as he paced closer. "Miss Talbot hit you, and Lord Alford appeared from nowhere, and then Fenton magically vanished. Did you see all of this in a puppet play, perhaps? Punch and Judy? Were you drunk?"

"I weren't drunk, boss, I swear! And I ain't lying, neither! I dunno where the young lord come from! We was watching for two hours and there weren't no sign of 'im! All I know is, one minute 'e weren't there, and the next 'e was!"

Wilkes snorted and adjusted one jeweled cufflink. "When I hired you, Gooley, it was with the expectation that you would help me with certain aspects of my London business. But you are a stupid, stupid man." He sighed. "And now I shall have to deal with Lord Alford alone, without your help."

"I know I cocked up, boss! But I ain't lying! I can still 'elp you!"

"Well, you leave me in a pickle, Gooley. A pickle indeed." Wilkes cracked his knuckles. "Tomorrow night I shall, of course, make Lord Alford pay dearly. But it has become more and more clear that not only are you not an asset—you are an actual liability. No, no. I'm afraid that it simply will not fadge." He tsked.

"I'll do better! I swear!"

Wilkes stared thoughtfully at him for a long moment. "Oh, I wish I could believe that, Gooley. I do indeed."

He nodded to the men standing behind Gooley. One went to a big metal winch and threw the handle forward. The gears clicked. "No!" screamed Gooley, as he recognized the sound. "No, boss! I never did you dirty! I'll make it up to you!"

The double doors in the warehouse floor began to open. The reek of the dark water rose even more strongly. Wilkes nodded to the other man. He put his foot in the small of Gooley's back and shoved. Now Gooley was at the lip of the hatch.

The little man was breathing hard, sniveling. "Boss! No! Please! I swear I'll—"

Wilkes made a small gesture. The man kicked Gooley forward. One moment he was there—a miserable heap of sniveling terror. The next, there was a scream that cut off abruptly as he splashed into the water. Then there was nothing.

Wilkes stood a moment, listening to the gurgle of the Thames rushing through the piers that supported the building. Then he turned, walked back out into the evening and took a deep lungful of river-tainted air.

The time had come for him to rid himself of everyone who'd been holding him back. He couldn't do it overnight, of course. But he'd made a start. Fenton was next. He'd run away—but he wouldn't get far.

And of course, there was Celia. It was her unexpected defiance that had caused all of this. There was only so much that he would tolerate from a lady, and she had put him to trouble and expense.

If any of what Gooley had said was true, the young lord had come to her rescue once again. It was beyond a coincidence now. She must have arrived with him—though his men had been too incompetent to notice.

And that meant that she was living under his protection somewhere. The little whore. He ought to have known that she was just like all the others.

Miss Talbot still had a minor part to play. But after that she could join her late sire in hell.

Church bells near and far were striking eight. As he climbed back into his carriage, Wilkes felt almost light-hearted.

* * *

At six o'clock on the morning of the ball, the housemaids had been hard at work for an hour, scrubbing the front hall and stairs. Delicate red clouds floated in the east as the morning star faded with the sunrise. The mews was already almost impassable. Tradespeople hurried back and forth between the house and their wagons, carrying boxes of strawberries, crates of champagne, prawns packed in ice, baskets of asparagus, and myriad other last-minute deliveries.

By eight o'clock, the delicate red clouds had bloated to three times their original size and turned grey. The gardeners using plumb bobs and spirit levels to trim the hedges into geometric perfection looked at the sky and shook their heads.

At ten o'clock, Lady Alford was drinking her chocolate in the breakfast room when the first fat drops struck the windows. She set the delicate Minton cup down in disbelief. "That *cannot* be rain!"

The pair of footmen standing against the wall glanced at each other.

"It cannot be! We *cannot* have rain today! Everyone

said that the rain had passed and we should have fine weather for the ball. *Everyone*!"

She pushed back her chair without waiting for a footman to pull it out and rushed to the window just as a flash of lightning lit the surrounding rooftops and thunder boomed almost directly overhead. The skies opened. The gardeners dashed about collecting their tools and ladders before vanishing.

Lady Alford stared out at the downpour until another peal of thunder rattled the windows in their frames. "How is this possible? *How*? There can be only so much rain in the world! It must already have fallen over the past few days! This goes against... *science*!" She turned to the footmen. "Only last night the weather appeared to be clearing. Mrs. Dodd said so! You must have heard her say it, Martin! 'Appeared to be clearing!' Those were her very words! You heard her—did you not?"

Martin glanced nervously at the other footman. "Yes, your ladyship."

"Then how can this be?"

"I—I cannot say, your ladyship."

She whirled about and glared out the window again. The flagstones below were already covered with puddles. The balustrades dripped. The white roses in the urns that adorned the terrace drooped their full heads under the weight of raindrops. Soaked petals dropped sadly onto the steps.

"No." She turned her back upon the desolate scene. "*No*. This is merely a passing shower." She clasped her hands to her breast and took a few tottering steps back to the breakfast table. Martin rushed forward to push in her chair as she sat down again. She laid her palms flat upon the white linen cloth. "I am calm. I am *calm*." She took a deep breath. "The rain *will* stop. The roads and pavements will be quite dry. The evening will be fine and warm. We shall have the terrace doors open. The prince will *not* stay home. My ball will be the success of the season."

Her hand shook badly as she attempted to lift the chocolate pot. The china rattled.

"Shall I pour you some chocolate, your ladyship?"

She swatted his hand away. "Oh, stop *fussing*, Martin! *I am perfectly calm*!"

He bowed and retreated to stand against the wall, where the other footman gave him a swift look of commiseration. The rain beat against the panes.

The door opened.

Pomona was mid-stride, her face shining with joy, when she saw her mother. She stopped short. "Oh."

"*What*?" Lady Alford's voice was waspish.

"I... Good morning, mother. I did not expect to... You breakfast in your room."

"Well, today I am breakfasting here! In the breakfast room! I have been downstairs since the break of dawn, trying to get it through Cook's thick head that she ought to have made twice the number of salmon pies as she seems to think!"

Martin held the chair for Pomona as she sat down, and poured her a cup of coffee.

Lady Alford turned on her daughter. "You have no color at all. The earl will not look twice at you."

"What earl?"

"The Earl of Didsbury. He is to attend tonight."

"I do not understand. What has the Earl of Didsbury to do with me?"

"Provoking girl! The earl is a widower. It is a most eligible situation."

"But is he not at least forty?"

"What can *that* have to do with anything?" Lady Alford banged her fine china cup down into its saucer. "Really, Pomona. You are not some great beauty with all of London at her feet!"

Keynsham strolled in. "Good morning. What a surprise to find you downstairs, mother."

"*Good*? What is good about it? I had *counted* on having the terrace doors open. But of course, that is precisely the direction from which the rain is driving!"

Keynsham tried to catch Pomona's eye. The previous evening when he'd told her what the publisher had said, she'd been aglow. He'd been looking forward to a longer discussion with her over breakfast.

She didn't look at him. She was staring down at her plate, looking as though she were about to cry. The source of this misery was all too obvious.

He turned to their mother. "Well, ma'am. It is my honor to inform you that I am engaged to be married."

Lady Alford gasped. She clasped her hands to her bosom. "My son! Oh, my *son*! I *knew* that you should not fail me! You have *never* failed me. Thirty thousand pounds!" Her face was rapturous. "I *knew* that Miss Spry would accept your suit! I never doubted it for a single moment!"

"Ma'am, I fear that you have..."

"I could not have planned it more perfectly myself! The timing is perfect! When we announce your engagement tonight, the astonishment and envy will be so general that everyone will be talking of my ball this twelvemonth!"

Keynsham signaled the footmen, who discretely left the room. "Ma'am. I must explain that—"

"The most eligible bachelor, and the heiress of the season! What a match! *Thirty thousand pounds*!"

"Ma'am, I—"

"You must and shall order a new carriage immediately. I still do not understand what happened to the other one." She raised a finger. "A barouche! A barouche for the ride from the church! Nothing could be more *à la mode*."

"*Ma'am*." Keynsham held up a hand. "You have not allowed me to finish. I am not marrying Miss Spry. And I do not require advice on carriages."

Lady Alford froze. One hand went to her throat. "*What?*"

"The lady I am to marry is Miss Celia Talbot, of Hampshire."

"*Who?*"

"You will meet her tonight. At the ball."

"But... but..." Lady Alford had gone deathly pale. "*What about Miss Spry?*"

"Miss Spry has... cried off."

His mother gulped for air. "No! That is not possible! A young lady who is compromised may not *cry off*! She is *ruined*!"

"Not at all, ma'am," put in Pomona. "Miss Spry is said to have an understanding with the Marquess of Ladbrooke."

There was a terrible silence. Lady Alford rose from the table and threw her napkin onto the cloth. "I shall go lie down. After all that I have done, to be treated this way by that chit of a—a..."

Fortunately, whatever unladylike word she was

about to say was drowned out by a peal of thunder violent enough to rattle all the china on the table.

* * *

"Boss wants you dead." Comstock's tone was chillingly matter-of-fact.

Fenton felt the grip of fear around his heart but scoffed anyway. "Nah. 'E's just flown up in the boughs on account of this to-do over Miss Talbot."

Comstock glanced around the grimy-windowed riverside tavern as though someone might be listening and lowered his voice. "Shut your trap for a minute if you can manage it and listen to me. Gooley's dead. He killed 'im."

"*Killed* him?"

"I said keep your voice down!" Comstock's hand shot across the sticky tabletop and gripped Fenton's wrist. "I seen it myself. Now 'e's ranting and raving, saying as 'e'll do the same to you. But 'e's off to settle up with the young lord tonight."

Fenton eyed him. "Settle up?"

"Them rum culls is 'aving a party. Boss thinks 'e can go blend in with the gentry. Mayhap he can, too—with all them fine clothes of his."

Fenton was incredulous. "Wilkes is going after the young lord? In his *house*?"

Comstock snorted. "It ain't *your* concern now—believe you me. As soon as 'e's offed the young lord, 'e's coming for you. I'd say you got a day to get out of town."

Fenton felt as though he'd been punched in the chest. "But... I got no money."

"Well, that's your problem, innit?"

"I thought you was going to talk to Wilkes for me! Smooth things over, like."

Comstock stared at him, incredulous. "*Talk* to him for you?" He stood and threw some coins down on the table. "I shouldn't even 'ave come to warn you! If 'e finds out..." He drew his forefinger across his throat. "This is the last drink I buy you—and the last time I see you. Matter of fact, I *never* seen you. Understand?"

He turned, slipped between two other patrons, and was gone.

Fenton stared at the forest of masts that bristled along this reach of the river, trying to catch his breath. If only he'd taken ship for the Americas after he'd helped Wilkes dispose of Squire Talbot's body! That would've been the time to disappear. But he'd been afraid to leave everything he knew behind. And now the walls were closing in. He could feel it.

Wilkes had always blamed him for staging the carriage accident on the wrong road. He'd never forgiven him for it. Fenton had thought that he could earn his way back into Wilkes's good graces. He'd thought that he could prove to Wilkes that he was loyal.

But in the end, nobody was ever loyal enough for Wilkes.

He drained the dregs of his beer. Perhaps he should simply stay here, drinking, until Wilkes found him. What good could it do to run? If Wilkes could kill Lord Alford—in his own house, in the midst of an evening party—there was no force on earth that could stop him from killing Fenton. Or anyone else.

Grey rain blurred the river. He tried to think. Wilkes had been trying to pass for a gentleman for years.

Certainly, he dressed like one. So Comstock was right—there was a chance that he could fool everyone, and walk right into the young lord's house. But none of his men could. Which meant that for once, Wilkes wouldn't be protected by the bodyguards who now accompanied him everywhere.

What if...

But no. What Fenton was considering was impossible. It was suicide.

On the other hand, if he were going to die anyway, maybe he should take Wilkes with him.

Chapter Twenty-One

"Now, do not be alarmed." Lady Sophronia, in a diamond and pearl tiara and white satin gloves, was wrapped in a pale blue velvet evening cloak. "I shall be with you. And of course, Keynsham will too—which I am certain is more to the point, as far as you are concerned." Her keen eyes sparkled with amusement. "You will do very well, my dear. I am certain that you will make a success."

Celia was less certain. But it was too late to back out now. Lady Sophronia's coachman opened the door and handed them down. A moment later, she was making her way across the forecourt of Alford House, clutching Lady Sophronia's arm for dear life as a footman held an umbrella over their heads.

The porticoed facade of Alford House, every window brilliantly lit, rose above a scene of chaos. A line of carriages waited to move forward. Some passengers had alighted early, leaving their carriages marooned in the unmoving traffic jam, and were hurrying through the rain toward the steps, dodging puddles and horse dung.

Hooves and wheels crunched on the gravel of the drive. Horses snorted, sending puffs of steam into the unseasonably chilly evening air. Coachmen forgot themselves and swore at each other. Servants held lanterns above important-looking guests.

"*Eighty people?*" They stopped abruptly as a carriage rolled ahead in front of them. Lady Sophronia looked about with narrowed eyes. "This is not *eighty people*. This is... this is a *mob*. Poor Pomona!"

Celia had no chance to ask what she meant before they were climbing the wet, torch-lit stone steps and passing through a tall pair of open doors. She found herself in a beautiful pale green entrance hall blazing with what seemed to be thousands of candles. Her stomach gave a nervous lurch. She had to remind herself that in another moment she would be on Keynsham's arm... and then none of her anxieties would matter.

Lady Sophronia's footman whispered to the Alford House footman. "The Dowager Viscountess Alford and Miss... Talbot!" he boomed. Celia felt a smile already beginning on her face, anticipating the moment that she would see Keynsham coming toward her.

But he didn't appear. She was surrounded by unfamiliar faces—a few gawking, some eyeing her gown and studying her person, but most indifferent. Her heart sank.

She told herself that she was being ridiculous. Keynsham was the host of the ball. There was no reason to think that he would be waiting to meet her at the door! She would see him in a moment or two... though how she was to see anyone in this crowd, she wasn't certain.

Lady Sophronia was frowning. "This is worse than I could have imagined. Why..." She didn't manage to complete her sentence, because they were jostled by a large group of new arrivals. Celia tried not to wince as the footman bawled out their names at earsplitting volume. Lady Sophronia looked pained too. "Who *are* these people? I do not recognize a soul here! Do *you* see anyone *you* know, Miss Talbot?"

Celia managed to shake her head slightly. "I am afraid that I do not, ma'am."

Though her formidable appearance didn't suggest it, Lady Sophronia was kindhearted. Unfortunately, however, she seemed to think that Celia was a member of London society, and that they must have acquaintances in common. "*Talbot*," she'd said that morning, as she'd been helping Celia choose a gown from her extensive collection. "A cadet branch of the Shrewsbury family, I take it?"

"I—I am afraid that I do not know, your ladyship."

"Well, perhaps the fifteenth earl will be in attendance. He will know."

The fifteenth earl? But just then the seamstress had been shown in, and the discussion moved on to which gown could be most speedily altered in time for the ball, and Celia hadn't had a chance to ask Lady Sophronia who she meant. And now they were here, and though on the outside she was gowned and coiffed as elegantly as any other lady, on the inside she was quaking.

A moment later they were jostled again, and a cold gust of wind through the opened doors spattered them both with raindrops. Lady Sophronia drew herself up. "We must move away from the doors. This is most unpleasant." She took Celia's arm. "Let us go through to the ballroom. Do not let go of me, whatever happens."

As they made their way deeper into the chaos it became more and more difficult even to speak. A foot or so away, a red-faced man was shouting at an acquaintance, simply to be heard over the din. Celia glimpsed the tops of enormous floral arrangements over the heads of the other guests. People packed a curving marble staircase above, waving drinks and throwing back their heads in raucous laughter.

"My dear, you look quite terrified." Lady Sophronia had to raise her voice above the uproar. "Unless you are about to faint?"

"No, your ladyship." Celia hadn't realized how much her face betrayed her anxiety. Her only previous experience of a London ball—which fortunately, Lady Sophronia didn't seem to recall—had been disastrous.

"Good." She gave Celia's arm an approving squeeze. "That cream satin suits you very well. And one can never go wrong with ostrich plumes, of course. If you are nervous, remind yourself of the perfection of your costume. That is what I do."

They managed to advance another few paces. Celia tried, and failed, to imagine any situation in which Lady Sophronia might feel anxious. "And I have been meaning to say—when we find Lady Alford, you need not answer any impertinent questions," she added.

Impertinent questions? Celia's heart skipped another nervous beat. If only Keynsham were with them! He had a way of reassuring her with just a glance or touch. How she longed to take his arm and see the humor glinting in his eyes! With him by her side she would be equal to facing anyone.

They entered the ballroom—or so Celia assumed. The hubbub increased to deafening volume. The heat, too, was overpowering. All that she was able to see of the room was a vaulted ceiling with gold and white plasterwork, a double row of chandeliers, and the arched tops of high windows along one wall. She was forced to raise the elbow of her free arm to protect her chest from unpleasant contact with gentlemen's arms, and more than once she felt something brush her hair.

Lady Sophronia pursed her lips. "This is *quite* the most unpleasant entertainment that I have attended in years!" she proclaimed, into Celia's ear. "My dear, we must—"

But whatever she'd been about to say was lost when a drunken gentleman stumbled directly into them. Lady Sophronia let go of Celia's arm. Indeed, for a moment Celia thought that she herself might fall. She managed to catch her balance, though the ostrich plumes in her coiffure were buffeted and tugged at her hair. She put her hand to her head. "Lady Sophronia? Lady Sophronia!"

Lady Sophronia was only a few feet away. But though Celia stretched a hand toward her, she was powerless to reach her. She watched, helpless, as Lady Sophronia was borne away by the crowd. "Lady Sophronia!" But it was no use. Her last glimpse of her chaperone was of the flash of the diamonds in her tiara.

She dropped her arm and tried to assume an expression of calm, fearing that she looked foolish. She hadn't seriously considered that she and Lady Sophronia might be separated. But then, she'd never experienced a crowd like this one.

And then—a little more than a yard or so away—she glimpsed a man's back.

Her body reacted first. Her heart began to pound. If she'd been able to move, she would have run. But there was nowhere for her to go. All she could do was freeze.

No. It was impossible. That fair, pomaded head must belong to a gentleman who simply bore a resemblance to...

Wilkes. The man turned slightly as he angled smoothly through the crowd. She glimpsed a little more of his ear and cheekbone. She was almost certain... And then he was gone.

No. It couldn't have been him. Besides, she'd only seen part of the side of his face. And of course, Wilkes wouldn't have been invited. He couldn't have simply walked in. She was being ridiculous.

Someone bumped into her, startling her out of her trance.

Keynsham. Keynsham would take this situation seriously. No doubt he'd reassure her that Wilkes couldn't possibly be here. But... well, he could also order the servants to search the house. If she'd really seen Wilkes, he would be found and thrown out.

She must find Keynsham. She tried to edge past a tall lady in a gown of figured primrose silk and a gentleman in grey damask, and was rebuffed with an angry "I *beg* your pardon!"

"I beg your pardon, I..." But the couple had already turned their backs. Celia looked about in near-despair. She was trapped by the crowd and could see almost nothing. And she couldn't continue to stand in the middle of the floor. If she'd really seen Wilkes... well, she ought to find somewhere where she was less likely to be seen herself.

She gathered the skirts of her gown and began to work her way toward the wall.

* * *

"I am the most persecuted woman *alive*!" Lady Alford cast herself onto the blue and white toile *chaise longue* and flung a hand over her eyes.

Her maids exchanged looks. A large glass of colorless liquid sat upon a tray on the white and gold dressing table. One of the maids offered it to her. "*Madame*, perhaps..."

Lady Alford sighed. "Oh, very well." She took the glass, drank it off with alarming speed, handed it back to the maid and closed her eyes again. "It will not touch my headache. Nothing ever does. My suffering is of a sort from which there is never any respite."

"Yes, *madame*." The maid refilled the glass from a crystal decanter of raspberry *eau de vie*.

"Everything is ruined! Keynsham will not marry Miss Spry! The rain will not stop! The prince will not come out in this weather. And there is not a man alive who will look twice at Pomona! Why have I been singled out for such misfortune?"

A housemaid hurried in with a cold cloth wrung out with a solution of ice water and vinegar. Lady Alford's French maid took it and laid it solicitously on her ladyship's forehead.

After a moment, her ladyship snatched it off. "It is dripping down the sides of my neck!"

"*Je m'excuse*, your ladyship."

"Not one person in this house is capable of doing a single thing properly! Not one! Cook has made but twenty-four of the salmon pies and eighteen of the turbot! And my son is marrying the wrong woman!"

The maids exchanged a look. "*Un autre* glass, perhaps, madame? To settle the nerves?" Berthe, the French maid, could sometimes coax her ladyship into a better humor when no one else could.

Lady Alford accepted the second tumblerful of liquor with alacrity. "*Madame* looks very beautiful this evening," ventured Berthe. "Perhaps we try the emerald and diamond *boucles d'oreilles?*"

"*Earbobs*? What *possible* difference can *earbobs* make? Have some *compassion,* Berthe! Is that too much to ask?"

There was a knock at the door. "Ma'am?" It was Keynsham's voice.

Her ladyship hastily slid the glass under the *chaise longue*, lay back, and replaced the cloth over her eyes. "I cannot see anyone at present. I have a headache."

Keynsham opened the door and stepped inside. "Ma'am. There are, I am informed, *four hundred people* in this house."

Lady Alford spoke in a small, weak voice. "I am powerless to move. My head is throbbing. Someone else must do it. I am too old."

Keynsham folded his arms. "I came to see why you and Pomona are not downstairs. This is her ball, and you are her chaperone."

"Oh, why can you not *understand*!" said her ladyship, from beneath the compress. "Everything is a disaster! There may as well not *be* a ball."

"Nevertheless, ma'am, I can assure you that there

very much is one. The house is all but impassable." Keynsham glanced at his watch again. He hadn't seen Celia since the previous evening. Being apart from her was causing a strange ache to develop in his chest. He longed to take her arm, to share private jokes with her, and to proudly introduce her to everyone as his future wife.

And, if she'd already arrived, she couldn't possibly be finding this overcrowded entertainment at all pleasant.

But his mother still hadn't moved. "Please get up. I must go back downstairs and find Lady Sophronia and Miss Talbot."

"Oh, *Miss Talbot*!" moaned Lady Alford. "If I never hear that name again it will be too soon! I have not the slightest notion who this—this *girl* is. You were to marry an heiress! And now you have been taken in by a *nobody*, and everything is *ruined*, and Pomona will never marry well, as if it were not bad enough already that I have spent years trying to hush up her—"

"*Ma'am!*" exploded Keynsham. His mother snatched the compress off her eyes and stared at him in disbelief. "You *will* stop speaking!"

"All I was saying was—"

"Be *silent*." He turned to the maids. "Out. *Now*."

The maids scuttled out. Keynsham had never spoken in that tone before. "Now. You will never mention that—that *matter* again. *Ever*. Do I make myself clear?"

Lady Alford glared at her son. "How *dare* you! We both know what Pomona did! And we both know what would have happened!"

"Yes. Pomona would have married the man she

loved—a good man, a man who would have made her happy."

"*Happy?*" She snorted. "On two hundred a year? *That* is not likely!"

"Ma'am. Was there some part of what I said that was unclear?"

She folded her arms mutinously.

"Now. I have not wished to trouble you with the details of our financial position, when you are recently widowed. But you were aware that it is not good. And I told you, in no uncertain terms, that we could not afford a large ball. It is now evident that I must exercise my authority as head of the household in a more direct manner."

His mother stared at him.

"You have made Pomona miserable enough already. It stops now. You will make no further... comments. And whether or not you find that you are suddenly 'too old,' you will get up, you will take your daughter downstairs, and you will greet your four hundred guests. And next week I strongly suggest that you begin a restful stay at Laversham Court."

At this, Lady Alford regained the power of speech. "What? *Old*!" She rose, tore off her wrapper and flung it onto the chaise. "I said nothing of the sort!"

Beneath the wrapper she was fully dressed in a shimmering column of silver gauze over an under dress of orchard green silk. A diamond necklace blazed at her throat. "*Old*! Why, I am only six and forty! Everyone says that I look not a day older than five and thirty! As to Laversham Court, that is out of the question. I am to chaperone Pomona's season." She tossed her head.

"We will discuss that tomorrow. Perhaps Pomona may prefer to return to Augsburg."

She sucked in her breath. "Is that so? Oh, I see it *all* now! No doubt Theodosia and Sophronia are up to their necks in this little scheme! Pomona has all of you wrapped around her finger. Well, you will see what a failure she will be without my guidance. She has inherited none of my beauty. She is plain, and awkward, and a bluestocking, and will never make a ma—"

There was a slight noise. Keynsham turned and saw Pomona standing in the door. How long had she been there? The answer, as he saw by the fact that her face was flaming and she looked about to cry, was long enough to have heard every cruel word that their mother had said.

She cleared her throat. "I… I came to see when we are to go down." The satin fabric of her gown was an unflattering stark white that turned her warm skin green. Multiple rows of padded piping and rosettes around the hem made the skirt stand out like a cone, rendering her slight figure sticklike under the stiffened fabric.

Lady Alford tossed her head. "I make no apologies for saying what everyone knows to be true."

"Ma'am. Hold your tongue." He tried to smile encouragingly at his sister. "We shall all go down together." He offered his arm to his mother. "Ma'am?"

"Oh *dear.*" Lady Alford rolled her eyes. "You cannot seriously mean for us to make an entrance *en famille*—like the Lord Mayor at his annual fête!" She stumbled.

Keynsham glanced around the room, saw the glass

under the chaise longue, picked it up, and smelled its contents. "I see." He set the glass on the dressing table.

Lady Alford drew herself up. "I am *not drunk*!"

Keynsham crossed to his sister and kissed her cheek. "You look beautiful," he whispered.

"No, I do not." Her teeth were gritted. "But for God's sake, let us just get this over with."

* * *

The rain was coming down harder than ever. But the back gate was open, and deliveries were still being rushed toward the service door. Fenton slipped inside.

In one way, the weather was lucky. There were no torches or lanterns illuminating the garden, or strolling lovebirds for him to dodge. He ducked behind a tall yew hedge and began making his way toward the house.

Around the side opposite to what he took to be the kitchens, he found what he was looking for: An unlatched lower window. He pulled it open as wide as it would go and wiggled through feet first, scraping his already sore ribs on the windowsill. The floor was farther down than he'd guessed. He lost his grip, fell a foot or so, and sat down hard on the flagstones, rubbing his ankle.

Curse Wilkes. No doubt he'd strolled straight in the front way—like the gentleman he'd always wished to become. He'd be up there mingling with the gorgers, tossing food and wine down his gullet. Fine cheeses... cold roast meats... pastries... hothouse fruits, cakes, and...

Fenton's stomach growled. He ordered himself not to think about food.

He'd landed in a storage room with open shelves on both sides. There were some brooms and buckets near the door—and a row of dark wool jackets hanging on pegs. Finally some luck! He struggled out of his own wet and dirty jacket. Surprisingly, amongst those on the pegs he found one that fit. Then again, he supposed that weeks of near starvation would thin a man down.

The jacket would help him blend in. It was also long enough to hide the pistol that he'd brought, once he'd tucked it into his waistband.

The shelves held household items: paper bundles full of beeswax candles, tinder boxes, clothes brushes, boot brushes... He pocketed several of the tinder boxes. They'd fetch a few bob. Then he brushed at his trousers until he'd got the dirt off—or at least as far as he could tell in the near darkness.

He didn't want to be here. He didn't want to be doing any of this. But Wilkes had left him no choice.

He turned the door handle and found himself in a bare, whitewashed basement corridor lit by tallow candles. At the far end, another door led to another corridor. The sound of pots and pans clanging warned him that the kitchen was near.

A kitchen—particularly during a large ball—meant plenty of servants.

Would he be caught? He paused. If he'd been clever, he would have... Well, that was just it, wasn't it? He wasn't clever. Not like Wilkes was clever. And besides—nobody was clever on one meal in two days.

He pushed the door open a few inches and peeked out. Someone was shouting orders. The rich fragrance of roasting meats billowed into the hallway. It was enough to make his stomach cramp with hunger. A footman rushed past, seemingly only inches from his nose, carrying a tray loaded with cups.

He let the door close. How on earth could he get past so many people? He couldn't. He couldn't do it. He took a breath and leaned against the cool wall. This had been a bad idea—like most of his ideas. He should leave now. Perhaps he could manage to squirm out the same window that he'd come in.

But... if he gave up, Wilkes would kill Lord Alford. Fenton didn't doubt that for a moment. And when the young lord was dead, Wilkes would come for him. He'd be dead inside of a week.

He took a breath and tried to steady his nerves. His plan might be suicide. Indeed, it scarcely even deserved to be called a plan. But somehow, he had to get upstairs and kill Wilkes before Wilkes could kill the viscount. After that, it would be too late.

He pushed the door open, stepped out, and—keeping his head down—followed a footman toward the back stairs.

A heavy hand fell on his shoulder. "Where do you think *you're* going?"

Fenton's heart dropped. It was over already—and he hadn't even got upstairs.

"Well?" The man was glowering at him. "Don't let me catch you empty-handed again! Get back to the kitchen and see what Cook has that needs taking up! Do I make myself clear?"

"Yes... sir."

Fenton stepped into the kitchen, trying to look as though he'd been doing it all evening.

There were several huge trays waiting on a table. He

picked one up, balanced it on his shoulder, and joined the procession of servants to the back stairs.

Chapter Twenty-Two

W*ell, well, well.* Lord Alford was an even greater fool than Wilkes had realized. There had to be several hundred people here. Whatever the young lord had spent to host this evening, Wilkes knew that he couldn't afford it.

The house seemed even larger from the inside than it did from the outside. Even so, it was uncomfortably crowded. And that had made it a simple matter to stroll in through the front door without any of the overwhelmed servants so much as glancing his way.

He paused, getting his bearings. Enormous floral arrangements perfumed the air with their heady scent. Within a few hours, all of these blossoms would fade and wilt in the heat of hundreds of bodies and thousands of candles. All the money that they represented would be taken away in the back of the dustman's cart tomorrow.

Celia had had her head turned by a man so stupid that he'd borrowed money for flowers.

Rage made the blood pound in his ears. Until Lord

Alford had happened along, Wilkes' only serious problem with Celia had been finding her—and bringing her to heel. Perhaps one day, he'd overcome her dislike for him—not that it mattered. She couldn't survive on her own. She'd have to marry him.

But now—because this idle, overbred fool had meddled in his affairs—the dreams that he'd once cherished lay in ruins. No matter what he did now, Celia had been tarnished. She probably fancied herself in love with the viscount. Well, he'd settle accounts with Lord Alford tonight—fatally. But he could never think of Celia in the same way again.

A few feet away was a long table laden with silver platters full of sweets—raspberry tarts, *petit fours* topped with tiny wild strawberries and candied violets, pyramids of sugared cherries and nectarines, crisp rolled wafers and shortbread biscuits stamped with the emblem of the three ostrich plumes of the Prince of Wales. He popped a *petit four* into his mouth and looked about. What his father would have given simply to walk in the door of this house! How quickly he would have made the silverware disappear into his pockets!

But then, his father had been content to make a living stealing chickens and horses. He'd lacked ambition. He'd lacked... *vision.* Wilkes had always known that he was meant for bigger things.

He rejoined the throng. The press of people carried him into the ballroom. Rich men—heavy with scent, loud with liquor, and filled with unearned self-confidence—pushed past him. How he hated them. Like Lord Alford, they'd had everything handed to them—including power.

His covetous eye was caught by a lavishly embroidered silk waistcoat. The man who was wearing it saw him—and froze for a moment. Wilkes nodded. The man's eyes bulged with fear and his mouth fell open as the elegant lady on his arm prattled on, oblivious.

A surge of confidence filled Wilkes. Perhaps he wasn't the one who ought to be afraid after all. He wasn't a member of society... yet. But he pulled the hidden strings that controlled it. The gentleman in the embroidered waistcoat was highly influential. He also owed Wilkes a great deal of money. He'd also been involved in several interesting and very illegal ventures in his efforts to pay it off. If their association were to become known, it would spell the end of his parliamentary career.

So. Would he alert anyone to Wilkes's presence here tonight? No. He wouldn't. He'd keep his mouth shut.

The tightness in Wilkes's chest eased. As he made his way through the crowd he began keeping a running tally of the men present with whom he'd had dealings. Some pretended not to see him, of course. Still, he saw enough eyes widen to know that they found his presence unnerving.

Suddenly, he felt powerful—even invincible. He was a wolf, slipping through a flock of sheep... any number of whom he'd already fleeced. He smiled to himself. This evening was already proving more amusing than he could have anticipated.

It was time to get his plan underway. It was time to send the viscount a message.

All he had to do was find someone stupid enough to carry it.

* * *

"Damme, but Alford *has* pushed the boat out!" Bartlett whistled between his teeth. "Look at this spread." He downed several raspberry tarts, licking his fingers and smacking his lips. "And these shortbread biscuits are from Gunter, I should say. Very good. Very good indeed! Well, let us find the card room, Townley. It will be a long night."

He looked about. "Townley?" He waved above the heads of a cluster of ladies. "Townley!"

Townley reappeared, staggering back towards Bartlett. They'd only been separated for a few minutes, but clapped each other's backs as though they hadn't met for a year.

"It is as hot as Hades in this ballroom! Damme, but I am parched already." Bartlett stood on tiptoe and craned his neck. "Ah—here we are." He lifted two glasses of champagne off a passing tray. After guzzling the liquid, they abandoned the empty glasses on a chair against the wall for some unsuspecting lady to sit upon.

They set off again—stepping on heels and knocking plumed headpieces askew as they went. "The viscount and I are great friends, you know! We spar together at Jackson's! I am quite a favorite with the family! I have already promised two dances to his sister!" Bartlett's voice was loud, even considering the hubbub around them. Heads began to turn.

Townley mumbled something incoherent.

"No, no. Certainly not a beauty! Still, a tolerable enough looking girl, for all that. And it is an eligible situation, to be sure! The viscount told me in confidence that the condition of the estate is far better than popular report has it! Ah! Punch!" He lifted two silver cups from a tray and handed one to Townley. "And of course, there is the thirty thousand pounds from Miss Spry's marriage portion! The engagement is to be announced tonight, of course!"

A gentleman, overhearing this, leaned toward a lady and whispered something in her ear. Her eyes widened. As the oblivious Bartlett and Townley lurched onward, a ripple of gossip spread outward from them, like the wave from a pebble tossed into a pond.

"Give it to me, Townley. No, to *me*. No, the *cup*." Bartlett glanced about and hastily slid the empty cups onto the dirt beneath a potted palm tree. "Now, what do you think of this? 'Miss Keynsham,' I shall say to her. 'Miss Keynsham, I hope that you will not break my heart by saying that you do not remember that we was to dance!' Eh? Damme, but that *will* be very pretty! Am I not a very silver-tongued devil? She cannot say no to a speech like that—can she? Townley?"

He paused to wait for Townley, who'd stumbled into a lady and become entangled in her reticule. When they were both fully vertical again—Townley taking a few well-deserved blows in the process—the men resumed their progress.

Townley slurred something. Bartlett frowned. "Well, I expect that it is because they are waiting for the prince to arrive to begin the dancing. And he is late, of course! And that is if he is coming at all. He is always a deuced awkward sort of fellow to invite to anything!" He looked around. "Townley? Townley! Damme, you must try to keep up!"

Townley wove toward him. His face was ashen. He mumbled something.

"Note? What note? What are you talking about?"

Townley mumbled again.

"What man? Where?" Bartlett looked around, frowning. "Damme, Townley, we are in the middle of a ballroom! There is no one here who could have *threatened* you. You are hysterical—and it is not the first time, either."

Townley's hands were shaking as he produced a slip of paper.

"Well, give it to me, then!" Bartlett snatched it. "No, of course I will not. I am a gentleman! Really, Townley! You must calm yourself."

Townley began to cry.

"Now, now." Bartlett patted him awkwardly on the shoulder. "You need another drink—that is all. There's a good fellow." He glanced around for a footman, but there were none in sight. "You are in no danger. *Moneylender*! Do not be ridiculous! No one like *that* would be present tonight. Here."

He gave Townley his handkerchief. "Now. Pull yourself together. We shall find Lord Alford and give him this note, and that will be the end of the matter."

* * *

As he crossed the entrance hall with his mother and Pomona, Keynsham couldn't see Celia anywhere. Had she arrived yet? Where would she and Lady Sophronia have gone? Everywhere he looked, some drunken stranger had his or her head thrown back, braying with laughter. This was his own home—and yet he felt like an unwelcome and all too sober intruder amidst the revelers.

Pomona, clutching his arm, looked about in dismay. "This is simply dreadful! It reminds me of the part in *A Midsummer Night's Dream* when everyone is lost in the wood. We shall never find grandmama in this crush!"

"Hush, you ungrateful girl!" Lady Alford, on Keynsham's other arm, glared at her daughter. "It is *not* dreadful! It is the ball of the season! And you will keep your... your *bluestocking* remarks to yourself!"

"Ma'am." Keynsham had to raise his voice over the din. "*Ma'am*. My sister may say what she likes, when she likes. Am I clear?"

Pomona shot him a grateful look, but Lady Alford pretended not to hear. "We shall go through to the ballroom. Come, Pomona. Keynsham may stay to greet the prince when he arrives."

She tugged Pomona away. They vanished into the mob and were gone before he could say anything further.

Keynsham didn't have the slightest intention of lingering in the entrance hall waiting for the prince, like a majordomo at a Continental hotel anticipating a wealthy guest. Indeed, he doubted that the prince would come at all. Every time the doors opened the fierce downpour outside was visible, the rain streaking down through the lantern light as stragglers continued to arrive.

All he wanted was to find Celia. He'd been counting the minutes until he could see her again. Had she and Lady Sophronia arrived while he'd been upstairs, trying to cajole his mother to attend her own ball?

He began making his way to the ballroom. But everything seemed off kilter somehow. There was no logical reason for him to feel uneasy, he told himself. He was in his own home, for God's sake! None of the people who surrounded him were threatening. They were simply members of the *ton* who his mother—anxious to impress strangers at the expense of her own family—had invited in order to make a show of importance and popularity.

"Alford!" Someone touched his arm. He jumped.

"Ha ha ha! You are certainly on edge, sir! Why, you look as though you do not know me! Bartlett, of course! And you know Townley, I am certain."

It was the gentleman who'd accosted him at the gymnasium. Keynsham shook hands, pretending not to notice that Bartlett's friend miscalculated where his hand was on the first and second attempts. "How kind of you both to come tonight."

Bartlett blew out a puff of alcohol-laden breath. "Wouldn't have missed it! Would we, Townley?"

Townley, who seemed unable to focus his eyes, mumbled something incoherent. Keynsham frowned. "Is your friend, er…? Perhaps some air?"

"Townley?" Bartlett emitted such a loud bark of laughter that even in the din of the ballroom, heads turned. "Oh no! No, sir! Townley is quite at his best! Merely half seas over! No worse than any other night! As long as he don't start crying again—eh, Townley?"

Townley stared glassy-eyed at Keynsham, apparently unable to formulate a response.

Keynsham tried to see past him. Good God. The house would have been packed with two hundred people—let alone double the number. He couldn't find his own fiancée, the clamor of the crowd was almost painful, and someone seemed to be bumping into him every other minute. It was not so much a ball as a crush. It was not at all an appropriate event for the come-out of a viscount's daughter.

And then the prickle of danger raced up his neck again. *There*! Out of the corner of his eye, he saw a man carrying a tray. It was the big thug who'd nearly killed him in the woods—and who'd tried to grab Celia only yesterday!

He lunged. But a boisterous group pushed between them. He was forced to issue quick apologies before he could dodge past and seize the man's arm.

The man turned, somehow continuing to balance the tray. And... he wasn't Wilkes's thug after all, but a tall footman: Peters. "I—I beg your pardon, your lordship! Have I...?" His face was horror-struck.

"Oh. No." Keynsham backed away, his heart thudding. "It is I who... that is, I beg your pardon, Peters. I thought..."

He wiped his forehead. Had he gone mad? He would have sworn that... Perhaps he ought to get some air himself.

But of course, Bartlett was right there on his heels, propping up his friend and smiling obsequiously. "Your lordship, I have a—"

"Please. Excuse me." He couldn't listen to this rattle a moment longer. He must find Celia.

"One moment, please. I have been charged with giving you this note." Bartlett handed him a folded piece of paper.

Keynsham stared at it, frowning. "What is this?"

"A gentleman gave it to Townley, with instructions to give it to you. When I asked Townley which gentleman it was, he could not point him out."

That didn't surprise Keynsham. He doubted that Townley could have pointed out the king himself.

"No doubt it is the scheme of some young lady." Bartlett rocked back on his heels, plainly pleased to have become part of an intrigue. "I advise you, your lordship —do not be taken in! It is the very worst thing to be taken in by a young lady! If this is an attempt to arrange a private meeting, I advise you not to go. Miss Spry would be bound to hear of it!"

Townley mumbled a long incoherent statement.

"Oh, do not mind Townley. He is still in love with Miss Spry himself—ain't you, Townley? But Lord Lotion is against the match. It seems that the old fellow disapproves of drink, and has got hold of some notion that Townley is a toss pot."

"Imagine that." Why Bartlett was babbling about Miss Spry, Keynsham neither knew nor cared to find out. He unfolded the note to find a hasty scrawl: *Come alone to the library at eleven o'clock—or you will regret it.*

"*Regret* it!" Bartlett was craning his neck to read over his shoulder. "Good God! What have you done? The young lady must be in a rare pelt indeed!"

"Sir, this is a private communication." Keynsham had memorized the note that Celia had left him at the inn, and this was certainly not her handwriting. Besides, she wouldn't have sent such a ridiculous message.

"Never fear! I am as silent as the grave. I am a positive vault!" Bartlett mimed buttoning his lips together. "I am the soul of discretion!"

Keynsham wasn't listening. He was trying to think. He'd been unable to find Celia anywhere. He was trapped by these drunk buffoons. And something—he didn't know what, exactly—was wrong.

A flash of lightning so bright that it cast the packed guests into a frozen tableau was followed almost immediately by a long rumble of thunder. Bartlett shuddered theatrically. "Damme if this storm has not lingered directly overhead since morning! It is most uncanny. I advise you to take it as an omen, your lordship! Do not go to the library! Do not risk the wrath of Miss Spry."

But Keynsham had had enough of Bartlett and his incoherent friend. "Excuse me," he said, curtly, and began forcing his way through the crowd.

"Your lordship! Your lordship! Do not go!" Out of the corner of his eye he could see Bartlett frantically waving at him over the heads of other guests.

Keynsham ignored him. He must find Celia. Only then could he be certain that his anxiety was unfounded.

Chapter Twenty-Three

Celia straightened her shoulders, lifted her chin, and began to struggle through the crowd alone. If there was one thing that she'd learned since Wilkes had forced her to leave home, it was that it was important to look as though she knew where she was going—especially when she didn't.

She pushed her anxiety down. Of course Keynsham was here. This was his house! They would be reunited at any moment. And then her fears would fade into nothing. The whole tone of the evening would change. Her worst problem would become something trivial... like... like trying not to forget anyone's name.

No doubt, when she looked back, she would feel very foolish at how she'd allowed herself to panic—and how she'd allowed her imagination to run away with her, and fancied that she'd seen Wilkes.

She tried to edge past a large group of chattering people. "It is quite intolerable!" cried a lady. "One feels as though one was invited simply to make up numbers!

I should like to leave. Indeed, if I can ever locate Lord Gray, I shall ask him to order our carriage immediately!"

"I must admit that I should like to see the daughter, now that she is returned from Germany," said another lady. "It is said that she is a bluestocking—and *quite* plain."

What an unkind thing to say of Keynsham's sister! Celia wished that she were not being forced to eavesdrop. But she seemed to be trapped.

The first lady tutted. "No doubt Lady Alford wished as many people as possible to be here for the announcement of her son's engagement. Though of course, everyone knows that it is a patched-up affair that has dragged on far too long."

Celia's heart began to pound. *Patched up? Dragged on far too long?* That seemed very unfair!

"It is indelicate," pronounced a gentleman. "Everyone is perfectly aware that she would not be marrying Alford at all if the old duke had not interfered—or if Lord Lotion hadn't objected to the other fellow."

Old duke? Lord Lotion?

"Are you certain that it is back on?"

"Well, she would hardly be here otherwise. I saw her not five minutes ago. Togged out in pink, with too many jewels, as usual." The others laughed.

Celia began to feel sick. Surely they couldn't mean...

"Ah, well," sighed the first lady. "People have short memories. The scandal will be forgot soon enough. And Alford will need every penny of Miss Spry's thirty thousand pounds, from the looks of this ball."

They all laughed again, and began to move away.

Celia stood frozen to the floor. *No*. Keynsham had made promises. He'd talked of the future. He'd asked her to marry him! He was too honorable to treat her in such a way.

But... was he? What might have happened at the inn, if she hadn't discovered the engagement ring? The engagement ring that had been meant for... Miss Spry? He'd admitted that he'd been under an obligation to her. Then yesterday, he'd claimed that he scarcely knew her.

It had seemed plausible at the time. But had he been telling the truth? If only she could find him, and ask him for an explanation.

But what if the very fact that she couldn't find him was all the explanation that she needed? If Miss Spry was here, Keynsham would be with her. He would not be looking for Celia.

And the gossiping gentleman had been quite certain that she was here. And, as he'd pointed out, Miss Spry wouldn't have come unless she and Keynsham were still engaged. That was the most damning argument of all.

Celia's heart was racing faster and faster. A drunken man bumped into her and stepped heavily on her toe. She wanted to burst into tears. She bit her lip and limped toward the nearest wall. If only she could have a moment's peace and quiet in which to think through all of this! There had to be some misunderstanding. She didn't see how, but... well, there simply had to be. Keynsham had talked of fate bringing them together. She would have known if he'd been lying.

And yet... for the first eighteen years of her life she'd lived in a web of lies. And she hadn't known that, had she? She'd never suspected that her father had been cheating Wilkes—or that he'd tried to steal her inheritance. How could she trust her judgment when she hadn't seen the truth about her own father?

Perhaps, with Keynsham too, she'd been seeing only what she wanted to see.

The noise, the heat, the lack of air... her head was beginning to pound. She leaned against the wall for a moment and tried to collect herself. But it was no use. Whatever else she told herself, she couldn't explain away the fact that the other lady—Miss Spry—was present tonight. She didn't think that she could bear to see Keynsham with Miss Spry. Her heart would break.

If only she could think! If only she could leave the party! But she was trapped, in a short-sleeved cream-colored satin ballgown that didn't belong to her, with a thunderstorm outside.

By creeping along the wall, her foot still throbbing, she made her way back to the entrance hall. Fortunately it was less crowded than it had been before. She looked around, at a loss. Opposite the front door, where latecomers were still arriving, was another door. She made her way to it and—checking to be sure that nobody was watching—slipped through it and into an empty corridor.

She took deep gulps of cooler air. But she could feel a sob rising in her throat. She tiptoed across the corridor and opened a door. It opened into a large room set with tables, where a servant was placing a tray upon a crowded sideboard. She shut the door quickly, before he could turn around.

Fortunately, there was another pair of doors farther

down the corridor. She hurried to them and tried the handle. The doors were unlocked. And they led exactly where she'd most hoped that they would: the quiet dimness of a library.

She slipped inside, shut the doors as silently as possible and leaned against them, no longer able to hold back the tears that overflowed from her eyes.

She'd had to discover the ring for herself—and only then had Keynsham admitted that he was all but engaged. Then he'd claimed that Miss Spry had thrown him over—despite the fact that he'd compromised her. But she was at this very ball, and people were gossiping about the forthcoming announcement of their engagement.

If Celia weren't capable of putting such large and obvious pieces together for herself, then she was a fool indeed.

She must find some way to leave—ballgown or no ballgown. "You have developed a certain expertise at running away," Keynsham had said to her, only yesterday. Well, now she'd have to use that expertise.

She rested her forehead on the door for a moment, took a steadying breath, and was reaching for the handle when there was a noise behind her. She whirled around, her hand at her throat.

And out from the shadows, into the firelight, stepped Wilkes.

"Good evening, Miss Talbot." His face twisted into a smirk. "I did not expect to see *you* here tonight. Are you not enjoying the ball?"

* * *

If Keynsham had learned anything at all, he'd learned that it wasn't wise to go to a library on the invitation of an anonymous note. He turned the piece of paper over in his hand. "*Come alone to the library at eleven o'clock—or you will regret it.*"

He didn't have time for this nonsense. And he didn't see what else this ridiculous threat could be. He was already late to find Celia, and his feeling of dread was growing. He was about to crumple the paper in his hand when he saw... Miss Spry.

With her dark hair curled into ringlets and piled high, she strolled through the crowd as though she were the only person in the packed ballroom. People stepped out of her way, and she appeared to be unaccompanied.

Of course, her chaperone—as Keynsham knew all too well—was always conveniently somewhere else. The self-satisfied expression on Miss Spry's face was the only sign that she was aware of the stares and gasps and whispers that followed her. She was shocking the *ton*—and she was reveling in it.

His mother must have invited her. But then, she'd invited most of London. And it was possible that the invitation had been sent before Miss Spry had thrown him over.

Still, Miss Spry herself must know that it was in the worst possible taste for her to attend this ball after she'd cried off from their engagement. She must know that her appearance here, tonight, would cause talk—and that it would make everyone think that they were engaged. There could be no innocent explanation for her behavior.

The only saving grace was that she was so busy

being the center of attention that she hadn't yet seen him.

Somehow, he must make her leave. Because the second she put on some display of rushing to him, or whatever she was scheming to do—everything that he had with Celia would be in jeopardy. And he couldn't allow that.

A public confrontation with Miss Spry would accomplish nothing except to cause further talk. Besides, she'd twist anything that he said to make him look like a brute, and gain the sympathy of bystanders. A private meeting, however...

Oh. Of course. The realization struck him like lightning. It was Miss Spry who'd written the note. *Or you will regret it.* Yes, that was *precisely* the sort of language that a young lady of her dramatic tendencies *would* use.

Anger began to build in him. He couldn't be rude to her, of course. That would be ungentlemanly. But Miss Spry must truly think him a fool if she thought that she could use exactly the same trick that she'd used to dupe him before.

He'd held back before. But now he had Celia's peace of mind to consider. If Miss Spry wanted a meeting, she'd get one. It just wouldn't go the way that she expected it to. He'd leave the library door open—so that she couldn't claim that he'd tried to kiss her, or any other nonsense—and he'd have her carriage brought round to the mews, so that she couldn't turn her departure into a dramatic scene.

He began shouldering his way through the crowd, back toward the entrance to the ballroom. The only person who would regret this meeting would be Miss Spry.

* * *

"Good man. Set them down there, on the sideboard."

Good man? Fenton, who'd just carried two heavy trays of cold roast pheasant in aspic up to the dining room, was warmed by the praise. He couldn't remember the last appreciative word he'd had from Wilkes.

Or if he'd ever had one.

He rubbed his shoulder and gazed at the buffet table. He'd never seen anything to beat this spread. Meat pies, fish pies, pigeon pies, cold ham, cold roast fowl, cold roast beef, cold sides of salmon, salmagundis, blanched asparagus... all of the dishes that weren't served hot had been brought up from the kitchens and arranged along the sides of the room on huge white linen-draped tables.

His stomach growled. Despite the fact that he'd had nothing to eat today, he'd worked nonstop. He wiped the back of his hand across his brow. The long buffet of desserts at the far end of the room was crammed with pistachio macaroons, almond biscuits, ratafia cakes and cherry biscuits, towering cones of pastry puff balls encased in clouds of caramelized spun sugar, syllabubs, thousand-layer cakes and raspberry creams, almond pastries, savoy cakes, apricot tarts, chocolate tarts, dishes of almond prawlongs... Or at least, that was what he'd been told they were called. There wasn't room for even one more plate.

Supervised by Mr. Brock, the butler, the footmen had arranged all of it into a sumptuous display that made anything that Fenton had ever seen in a confectioner's window look pitiful by comparison. Towering above it was a large molded sugar ornament, tinted and gilded, that bore the legend WATERLOO.

What Waterloo had to do with dessert, Fenton couldn't imagine. But he considered himself a patriot, and appreciated the sentiment.

The footman slapped him on the shoulder. "Well, we shall have a grand supper of our own, once this is over! Cook says we have double the food that's needed. But of course, there was no telling her ladyship that." He leaned closer and laid one index finger beside his nose. "Now, a word to the wise: Whatever you do, if you see her ladyship, don't say a word. Don't even *look* at her. And *stay out of her way*."

This sounded ominous. The young lord's fists were bad enough. "Is—is her ladyship the... the young lord's wife?"

"Young lord...?" The footman frowned. "Of course not! Lady Alford—the dowager viscountess, that is to say—is Lord Alford's *mother*." He glanced about and lowered his voice. "And a perfect termagant she is too! We've had to rearrange the house three times—just so her ladyship could invite more people to this ball. You see this room? It's the state drawing room."

"But..." Fenton looked about. There was no indication that it had ever been a drawing room.

"She's been at it for a month! She had us remove every stick of furniture. All these dining chairs are rented. We had to carry them in yesterday—in the rain." He sighed and rubbed his lower back. "But it might have been worse. She'd talked of emptying the library as well and putting more tables in it. It's just through there, you see." He motioned at what appeared to be a solid wall. "We were only saved because Lord Alford had objected to furniture being placed in his room, and she knew that he'd catch on if she started crating up the books."

Fenton was still trying to imagine all of this. "*Rented chairs?*"

"Three hundred of them!"

The idea of rearranging an entire house for an evening party would never have occurred to Fenton. What these gorgers got up to!

"I don't mind telling you that we shall all be very glad when this is over." The footman folded his arms and sighed. "Well, we are only waiting for the prince now. Once he arrives, the dancing will start. And then at one o'clock, supper will be served."

"The *prince*?" This tale just got more and more astounding. "You mean the *real* one? Or one of them foreigners?"

The footman frowned. "The *real one*. I assure you that His Royal Highness the Prince Regent will *not* snub an invitation to Alford House!"

"Our own prince! Think of that!" Fenton was a great admirer of the royal family. "I shall be pleased to drink his very good health!"

The footman was called away to do something with the wines, and for the first time since Mr.Brock had mistaken him for one of the extra servants hired for the evening, Fenton was left without a task.

Which meant that he must stop wasting time, and do what he'd come here to do: Kill Wilkes.

The only problem was... how?

The one thing that he knew was that there hadn't

been any outcry. Which meant that Wilkes hadn't killed the young lord... yet.

But how could he find Wilkes? He hadn't expected that there would be so many people crammed into the house—though the place was more like a palace than a house, in his opinion. Even if he'd had a plan in the first place, it wouldn't have worked. And he'd never had a plan.

But then, that was just like him, wasn't it? Dick Fenton—the man who could never manage to finish any job. The man who couldn't do anything right. The man who'd staged a carriage accident on the wrong road. The man who'd let Wilkes tell him what to do and when to do it, because he was too weak to think for himself.

It was time to face facts: He had another week of life ahead of him at best. Then it would be a knife in the ribs—or worse.

Alone in this heavenly room, with its celestial blue walls and high white plaster ceiling, he could have wept. He'd done a lot of bad, bad things... and in a few short days, he was going to pay for them with his life.

It was time to get out of this house. At least the footmen thought that he'd done a good job. He should leave before he could disappoint them, too—the same way as he'd been disappointing everyone his whole life.

His stomach growled as he turned away. He paused. Since he was nothing but a thief and a failure anyway—not to mention as good as dead—there could be no harm in stealing some of this food.

He glanced around to be certain that he was still alone. Then he snatched a choux pastry filled with almond cream from a silver tray, stuffed it whole into his mouth, bit down, and closed his eyes in rapture as the rich, silky filling exploded into his mouth. It was the best thing he'd ever tasted.

He ate another... and another. He crammed an apricot tart into his mouth. He wolfed down shortbread biscuits. He eyed the cakes, trying to decide what to try next. It almost seemed that the more pastries he ate, the worse his hunger got. He longed to cut himself a substantial slice of one of the meat pies. But that would ruin the display that the footmen had worked so hard to assemble.

He surveyed the dessert table again, and reached for the almond prawlongs.

And then he heard a voice.

For a moment, it seemed to be coming from nowhere. Then he remembered that the footman had told him that the panels behind the dessert buffet were doors that led into the library. He shrugged to himself, and was about pour as many of the prawlongs out of a silver bowl as would fit into his jacket pocket, when the voice rose.

The voice was both angry and familiar. He trained his attention on it.

The voice belonged to... Wilkes.

* * *

Celia was too terrified to move or speak.

"Well, well." Wilkes looked her up and down. "I did not expect to see you here tonight. I must compliment you on that lovely gown. It is even finer than the clothes that you used to wear in your father's house. Not that it was his money that was paying for them. Practically speaking, it was mine."

It was as though she were looking at two different people superimposed onto one. The outline was the old Wilkes: tall, fair-haired, smirking, dandyish... and a thug to the bone. The details were the new Wilkes: the expert London tailoring, the jeweled fobs and ring and stick-pin, the fashionable hairstyle, the languid manners of a habitué of the *ton*.

"I—I *knew* that it was you." Her voice came out as a croak.

"You knew that it was me? What *are* you babbling about?" He leaned against a bookcase and examined his fingernails. "Well. Never mind. It cannot be at all interesting. And I must say, your arrival in this library is particularly ill-timed."

She put her hands behind herself and felt for the door. If she could just turn the handle...

"Why, Miss Talbot! Surely you cannot wish to leave before we have a little chat—now, can you? You will hurt my feelings." He smirked.

Her mouth and throat had gone dry. She stopped feeling for the door handle. "Why... why are you here?"

Instead of answering, he pulled out an expensive-looking watch and consulted it. "Ah, you see? The mantel clock is slow by a good five minutes. I thought so." He tucked his watch away again. "Well. As it happens, I am expecting your friend Lord Alford to join us at eleven o'clock. There is a matter that he and I must... discuss."

He was here to kill Keynsham.

She knew it. He wouldn't have risked everything to come here otherwise. And if he'd arranged to lure him to the library... then he must be intending to murder him here.

"Lord Alford *is* your friend—is he not?" Wilkes studied her. "Dear me! I do hope that he is not the reason that you are crying. You have never been quick-witted, Miss Talbot, but even *you* must have known that he would not marry you. Why, he is to marry the heiress! Everyone is talking of it."

He shook his head, tsking. "And yet, here you are in a silk gown. Why, anyone who did not know the truth would think that you are a lady."

She forced out a quavering sentence. "I *am* a lady."

"But are you really?" He strolled casually to the fireplace and stuck out his chin as he turned his face from side to side in the mirror over the mantel. "It is an interesting question. After all, your father was no gentleman."

He sighed. "It is a hard world—is it not, Miss Talbot? So often, people are not what they seem. Take this ball, for instance. Any number of gentlemen present tonight are believed to be rich! Yet as it happens, *they* owe *me* money. The rich man is me."

He leaned closer to the glass and adjusted the large diamond stickpin amidst the snowy folds of his neckcloth. "What a mistake you made, Miss Talbot, when you rejected my offer of marriage."

She tried to conceal her surprise. Was it possible that she'd wounded his pride? His bragging about his money made her suspect so.

In that case she must flatter and soothe him. She'd done it with Mrs. Ellesmere, after all. She could do it now. "I beg your pardon if that was your impression, Mr. Wilkes."

He froze for a moment. "*Impression*?" He gave a short laugh. "Oh, I recall it perfectly well, Miss Talbot. You fobbed me off with some cant about my proposal being flattering—but so very *unexpected*. But what you really meant was that you thought yourself better than me. And yet look at you now—cast off by the viscount."

She must not take his bait. "Of course I was flattered by your offer of marriage, Mr. Wilkes. But I had suffered the sudden blow of losing my father. I… I believe that I was in a state of shock."

He stared at her for a moment, his expression unreadable. The only sound was the rain lashing the windows. Then he turned back to his own reflection and made another minute adjustment to the jeweled pin. "Oh, Miss Talbot. Oh dear." He studied himself, his eyebrows raised. "How awkward this is. I find myself embarrassed for you. You are not even a good liar."

He sighed. "Your claim that Squire Talbot's death caused you to be overset by grief is…" He shook his head. "Well, the sentiment is very pretty, but it is also quite ridiculous. Even *I* knew what your father was—and that he had not wanted a daughter, and had not the slightest regard for you."

He leaned closer to the glass. "Why, he resented you. You, his own child! And if you had not been such a simpering little ninny, you would have seen that for yourself."

Did Wilkes expect that his words would crush her? That she was still the spiritless girl that she'd once been? He didn't know that she'd been to see her father's solicitor, and that any illusions that she'd had had already been shattered.

But Wilkes thought that she was stupid. If she

could use that blindness against him… if she could get him out of this house before he could kill Keynsham…

He'd already destroyed her future. She wouldn't let him ruin even one more life. "It is your own behavior, Mr. Wilkes, that has caused me to avoid your courtship."

For a moment he seemed caught off guard. "*Courtship*, Miss Talbot?"

Her heart was beginning to pound—but with fury, not fear. She struggled to push down her anger and keep her voice even. "I refer, of course, to your thugs chasing me in the public streets."

He recovered his composure and smirked. "'Thugs?' I prefer the term 'associates.'"

"I have no doubt that you do."

His self-satisfied smirk faded slightly. He seemed to be trying to work out whether she'd just insulted him. She must be more careful. But she was running out of time. It was almost eleven o'clock. "However, I shall accept your proposal, Mr. Wilkes."

He stared at her. "You mean…?" Lightning flickered outside, casting ghastly shadows across the scene. "Well." He cleared his throat. "This *is* a surprise. I never imagined that you could be so… so flinty-eyed, Miss Talbot. It does not accord with my idea of you."

"Flinty-eyed, Mr. Wilkes?"

He continued to frown. "Miss Talbot, I… What I mean to say is that I should have thought that you had the, er… conventional feminine notions about love."

She smoothed down the skirts of her gown. "Conventional, Mr. Wilkes? Why, I believe that I do. After all, most ladies understand that marriages are business arrangements, even if they do not say so aloud. I have had time to consider your proposal, and I am now minded to accept it."

There was a silence, underlined by the muted hubbub of the ball and the rattle of rain on the library windows. He blinked. "You... you... This is not..." He stopped.

He'd wanted her to blush, and be flustered and shy. He'd wanted to feel that he'd overcome her girlish reluctance. The idea made her feel sick.

"I suppose that I find it difficult to believe that you have had such a drastic change of heart, Miss Talbot. Are you certain that it is what you want?"

"Oh, Mr. Wilkes. We both know that what a lady wants is unlikely to matter much in *this* world." She tried to keep the bitterness out of her voice. "What I want is to have some peace. Indeed, I should like you to escort me out of this ball. It is far too crowded, and I find myself with a terrible headache."

"Hm." He clasped his own elbows and rocked back on his heels. "I see. You wish to leave immediately. With me."

She tried to force her face into smoothness. She felt as though he must be able to hear her heart pounding and see her knees shaking beneath the skirts of the borrowed satin gown. "Yes."

"But Miss Talbot, I have told you that I have important business here tonight. You seem in a great hurry to leave before I am able to... conclude it." A smirk began to play around his mouth again. "Why is that?"

He didn't believe her. "Surely your business may be postponed. After all, if you are to be my husband, I must be able rely upon you to care for me when I am unwell."

"Ah. I see. In sickness and in health. Is that it?"

She put a hand to her forehead. It wasn't even a lie. Her head was pounding.

"You do look very pale." He moved closer. Her skin began to crawl. "But you see, Miss Talbot, there is something missing. I had always imagined that this moment would include—oh, tender kisses, I suppose. Murmurs of passion. That sort of thing." Now he was beginning to smirk again. "Unless, of course, you are lying."

He reached out and caressed her cheek with his fingertips. Involuntarily she jerked away.

"Well, well, well." His smirk faded. "I begin to suspect that the apple does not fall far from the tree after all. Although I must say that your dear papa was far more convincing."

"Mr. Wilkes"—

He tut-tutted. "Oh, Miss Talbot. Were you really attempting to sacrifice yourself for the viscount? You have never been clever, but... well, that is simply pathetic. The viscount does not want you. Why, you are not even a lady."

Not a lady. It was the same thing that she'd been telling herself. Yet as the poisonous words came from Wilkes' mouth, she realized that they were lies.

"Is that so? Well, your views on who is and who is not a lady are certainly interesting, Mr. Wilkes, particularly when we both know that you are not a gentleman —and never will be one."

It wasn't much of a retort. But to her surprise, Wilkes's face twisted with rage. "Why, you little... How dare you! You think that because you were born into your position that you are *better than me*?"

She drew herself up. "No. I think that I am better than you because I am not a criminal."

He grabbed her arm. "Oh yes? Well, your dear papa *Squire Talbot* was one. And look where that got *him*!"

His hand tightened. She tried to pull away. "Let go! You are hurting me!"

Wilkes' smirk widened. His fingers dug into her arm. The clock on the mantel began to strike eleven.

Chapter Twenty-Four

"Your dear papa *Squire Talbot* was one. And look where that got *him*!"

Wilkes had Celia Talbot. And Fenton knew what Wilkes had done to her father.

The pistol was in his hand before he even had time to think. He grabbed a corner of the heavily laden dessert table and pulled it, thinking to slide it gently and quietly away from the doors. It scarcely moved.

"... gave *specific* instructions that the syllabubs and the Chantilly cream were *not* to be brought up until after the first remove. It is far too hot."

"But your ladyship..."

"*What* is that man doing?"

Fenton let go of the table and whirled to find himself facing a haughty, middle-aged blonde who seemed to be encrusted in diamonds. She was flanked by Mr. Brock and the senior footman. All three of them were staring at him, aghast.

He blinked. It took him far too long to realize that

her eyes were upon the... "*Gun*!" shrieked the lady. "He has a *gun*!"

From the other side of the library doors Fenton heard the sound that he'd been dreading: The report of a pistol. Wilkes had shot poor Miss Talbot.

He didn't need a plan after all. He seized the table and flipped it over.

* * *

Keynsham flung the library door open. This time, he wouldn't let Miss Spry divert the conversation with her lies and playacting. This time, he'd tell her exactly what he...

Instead of Miss Spry, he saw Wilkes, struggling with Celia.

Keynsham lunged.

The gangster stepped back, jerking Celia against him. Now he was facing Keynsham, holding Celia in front of himself as a human shield, his forearm around her neck. "Ah. Lord Alford. I expected that you would be along presently."

Celia's eyes met Keynsham's. They were full of terror and misery.

"You were expecting someone else? The pretty little heiress, perhaps?" Wilkes smirked. "Why, everyone at this soirée is simply *abuzz* with talk of your engagement! I have just explained to Miss Talbot here"—he jerked her tighter against him—"that she is not *quite* viscountess material."

He must not let Wilkes goad him into a mistake. "What an odd thing for you to say. Are you quite... *well*? Miss Talbot and I are engaged to be married."

Wilkes's smirk slipped for a moment. "Oh, is that so? Well, you may be interested to know that Miss Talbot's dear papa was—not to put too fine a point on it—a thief. He cheated me out of a very large sum of money. No, no, I am afraid that Miss Talbot is... not quite the thing."

Keynsham kept his voice even. "Let go of her now."

"Oh, I think not." Suddenly there was a pistol in his hand. "You see, *viscount*, I invited you here because it is time that I settle a score with you."

"Oh, stop *crying*, Townley!" A braying voice came from the corridor. "Mark my words, Alford took my advice! He will not have been so foolish as to come to the *library*."

Two figures stumbled through the door. One was Bartlett. The other—Townley—lifted a shaking hand to point at Wilkes.

"What the devil...?" Bartlett lurched forward, his fists raised. "Who are you? I warn you, sir! I am a trained practitioner of the pugilistic arts! Unhand this lady!"

Wilkes drew back, collided with an armchair, and stumbled. The pistol went off. Townley screamed and clutched his arm.

Regaining his balance, the gangster shoved Celia aside and lunged at Keynsham. A flailing blow caught Keynsham above his left eye. His head rang. "You overbred, interfering..." *Wham*! Another punch caught him in the stomach, knocking the wind out of him.

A thunderous crash seemed to shake the foundations of the house. The doors to the adjacent room were torn open. Light spilled into the library. A man was shouting over the sound of smashing china. "It's him! It's him! Stop him!"

Wilkes looked toward the noise. Keynsham, gasping for breath, managed to swing. His right cross caught the gangster across the jaw. Wilkes spun sideways. He reached for Celia, his fingers spread like a claw.

"Never! Touch! Her! Again!" Keynsham's fist slammed into Wilkes's face.

Wilkes staggered. His pomaded hair was hanging into his sweaty face. Blood from his cut lip spattered onto his lace-trimmed neckcloth and his grey silk jacket. Still clawing at Celia's skirts, he crumpled slowly to the floor.

Bellowing like an enraged bull and clutching his injured arm, Townley charged forward and collapsed on top of Wilkes.

In the background someone was screaming. "Keynsham! *Keynsham!* The ball is ruined! *The ball is ruined*!"

Keynsham gathered Celia into his arms. "Darling! Darling! Did he hurt you?"

She was shaking. Her eyes brimmed with tears. "I—I shall not hold you to your promise."

He squinted at her. He really wished that people wouldn't keep punching him in the face. "What on *earth* are you talking about?"

* * *

Celia's knees were shaking so badly that she wasn't certain if she could continue standing. Her thoughts were jumbled. Chaos surrounded her.

"He shot Townley!" shouted one of the men who'd burst into the library. "*He shot Townley*!"

Keynsham pulled her closer. "Please tell me that you are unhurt."

And then Dick Fenton was standing before them. "He did it! Wilkes did it, Miss Talbot! He murdered your old dad! He's guilty as sin!"

Dick Fenton? How could he be here? She shrank back.

"Don't worry, Miss Talbot! I ain't here to hurt you!" He stretched a pleading hand toward her. "Wilkes did it, Miss Talbot! He killed your dad! It weren't no carriage accident! I came here to stop him afore he could kill the young lord!"

"Stop where you are." Keynsham raised a warning hand. "Keep away from her. And me." He pointed at the footmen who stood frozen in the other room. "You and you! Come into the library and light all the candles."

Celia stared at the big thug. There was a smear of... *whipped cream*? on his face. Her eyes traveled to the pistol in his hand. "Oh!" He reddened. "Sorry about that!" He stashed the gun in the back of his waistband. "Always putting me foot in it!"

Her eyes went to Wilkes—face down on the library floor, and half under the dead weight of the larger of the two men who'd burst into the library.

"Darling?" Keynsham's hand tightened on her upper arm. "You are safe. Wilkes will never hurt you again. Nobody will ever hurt you again."

"I—I think that I always knew it." Everything seemed to be spinning through her mind. She tried to clear her throat. "Somehow I knew it."

“You have had a terrible shock. Now is not the time to” —

“The ball is ruined! *The ball is ruined!*” The shrill voice broke through whatever he’d been going to say. An elegant blonde lady in an icy green gown was struggling toward them through the mounds of smashed cakes, biscuits and creams that covered the floor. She swatted away a footman who was trying to assist her. “Keynsham! *Keynsham*!”

Keynsham turned. “Ma’am.” He made her a bow. “Miss Talbot, my mother—Lady Alford. Mother, allow me to present my fiancée, Miss Talbot.”

Fiancée. He’d said fiancée.

Lady Alford’s eyes were narrow with fury. “*But what about Miss Spry*?”

Through the doors that connected the library to the other room was a growing crowd of spectators. Celia glimpsed a pretty young woman in a bright pink gown elbowing her way toward them. But at that moment, a trumpet flourish sounded.

Everyone looked around in surprise.

Lady Alford clasped her hands, her expression agonized. “It is the prince! The prince has come! *Someone clean up this mess*!”

The servants looked at each other. Before anyone could move, the prince himself—middle aged and leaning on a cane—entered the other room, smiling broadly. He was accompanied by an entourage of fashionable gentlemen. The crowd fell back out of his way. Everyone made deep bows and curtsies—except Lady Alford, who seemed too frozen in horror to move.

“Lady Alford! You are as exquisite as usual.” The prince was splendidly dressed in a high-collared evening suit of darkest plum damask. His snowy neckcloth was surmounted by the bright ribbon and heavy gold pendant of the Order of the Golden Fleece. And there was a gleam in his eye that Celia could only call... glee.

"Why, what have we here?" He raised a quizzing glass and surveyed the room. "Dear me! It looks like an explosion in a pastry cook's shop!"

His entourage snickered. The laughter spread to the crowd. Red with fury, Lady Alford recollected herself and sank into a curtsey. "Your royal highness."

The prince motioned for everyone to stand. "Yes, yes, that will do." His sharp blue eyes were sparkling with curiosity. "Now, what has happened?"

Before Lady Alford could answer, Fenton waded through the sea of smashed desserts, seized the prince's hand, and shook it. "What *happened*, your highness? He murdered her old dad! *That's* what happened!"

A gasp went up from the crowd. "Indeed?" The prince studied him through his quizzing glass. "And whose 'old dad' would that be?"

"Miss Talbot's dad!" Fenton gestured at Celia. "Squire Talbot, as was! Oh, aye! He killed him with his bare hands!"

Another gasp went up.

"I see." The prince frowned. "And who is this, er... alleged murderer?"

"Wilkes! Andrew Wilkes! Right there!" Fenton pointed at the unconscious gangster. "Oh, he's done a great many wicked things, has Andrew Wilkes! That's him! That's him right there!"

Lady Alford was motioning frantically at the footmen, apparently trying to get them to silence Fenton or remove him from the room. They all studiously gazed at the floor.

One of two gentlemen who'd burst into the library hurried forward. "Bartlett, your highness!" He made an unsteady bow. "And damme if that damned... damned *tulip* did not shoot Townley! *Winged* him! Without the slightest provocation!"

"I see." The prince frowned. "And who is *Townley*?"

"Cecil Townley, MP, your highness! But he has pinned the villain to the floor, as you see."

Townley, sprawled comfortably on top of Wilkes, let out a loud drunken snore.

"*Shot*, your highness! And it may prove more serious than it looks, for it has been scarcely a fortnight since the poor fellow took a ball in the *other* arm—when he and young Ladbrooke met to settle their dispute over Miss Spry!" He gestured in the direction of the young lady in the pink gown, who was still determinedly making her way toward Keynsham.

She froze. Everyone gasped.

The prince gave Bartlett a quelling look. "Sir! May I remind you that there are *ladies* present, and that such a topic is not suitable." He turned to one of the members of his entourage. "Fetch a surgeon for Mr., er... Townley. And for heaven's sake, take this—this other fellow into custody!"

The crowd fell back as two footmen did their best to support an incoherent and resentful Mr. Townley toward the door.

Then, as Celia held her breath, two more footmen and one of the members of the prince's entourage hoisted Wilkes' limp body between them. Her hand was over her mouth and her eyes were filled with tears as they carried him from the room.

He was gone.

One moment Wilkes was there—seemingly still capable of waking, springing up and terrorizing her. The next... he was gone.

It happened almost too quickly for her to believe that it was real. He'd murdered her father. He'd forced her to flee from her home. She'd been running from him for over a year. And then, in the space of a few minutes, he'd been lugged away like yesterday's rubbish.

The tears were tears of relief. Her knees were shaking so violently that she put a hand out for Keynsham. He slipped his arm about her waist to help support her.

"Ah. Lord Alford!" The prince applied his quizzing glass to his eye again. "There you are! Do you know, no one has yet explained how all this, er... tragic destruction occurred." Despite his cane he made his way through the sea of smashed desserts.

"Good evening, your highness." Keynsham bowed. "May I present my fiancée, Miss Talbot?"

"Charmed, charmed." The prince bent over Celia's hand as she sank into a curtsey. He squinted at Keynsham. "Somehow I am not surprised to see that you were involved in this, er... *contretemps*."

"Only in a minor way, your highness."

"*Minor*. I see. Well, no doubt that explains that nasty gash in your forehead." He glanced at Fenton. "And this... big fellow? Is he employed by you? He will have to swear out a statement, of course."

Fenton, still gazing in rapture at the prince, took this as a cue to seize his manicured hand again and shake it some more. “Blimey, what an honor this is, your highness! *What* an honor!”

“Your highness, this is all a dreadful misunderstanding!” Lady Alford hurried toward them. “This—this young woman is *not* my son’s fiancée.”

“*Ma’am.*” Keynsham’s tone was uncharacteristically sharp. “You have said quite enough this evening.”

The prince was trying to extricate his hand from Fenton’s grasp. “Yes, yes. That will do. I said, *that will do. Thank* you.” He turned to Lady Alford. “My dear, after the events of tonight, it is only natural that you find yourself... overwrought.”

"But your highness”—

The prince held up a be-ringed hand. “Consider the matter logically: Any man of Lord Alford’s fighting ability must certainly be able to see clearly enough to recognize his own future wife.”

His entourage began to titter. The laughter spread to the crowd. The prince basked in the admiration of his wit. Then he stooped, reached into the wreckage of the dessert table, and lifted something out of it. “Well, well.” His smile broadened. “What have we here?”

He was holding a sugar paste decoration molded in the shape of the word “Waterloo.” Somehow it had survived intact. “How very apt.” The prince held it up so that everyone could see it. “One might say that *several* people present this evening have met their Waterloos.”

“Very good, your royal highness,” said a gentleman. “A Waterloo indeed! Most witty. Most witty.”

Guests began to applaud. And at that exact moment, Celia saw a flash of pink silk disappearing from the back of the room...

The prince waved a hand. Everyone stopped clapping. "Now. You. Stop. Yes, *you*. Stop." He was speaking to Fenton, who'd been edging toward the door. "It will be your duty to give king's evidence."

Fenton stopped and gazed adoringly at the prince. "Yes, your highness."

The prince handed the ornament to a member of his entourage and dusted off his hands. "Well! And I had feared that this might be a dull evening! But after dear Lady Sophronia's ball last year, I ought to have suspected that the Alfords might provide a little scandal."

At this, Lady Alford made a faint moaning noise. The prince lifted one of her limp, gloved hands to his lips. "*Dear* Lady Alford! I jest, of course." He looked about. "Still, considering that—well, a man has been shot—it would be in poor taste to continue with the ball. And one can only hope that your innocent young daughter Miss Keynsham did not witness any of these dreadful events."

Lady Alford gaped at him. "But... but..." Her voice was faint. "The ices. The ices have not been delivered."

The prince frowned. "*Decidedly* poor taste."

His highness had just canceled the ball. As this sunk in, the guests took their cues and began pushing toward the front door. "The ices." Lady Alford pressed a hand to her breastbone. "*The ices*!"

The prince made her a bow that had an air of finality. Then he, too, turned and exited, followed by his entourage.

Lady Alford stood rigid for a moment. Then, red with fury and humiliation, she turned on Fenton. "You!

You are the one who ruined everything! *You* are the cause of all of this!"

Fenton froze. His eyes widened and his jaw dropped. For once, his blank face registered an emotion... and that emotion was terror.

He turned and ran after the prince. "Your highness. *Your highness*!"

* * *

Lady Alford stormed off. Celia looked about, dazed. In what seemed like only moments, everything around her had transformed. The guests were all but trampling each other in their eagerness to leave, and a chilly draft found its way along the floors from the open front door.

Yawning footmen were stacking dining chairs against the walls. Some of the housemaids collected broken china into buckets and baskets, while others lugged in pails of water and began mopping up the remains of icing and whipped cream.

Celia and Keynsham were seemingly forgotten by everyone. The prince had pronounced the dreaded word "scandal" over the ball. Members of the *ton* were fleeing the house as fast as they could. Keynsham's mother had been rude to her, and their engagement hadn't been announced.

And... she had never been so happy in her life. Keynsham's hand still rested on her back. Warmth seemed to flow into her from his touch. Warmth... and hope. She didn't have to run away ever again. She was finally free to be with the man she'd loved almost since he'd rescued her in Whitechapel.

She reached up and gently touched the fresh cut on his forehead. "You are still handy with your fives."

He winced, caught her hand, planted a kiss in her palm and smiled. "I beg your pardon, darling?"

"On the night we met, you told me that a gentleman might be as handy with his fives as any ruffian."

His eyes kindled. "You remembered that?"

"Of course I remembered it. I remembered everything." She met his gaze. And for a long, long moment she was lost in it.

"Well." He cleared his throat. "Now you have seen what you are getting yourself into. You will be allying yourself with what is currently the most scandal-ridden family in London." He took her other hand and held both of them in his. "My mother is bound to make our wedding as awkward as she can manage. My face will be covered in bruises at the ceremony. I should not blame you in the slightest for making a run for the stagecoach—any stagecoach—while you still can. In fact, perhaps I will join you."

The happiness she felt was like a sunrise in her chest. "Oh, I am almost used to your bruises by now." She glanced around to check that everyone was still ignoring them, then reached up and placed a quick kiss on the unbruised side of his mouth. "And I do not plan on going anywhere."

Epilogue

TWO MONTHS LATER

"Well, Mr. Townley has won reelection to Parliament." Keynsham clucked to the horses. "Not only that, but his name is being mentioned for a cabinet position. Being shot at Pomona's ball was a great boost to his political career."

He turned the gig off the main London road into a dusty country lane. "He gave all his campaign speeches with his arm in a sling, and whipped up public fears about the dreadful problem of crime in the nation."

Celia sighed. "But I cannot help but feel that it is my fault that Wilkes was at the ball at all."

"*Your* fault?" Keynsham glanced over at her. "Of course it was not your fault! He is a madman! A madman who has confessed to two murders—though there are very likely more than that." He reached over and squeezed her hand. "You must stop blaming yourself. Wilkes went to the ball intending to kill *me*, without even knowing that you would be there."

Celia smiled at her handsome husband. Somehow he always managed to make her feel better. "Well, I wish

Mr. Townley at the devil. He has talked of the incident at the ball so much—and so publicly!—that your poor sister's season has been ruined by the scandal. She was not even given vouchers for Almack's."

"Yes. It is most unfair. Of course, Lady Theodosia still feels that it will all blow over by next season—and that she will be able to persuade Countess Lieven to intervene in the, er... voucher situation. Ah. Here it is."

"Here" was a pair of towering stone gateposts supporting a huge iron gate. Keynsham turned into the driveway that they marked, and in moments they were driving through the cool shade of a dense wood. "All that said, if Pomona wishes to return to Augsburg with Lady Theodosia, that is her decision alone."

"She would also be most welcome to return to Alford House, of course." Celia still felt shy about issuing invitations to her new home—especially so soon after Lady Alford's contentious departure from it.

Keynsham squeezed her hand again. "She is very fond of you already—but now that Lady Theodosia is here, Pomona seems determined not to be parted from her again."

Lady Theodosia's return to London was yet another upheaval in the family. She'd shocked everyone when she'd walked into the family drawing room of Alford House only the day after the ruined ball.

"What on *earth*... ?" had been Lady Alford's ungracious words on first seeing her mother-in-law's sister. "How... how did *you* get here?"

"In my carriage, of course." Lady Theodosia swept up to Lady Alford and kissed her on both cheeks in the Continental manner. "I had it put aboard ship in Ostend. You *know* how I abhor public conveyances."

Celia curtseyed to her. She embraced Lady Sophronia and looked around the room. "Then I take it that my letters have not arrived?"

Even Lady Sophronia seemed at a loss for words. Lady Theodosia's eyebrows went up. She was a tall lady with the same silver-streaked blonde hair as her sister, and wore a deep blue silk carriage gown of such stunning elegance that she appeared to have stepped straight from a Parisian modiste's salon into Lady Alford's drawing room—without an uncomfortable journey in the middle.

"I had intended to be here at least a week ago—in time for Pomona's ball, of course—but the weather on the North Sea was so shocking that we could not put out from port." She glanced around at the extra furniture that hadn't yet been carried back downstairs. "But where *is* my darling girl?"

At that moment a disheveled and red-eyed Pomona rushed into the room, threw herself into her great aunt's arms, and silently clung to her. "Good heavens! You are very pale." Lady Theodosia patted her on the back. "Indeed, you are *all* rather pale. Tell me—how was the ball?"

Pomona burst into tears.

After this there was a family discussion that quickly grew heated Despite the presence of Celia, an outsider to the family, Lady Alford had a great many inappropriate things to say.

It turned out that Lady Theodosia had arranged to rent a house for the time of her visit to London. Pomona would have packed her things and left with her great aunt that very moment, but Lady Alford said that it was out of the question. She became shrill, and accused everyone of conspiring against her. Nothing was resolved. Pomona left the room in tears again.

And then, the next day, a miracle occurred—in the form of Mrs. Townley, Mr. Townley's rich and influential mother. She happened to be shopping in Bond Street with two of her friends when they saw Lady Alford. All three cut her dead.

On her way home, Lady Alford had a sudden epiphany: She needed a long rest in the country. "*None* of you appreciate anything I do. It is pointless for me to stay in town when Pomona has received not a single invitation since the ball! Well, let her go be unpopular with Theodosia—since that is what she wants. I wash my hands of her. And she had better not come crying to me when she fails to marry well—or at all!"

Had two months in the country improved her mother-in-law's sharp tongue? As the gig drew up before Laversham Court, Celia looked nervously up at the pale stone front of the Alford's country house.

Keynsham handed her down. "Well, here we are. At least we have the excuse of needing to continue our onward journey to keep our visit short."

* * *

"It is most disagreeable that you have involved yourself in *building houses*. Whatever will people say?"

"That we are solvent. And no one is likely to complain about that."

Lady Alford scowled at the wide lawn below the terrace. Where it ended, the sparkling curve of the river glinted in the afternoon sun. "You may be *quite* certain that your poor father never spoke to a bricklayer in his life!"

Now that fifth viscount had been dead and buried for over a year, Lady Alford had begun referring to him as "my poor late husband" and "your poor father." Anyone who didn't know how much she'd hated him could easily have mistaken her for a grieving widow.

Keynsham caught Celia's eye. "As I have explained, ma'am, it is not uncommon for gentlemen to involve themselves in land development. Indeed, it is the very means by which a number of our leading families became wealthy."

"Well then, they ought to be ashamed of themselves." Lady Alford fanned herself irritably. "Martin? *Martin!* Bring some orangeade. And adjust the umbrella at once. The sun is in my eyes."

The footman, sweating in powdered wig and gilt lace-encrusted livery, hurried to obey.

"And that still does not explain why you are returning to town *now*. *Nobody* who is *anybody* is in London at the end of August." Her jealous eyes rested on Celia's pretty new bonnet. "But then, I suppose that *you* do not mind."

Celia and Keynsham exchanged a look.

"I have set several meetings regarding Lady Alford's property," said Keynsham. "My foreman is in Hampshire going over the house, and we must discuss its condition and sale with Lady Alford's solicitor."

The dowager viscountess jerked upright and frowned. "*Property*? What *property*?"

"Why, Talbot Hall, of course, ma'am."

Before Lady Alford could ask the questions that she was all too obviously longing to ask, a parade of footmen began to lay out trays full of iced cakes, plain cakes, lacy rolled ginger biscuits filled with cream, orangeade, ratafia and tea.

A fathomless blue sky hung overhead. Bees buzzed in the lavender and roses that edged the terrace. The fragrance of new-mown grass was thick in the air. Somewhere deep in the trees a pheasant croaked.

"I have had a letter from Theodosia." Lady Alford motioned for the footman to refill her glass of ratafia. "She says that she is intending to stay on in England for some time. I really cannot think why!"

"She has been alone for the better part of five years, since the count was killed at Leipzig." Keynsham set his teacup down. "It is only natural that she wishes to renew old acquaintances in London, and visit with her sister—and of course, Pomona."

The dowager viscountess narrowed her eyes. "Renew acquaintances! If what I hear is true, she and Pomona go nowhere—except to lectures and literary salons. And now everyone is saying that Pomona is a bluestocking and will never get a husband. I told you how it would be. But no one listens to me. "

Keynsham cleared his throat. "My sister has been suffering from a lack of invitations, ma'am—as you must be aware."

"Oh, surely people are not *still* being tiresome about the ball." Lady Alford tossed her head. "Why, that was two months ago! And it is not as though anyone but Mr. *Townley* were shot!"

"Indeed, ma'am." Keynsham rose, held out his hand to Celia, and made his mother a bow. "A ball at which only one person was shot must certainly be accounted a success."

* * *

"Well, perhaps she will go to Bath, as she has been saying that she intends to do." Keynsham turned back onto the London road. "And perhaps the next time we spend time in the country, we will stay at Laversham Court ourselves."

She smiled up at him. "I was very happy to honeymoon in Devonshire."

He squeezed her hand. "And so was I."

In another hour, fields dotted with sheep and cows began to give way to strips of market gardens. For the first time, as she approached the ragged edges of the growing city, Celia felt almost as though she might be coming... home.

Wilkes was in prison awaiting trial. Mrs. Ellesmere had allowed Celia to collect her few possessions. Of course, she'd also made it clear that she didn't believe that Celia was really going to be a viscountess... so the call had ended awkwardly.

And finally, they'd gone on honeymoon, and at last Celia began to let go of the fears that had ruled her thoughts for so long. There were still times when she couldn't quite trust that that painful, uncertain, frightening era of her life was over. But gradually, she was learning to believe in a happy future.

And she was learning more pleasurable things, too. She glanced over at Keynsham again, thinking of what they'd been doing only the previous night. Her mind went to the way he'd...

"You are rather quiet." He glanced across at her. "What are you thinking about?"

Her face heated. "Oh, nothing."

"I hope that my mother has not upset you."

"Not at all." She met his eyes. "I am too happy to mind her ridiculous comments."

"*Really*!" His smile broadened into a grin. "I should like to hear more about why you are so happy, Lady Alford. Perhaps you could... describe some of the specific... er, *activities* that you have been enjoying since we married. In detail."

She would swear that he knew *exactly* what she'd been thinking.

"I am—I meant... Well." Now her face was burning. Changing the subject seemed the safest course. "What did Downey write to you about the condition of Talbot Hall?"

"Ah." He clucked to the horses as the London-bound traffic grew heavier and they had to slow their pace. "The fire damage to the stable block was relatively minor. He has hired a a local man to replace the floor and rafters. And the solicitor thinks that the sale of the property should realize perhaps four thousand pounds. You are still certain that you wish to sell it?"

"Yes." Even saying it lifted a weight from her. "Yes, I am certain. I never wish to see the place again, after... after..." She shuddered, and tried not to think of her father's end. "Well, you already know. Although of course I would like to visit Mrs. Ryder. And I would like to pay all the former servants proper annuities. My father made no provision for them."

"You are quite right to do so, of course. Indeed, you are a paragon. *My* paragon." He squeezed her hand again. "And a rather rich one, too. It will be interesting to see how my mother behaves when she discovers that I have married an heiress after all."

Ominous clouds were piling higher and higher in the sky over the city as they crossed Putney Bridge. But Celia's mood was lifting. "Some might say that you have a certain history of compromising ladies with money."

He shot her a swift sideways smile. "And some might say that you are more witty than a dull fellow like me has any right to expect his wife to be."

"Dull! Surely nobody who gets into as many fist fights as you do can be called *dull.* But I must admit that I should prefer it if our life together could be *very* dull from now on."

"Should you?" He squeezed her hand again. "Well. I will do my best."

* * *

As they drove past the southern boundary of Hyde Park a gust of wind roared through the trees, tossing the branches up and sending a few loose leaves skittering down Rotten Row.

Riders, carriages, and pedestrians looked at the threatening skies and hurried for the park exit. Lady Alford was correct that the end of August wasn't a fashionable time of year to be in London. Even so, the bottleneck that developed at Piccadilly left them waiting in traffic.

A few fat drops of rain spattered out of the darkening sky, and the hood of the gig provided little protection. They had not far to go now, but just as they drew up before Alford House the skies opened.

Keynsham's tiger leapt down to take the horses, and they hurried up the steps together. Just as they reached the door it was thrown open by a footman, who was so out of breath that it was plain that he had run to meet them. "Lord and Lady Alford! I do apologize! We did not expect you until tomorrow!"

"Good afternoon, Quentin. If you will bring up the trunks from the gig, we shall manage perfectly well." Keynsham turned to Celia. "We must have beat the luggage back to town after all."

Celia's maid and Keynsham's valet were accompanying the luggage in the big traveling carriage. They stepped into a very quiet entry hall. The dowager viscountess had poached a number of the servants and taken them with her to Laversham Court. Many others had given notice after the shooting. For now, the house was unusually empty.

"Ordinarily everyone would have assembled here to greet us." Keynsham tossed his hat and gloves onto a table. "But I am just as happy that they have not. All of that pomp can wait until later."

Celia looked up at the lofty ceiling of the entrance hall. "It is intimidating enough as it is. I still cannot quite manage to feel that this is my home."

"Intimidating?" Keynsham looked about. "Well, you will soon grow used to it." His cheekbones had the glow of their honeymoon by the sea, and his hair had acquired some golden streaks that it hadn't had before a month of salt water bathing. Surely it could not be normal for one's husband to set one's heart pounding and one's thoughts racing ahead to...

He caught her eye and his eyebrows went up a little. "Well, I must go through to my study. I asked for any letters of business that arrived in my absence to be left upon my desk. I must check to see if there is anything that appears to be urgent."

"Oh. Yes. Of course." She was suddenly and ridiculously disappointed that they could not go upstairs, where they could be alone... But then, she reminded herself, there was always later. After all, two of the many qualities that she appreciated about her husband were his practical nature and his attention to duty.

"Come with me a moment." He tucked her hand into the crook of his elbow, escorted her down the corridor past the library, and unlocked a door.

"*This* is your study? It is not as bleak as I expected, based upon your descriptions." He'd told her about the late nights he'd spent despairing over the estate's books. "Why, I pictured you shivering in a garret."

His eyes glinted. "I am certain that it was bleaker in those days."

"Indeed?" She eyed the thick carpet, carved desk, mahogany shelves, and gilt-framed Romney portrait of the fourth viscount. "Somehow I doubt that."

"Well, it seemed so to me, combing through the ledgers at one o'clock in the morning—when I thought that I had no hope of seeing you ever again." He returned to the door, looked both ways up and down the hall, and closed it.

"Now then, Lady Alford." He traced a tender finger along her jawline. "Here we are at last. Home. Together." He pulled her closer. His mouth found hers. "And I hope that our life here will not be *entirely* dull—despite what you said on the drive here. The long, *long* drive. During which I could not do *this*."

His lips, surrounded by light stubble, traced along her jawline to the hollow beneath her ear. His voice was suddenly low and intimate. "Do you know how difficult it was to refrain from kissing you? Kissing you properly, I mean. Like this."

She did know. His mouth recaptured hers and her lips parted and his tongue was playing with hers, stoking the desire that she'd had to repress all day. She gasped and pulled back. "Perhaps... perhaps we ought to go upstairs."

"Upstairs? Why?" A smile was beginning to play about the corners of his mouth.

Something low in her belly did a slow flip. "I—I meant..."

His smile widened into a wicked grin. "Perhaps I should tell you—or better yet, show you—how I kept up my spirits... and certain other parts of my body during those bleak hours." He backed her up against the desk until the wooden edge of it was against the back of her thighs. His hands tightened, and he lifted her easily onto the desk.

"I spent a good deal of time thinking about doing this." He reached down to her ankle, took a handful of the fine cambric of her gown, and began to ruck it up. "And also this."

She glanced involuntarily at the door. "But not here in the..."

"Oh, yes." He kissed her again. He kissed her until she was weak. His lips traveled down her neck. An involuntary sound came out of her throat.

His hand roamed over the stiffening peak of her breast, teasing it through the fine muslin. He pulled away her fichu and pushed his fingers under the neckline of her gown, teasing her nipple, then freeing it from the fabric and sucking it into his mouth until she had to stifle a cry. Shocks of pleasure flew across her skin.

Already, everything was tightening inside her in anticipation...

He pushed the skirts of her gown up still further. His fingers caressed the bare skin along the top of her stocking, slid higher to the sensitive skin of her inner thigh, and then making her gasp when he ran them unexpectedly and lightly along her cleft. She pushed against him with an inarticulate cry. His fingers found the taut bud there and began to circle.

It was all happening quickly... and yet not quickly enough. He unbuttoned the fall of his trousers. They slid to the floor. She heard papers falling from the top of the desk behind her as he pushed her farther back.

His fingers were still playing over the tight bundle of nerves between her legs. She was already poised helplessly on the edge of climax. "*Please.*" They were in his study. A servant might open the door.

He stroked her once... twice... and she gasped his name as every muscle fiber in her body pulled taut. As the first shudders of her release racked her, he pushed inside. Her spasming channel stretched around his member and she moaned.

As he began to move he seemed to be reaching a place inside her sensitized body that she hadn't known existed. Within moments she was aching for a deeper release.

He cupped her face against the palm of his hand and held her gaze in his with an intensity that she'd never seen before. His unhurried, deliberate thrusts seemed to hit every secret and sensitive place inside her. As many times as they'd made love on their honeymoon, this felt different. Her nerves wound tighter and tighter as his pace quickened.

Another climax was building inside her. Her channel tightened around him. "*Celia*," he groaned. He reached down and touched her, and she broke apart. Deep shudders racked her and she couldn't stifle her cries as her inner muscles gripped him. She felt him jerk inside her as she imploded into ecstasy.

Much later, it seemed, they were sprawled, still panting, on the desk. Celia drifted back to reality. Her gloves were on the floor, in two different places. Her skirts were up around her waist. She blinked. Her brain, still wrapped in a warm haze, didn't seem to be working properly.

Keynsham brushed his thumb over her cheek and as her eyes came back into focus she realized that he was smiling tenderly. "Well, Lady Alford, I hope that you did not find that *dull*."

"Dull, Lord Alford?"

He helped her gently off the desk, checked her gown for stray papers and straightened the back of her skirts. Then he drew her close against him. She took a long, contented breath. Outside the rainstorm was continuing. Inside, she could stand here, encircled in his arms, forever.

"Well, you did say that you wished that our lives together from now on could be dull."

"Oh. That. Yes. I suppose that I did."

He kissed the hollow beneath her ear. "Have I told you today how much I love you?"

"Hmm. I cannot recall."

"Well, in case I did not—I love you." He kissed the place on her temple that he so often kissed. "Indeed I adore you. And the more I think about it, the more I fear that while I may be able to be a *little* dull, I cannot promise to be *very* dull."

She thought that her heart might actually burst with love. "Can you not?"

"Well, I think that I can safely promise not to be chased through Grosvenor Square by gangsters. Just for instance. But beyond that—well, it will be difficult to feel dull, now that I am married to you." He dropped another kiss on her temple.

"I see." She was struggling to keep a straight face. "Well."

"In fact, Lady Alford, at this very moment I am feeling... how shall I put this? Not at all dull."

"Oh?"

"Yes. Almost extraordinarily not dull. In fact, I am wondering if you should like to go upstairs—where we may continue not being dull together."

"Do you know, Lord Alford... I think I might."

Afterword

Thank you for reading *Lord Something.* I hope you enjoyed it! It's the fourth book in the Unexpected Heirs series, but obviously can be read as a standalone. If you missed the prequel novella *Miss Nothing*, and are wondering how Celia and Keynsham originally met, it's available free here.

If you'd like to be the first to get updates and sneak peeks, as well as the chance to win merch, please sign up for my mailing list at loreahartwell.com.

Reviews are the main way that readers discover books. If you have a moment, please consider leaving a review for *Lord Something*, and help other readers and fans of Regency romance to discover it!

Notes

Grosvenor Square's Landscape

In 1677, Sir Thomas Grosvenor—Third Baronet and MP for Cheshire—acquired the land that was to become Mayfair and Belgravia when he married an heiress, Mary Davies. Her dowry included five hundred acres of mostly marshy land at what was then London's western boundary, stretching from Oxford Street south to Pimlico.

Sir Thomas realized that wealthy homeowners would want both larger houses and mews access for their carriages and horses—and so, as he began to develop this huge tract of land, he laid out wide streets and large lots that included these amenities. His projects included Hanover Square, the church of St George's, Hanover Square (where so many society weddings are held, both in real life and in Regency romances!), and Berkeley Square.

After Sir Thomas died in 1700, aged only 45, of a sudden fever, his son Sir Richard continued developing Mayfair as London's most exclusive neighborhood, with Grosvenor Square as its centerpiece. When the square was laid out in 1720, he hired John Alston, the most famous landscape designer of the time, to design a garden for it.

At six acres, the square is large, and Alston's design was meant to recreate the English countryside in the heart of London. No plans or drawings have survived to show what it looked like at that time, but besides an artificial hill that was apparently planted with trees, it contained winding paths, elm trees, large shrubs, and a gilded statue of George I.

In the 1770s the paths were straightened. In the 1810s, some of the paths were removed and replaced with lawn. The elm trees were cut down in the 1840s, and the statue was removed and replaced with a gazebo.

Because this story is set in 1818, I imagined the square without the hill, but with the statue, straight paths, and mature elm trees and large shrubs.

The Minerva Press

The Thetis Press that publishes Pomona's book, and where Mrs. Ellesmere sends Celia to borrow sensational novels, is based on the real-life Minerva Press. Founded by publisher William Lane, the Minerva Press was wildly successful and way ahead of its time. It not only published books, but also owned a network of lending libraries in fashionable towns across England. It was best known for publishing popular Gothic novels that tended to mix supernatural horror and crumbling castles with murderous relatives, secret babies and star-crossed romance.

The famous list of seven "horrid novels" that Isabella Thorpe recommends to Catherine Morland in

Jane Austen's *Northanger Abbey* were real books (until fairly recently, many people thought that Austen had invented the titles to mock the genre!) Six of the seven were published by the Minerva Press.

Many of the Minerva Press's authors were women —arguably the first time that mass entertainment was produced by and for women. This scandalous state of affairs led to complaints about the amount of time that women were spending reading for pleasure, and the moral decline that this surely represented.

About the Author

Lorea Hartwell loves a man in a well-tied neckcloth. She grew up reading paperbacks from the wire racks at the supermarket... and *Mad* magazine. Fortunately or unfortunately she later got a degree in English literature. She's worked in libraries and at newspapers and magazines, and aspires to become a lady of reserved charm, although that is unlikely.

Also by Lorea T. Hartwell

The Accidental Heiress

When Miss Phoebe Price, penniless spinster, unexpectedly becomes Miss Phoebe Price, heiress, the *ton* rejoices.

Just kidding. The *ton* explodes with malicious gossip.

Where did Phoebe's mysterious riches come from? Everyone wants to know—especially Phoebe! And when her new fortune drops her into the eye of a brewing storm of scandal, she doesn't know how she'll clear her name.

Certainly, the very last person she should turn to for help is Captain Anthony Grenville. The handsome war hero is back, and now he's the heir to an earldom. He's also the man who almost ruined her. It would be easy to give in to the desire he sparks with his hungry kisses—but Phoebe's had four years to think about the way he once betrayed her innocent heart.

Somehow, the newly-minted Heiress of Holborn must discover the truth about her money before her secret enemies can destroy her life. But can she do that while also staying away from Captain Grenville? And... does she want to?

The Unlikely Earl

When Miss Sophia Lightbourne's spoiled sister runs away from home, there's only one thing Sophia can do: follow her to London to try to save Kitty from being ruined. If only the trail didn't lead straight to Augustus Alleyne...

Alleyne is handsome, witty, and the stepson of a baronet.

He's painted the portraits of half the *ton*. Yet his wealthy and aristocratic friends are wastrels, and Sophia very much suspects that Alleyne is a rake. Too bad he's the only person who can help her find Kitty...

Augustus Alleyne doesn't have any use for family—his own has all but cast him out. And he certainly isn't looking for a wife. Yet as he and Sophia follow the trail of destruction left by the heedless Kitty, their connection grows passionate.

Does what happens in London stay in London? Sophia, who's always been forced to be practical, tells herself that her relationship with Alleyne can't last. But when Kitty turns up, Alleyne unexpectedly inherits a title, and Sophia's family tries to deny her dreams, she must learn to follow her heart.

Printed in Dunstable, United Kingdom

65939698R00204